Getaway Girl

TESSA BAILEY

TABLE OF CONTENTS

CHAPTER ONE

Addison

Scandal Erupts as Captain Du Pont Left in the Lurch at Church
—Charleston Courier

WHEN I WOKE up this morning, I didn't plan on crashing a wedding.

But here I am.

In leather pants and a faded T-shirt, I didn't even bother dressing up, which is drawing censorious raised eyebrows from the Charleston upper crust. There they are in their pressed pastels and bow ties, neatly divided into two sides of the aisle. Golden blondes on the left. Deep, rich brunettes to the right. Not a head of midnight-black hair among them.

None like mine.

Defiance rears back inside me and I toss that mane of inherited black hair now, letting it whip and settle around my shoulders. Perhaps it's the move that causes an older woman in the back row to recognize me—finally. Or recognize my mother, rather. I've grown up a lot since leaving this town, and since I own a mirror, I'm aware of the resemblance.

Green eyes, resting bitch face, stubborn chin, indecent curves.

I'm a Potts girl, head to toe.

Looking as if she's seen a ghost, the woman fingers her pearls

1

and leans over to start a gossip wildfire, no doubt. My mouth curls into a pleased smile and I go back to observing the congregation. Everyone is seated and waiting for the bride to walk down the aisle, except for me. I'm standing in the far back corner, cloaked in shadows. Appropriate, considering my cousin, Naomi, is getting married this afternoon and no one in my family was invited.

What family? You're the only one left now.

An invisible fist grinds into my chest and I push off the wall, intending to duck out for a breath of fresh air. No way I'm going to lose my composure in front of these people. *Especially* the blonde side of the room. When I turn to leave, however…that's when I see him.

Once, during a hurricane, I made the mistake of leaving my apartment in Brooklyn for a gallon of milk. Cereal makes up ninety percent of my diet, so I was desperate and tired of eating fistfuls of dry Cheerios. I didn't make it two steps out of the building when a hundred-mile-an-hour wind swept my feet out from under me, landing me on my back with a view of the dark thunderheads above. I still went and bought the milk, because I am a stubborn piece of work, but I remember that feeling of utter shock. The confirmation that forces more powerful than my iron will exist, just waiting to knock me on my butt.

That's how I feel when I see the groom. Naomi's groom.

My throat resists my attempts to swallow, coating itself in mud. Palms sweaty, pulse clamoring, knees buckling—yes, buckling—I fall back against the back wall of the church. I turn to find a full back row of blonde heads watching me and I lift my chin, commanding myself to pull it together. What in God's name is wrong with me?

As if induced by magic, my gaze lifts to the groom once more.

He's not the cookie-cutter trust fund boy I was expecting. No, he's...compelling. Hands clasped behind his back, he's the authority in the room without moving a single muscle. He must be six foot five, based on the way he towers over the groomsmen, and the breadth of his muscular chest is somehow *fierce*. Braced and ready for action. He has a thick head of tobacco hair, face shaven but already battling a beard. His blatant masculinity isn't what robs me of the ability to stand, though.

It's his eyes. For all this man's obvious power, they're heartbreakingly kind.

When I read the wedding announcement online, I scoffed at the description of Naomi's fiancé. I rush to recall it now. Elijah Montgomery DuPont. Citadel graduate. Served three tours overseas with the army. What else? There was something...else.

Oh. Right. Elijah is the son of Charleston's longest-sitting mayor. Plans to follow in his father's footsteps. Imminently. Would I expect anything less in a husband for impossibly polished, former pageant girl Naomi? Granted I haven't seen her sailing through town since we were teenagers, Naomi in her private school getup, me in ripped jeans and Salvation Army specials. I remember well, though. I remember the way her gaze skimmed over me and shut down, the whispers to her friends. *Her mother. Her mother is the one...*

I release a shaky laugh under my breath when I realize...I'm jealous of Naomi. Right now in this moment. *Actually* jealous over this man I've never met, who can't possibly be as kind as his eyes suggest. I don't even *like* kind men. Even as I tell myself that, I squint, trying to make out the color of those eyes. When I realize what I'm doing, I shake myself and turn to leave the church through a side exit. As much I wanted to shake up the proceedings and remind these people my side of the family existed, I can't stay now. The irony of me returning home only to develop this weird, instantaneous attraction for my cousin's fiancé is *way* too much.

Tomorrow, I will probably forget all about him. This afternoon will feel like a dream or a hallucination. But for right now I...I don't think I can watch him get married.

Steeped in disbelief, I press the handle of the exit down. Turning to take one last, stupid look over my shoulder, I pause when I see a woman jogging up the aisle. She's not the bride, but in that teal, ruffled nightmare of a dress, she screams bridesmaid. Her face is white as a sheet, a bouquet of flowers limp at one side, a folded note in the opposite hand. I take my fingers off the door handle, noting that everyone around me has started to murmur amongst themselves. What is going on?

The groom inclines his head, leaning down so the harried bridesmaid can reach his ear. Finished speaking, she hands him the note, closing her eyes as he unfolds and reads it. He's very still. Something is definitely wrong, but he seems more concerned about the bridesmaid's obvious upset, even patting her on the shoulder with a steady hand as he reads. *Gentle giant.*

I flinch at my own thoughts. They simply cannot be coming from me. Men are meant to be pleasant diversions from time to time. They all want one thing and I take a twisted pleasure in proving that. Proving *I* don't want anything more, either, and sending them on their way. Reminding myself of how I operate doesn't help now, though. As the groom—Elijah's—face turns more and more grave, I grow restless. I want everyone to stop whispering.

Finally, the bridesmaid turns and leaves the way she came, sniffling into her forearm. Elijah tucks the note into his pocket and faces the congregation alone, appearing almost thoughtful.

No one is whispering now. They're all made of stone, waiting to see what the robust military man in the tuxedo will say. "I'm very sorry you all came out on a Sunday. It would appear…no one is getting married today, after all," he drawls, his deep voice resonating with southern gentility. At his announcement, there are gasps from every corner of the aisle, women fanning themselves with almost fanatical fervor. Camera flashes go off. Elijah isn't immune to the sudden activity. Or the fact that he's just been jilted. No, he doesn't seem to know what to do with his hands, a forced, wry smile playing around his lips. "I hope your wedding gifts came with a good refund policy."

His attempt at a joke is met with a smatter of uncomfortable laughter, but mostly silence. I think. It's hard to hear anything over the wrenching in my breastbone. Yeah, I didn't want to watch him marry my cousin for some weird reason. But there's zero satisfaction in watching him get left at the altar. None. I've never seen someone look more alone in my life.

I watch as Elijah turns to his groomsmen and rolls a shoulder, his eyes averted. And in that tiny slice of time, I know exactly what he's going to do. Tomorrow, maybe I'll marvel over how easily I read Elijah in a room full of people who should know him better than me. But for now, I don't waste time slipping out the side exit, getting swallowed up in warm March wind and the scent of salt air. I weave through the parked cars to find my ancient Honda, breathing in time with my steps.

Moments later, I watch from my idle at the curb as Elijah strides out of the church, then comes to a dead stop. He looks straight ahead at nothing, the powerful cords of his neck standing out in the hazy, southern afternoon sun. Heartbroken? Angry? I can't tell a single thing, except that he wants to escape. Now. But before I apply my foot to the gas, I give myself a mental slap in the face. A cold, hard reality check.

Rich, powerful, handsome. Unattainable. This is the same kind of man my mother fell for. Fell *hard*. Everyone inside that church remembers how *that* ended, too. It tore apart two halves of a family, leaving one side to flourish in their wealth and the other to fall from grace.

Elijah Montgomery DuPont, the next mayor of Charleston, heir to southern immortality might have been left behind by his bride today, but someday soon? There will be another one.

She won't be a Potts girl. She will never, ever be me.

It costs me a surprising effort, but I paste on my most dazzling smile and pull up to the curb at the bottom of the church steps. By now, guests have begun filling the church doorways, slinking out one by one in the distance behind Elijah.

When I roll down the passenger side window, I get Elijah's attention all to myself for the first time and it hits me like that gale, hurricane wind—only nine times stronger. He's so *inviting* up close. A man who could double as a human shield. Or a furnace. He's just *radiating* warmth and capabilities, like he's someone to depend on. Oh God. I'm losing my freaking mind.

Sucking in a breath, I open the glove compartment and fish out the bottle of Grey Goose vodka, waving it at the jilted groom. "It's half empty, but you're welcome to it."

I was right about his eyes. That's my only coherent thought as he ducks into my Honda and straightens, his head resting against the ceiling. His gaze is made of the finest chocolate and just as fulfilling as it lands on me, grateful and weary. "Thank you, ma'am."

His thick burr rocks me down to the soles of my feet, making me think of cuddling. *Cuddling.* An activity I've never performed a day in my life. Hoping my shock isn't showing on my face, I twist open the bottle and hand it over. "All dressed up and nowhere to go?"

Humorless laughter leaves him in a slow rumble. "Something like that."

"I'm so sorry about what happened," I whisper, without thinking. "No one deserves that."

He cuts me a look, obviously just realizing I witnessed his humiliation. He becomes aware of more than that, though. Until right this second, I don't think he was really *seeing* me. I was just a blurry figure in a car. An escape hatch. Now, his attention travels down to my leather-clad thighs, before shooting back up to my face, alertness inching into his expression. "Who are you?"

"That's a long story." I tip the bottle up to his mouth. "For now, I'm Addison. And if you want to avoid the sympathy coming down the steps, I'm your girl."

Without turning to look at the church, he twists the bottle on his knee. "How so?"

"There are probably very few places you can hide in this town, am I right?"

Weary brown eyes focus back on me. "Yes."

So much weight and meaning packed into a single word. "I have a place. You can lay low for a little while."

His body language is still grateful, but hesitant now. "I mean no disrespect, Addison. I'm not assuming a damn thing, either, you understand." He waits for my nod. "But if you're thinking of offering me more than a place to lay low, I'm not sure I'm in the right frame of mind for it. Wouldn't be fair to you."

Just the suggestion of sex with this man makes me slippery between my legs. Which is pathetic considering he's just turned me down—not that I was offering. Still. What did I think? I would pull up in my old as hell, chipped paint steed and sweep him away like an avenging cowgirl? The man is reeling from being jilted. Any romantic notions I have that are coming to life against my will need to be put to rest. Immediately. Not so easy to do when I like him more with every genuine word that comes out of his mouth.

Ignoring the clang of doom in the back of my head, I pull away from the curb. "That's pretty noble of you. Most people wouldn't be concerned with fairness after something so shitty happened to them."

"Shitty things happen to people all the time," he answers, his tone conversational. Not in the least bit preachy. "It's no excuse to be selfish."

"No, I guess not." I barely manage to sound human after hearing him say *selfish* in relation to sex. Is that how he'd be with me beneath him, if we went to bed this afternoon? Rough and selfish and—*Lord.* I need to get a hold of myself, right now. Even if he was in the right mind frame for sex…Naomi is his type. Girls with a pedigree. Not a girl who was born out of wedlock and spends her life scraping by, week to week. I would be nothing more than a quick itch-scratcher.

That mental kick in the pants is exactly what I need. I know all too well what becomes of a woman who lets herself be a man's scratching post. "I'm not offering you anything but room-temperature Grey Goose and a place to watch television for a while." I take a turn onto the avenue, before flicking him a teasing look down my nose. "You think I want a man who got left out on the curb like yesterday's recycling?"

When Elijah throws back his head and laughs; the sound sends an appreciative shiver down my spine. *Ignore it.* "Something told me to get into this car." His big shoulders are still shaking. "I'm glad I listened." I pull up to a red light, startled when he takes my hand off the wheel, holding it in his warm grip. His head tilts, his brown eyes bursting with character. A torturously handsome, kind-hearted rake with an actual sense of humor. "Friends?"

Feeling as though I'm standing on the edge of a cliff, I roll a shoulder. "I'm reserving judgment."

His laughter defeats me this time and as I coast through the light, I smile.

CHAPTER TWO

Elijah

Special Report: Gift Return Policy Loopholes.
What the major department stores don't want you to know.
—Charleston Post

WALKING UP THE stairs to a second-floor apartment in an unfamiliar part of town feels like a dream. I don't know the girl in front of me from Adam, but I follow her in a trance. Laughter drifts from an unseen source, a baseball connects with a metal bat at the park across the street. Life as usual. Except for mine. When I woke up this morning, my entire life was plotted out on a strict timeline. Now it's like someone used their backhand to sweep my milestone markers off the table...and they're all left suspended in midair.

Was I really just left at the altar?

If I had my cell phone, it would be shrieking like a fire alarm in my pocket. But I didn't bring it to my wedding, since everyone I knew was going to be there. And they were. My parents, aunts, uncles, cousins, friends and colleagues came expecting to witness a union, before retiring to Gadsden House for dinner and cocktails. They bought clothes for the occasion, booked hotel rooms and purchased gifts. What are they going to eat for dinner now that their plans have changed? I pause on the stairs. Maybe I should have carried on with the reception. It wouldn't kill me to smile for a few hours and let everyone enjoy the party they were promised.

"Are you coming?"

Several steps ahead of me, Addison leans against the wobbling railing, inspecting her nails as if she couldn't care less whether I follow or not. Moving fast, I grip the unsteady wood in my left hand, in case it decides to give way behind her, little thing though she is. Her eyes cut to mine at the action, somewhat startled, before she goes back to examining her nails.

Lord. She's such a departure from the mayoral aides, campaign volunteers and Charleston residents who beam as I pass them in hallways and streets, addressing me as Captain Du Pont. Yes, Addison is indifferent. Insulting, even. When I drifted down the steps of the church, at a loss for the first time in my life about what to do, an invisible wind seemed to push me toward the car. An outlandish notion if I ever heard one. I was merely hoping to avoid making everyone feel awkward. Southern manners dictate that each and every guest pat me on the shoulder and tell me I'm better off without Naomi. Jumping into Addison's car was simply the easiest way to spare them from that obligation.

It has nothing to do with the instant…kinship I felt for her when she smiled and shook the half-empty bottle of Grey Goose at me.

"Yes. I'm coming." I clear my throat and continue up the steps, raising an eyebrow when Addison shrugs, as if she can take me or leave me. It's not a reaction I'm accustomed to—and it's somehow exactly what I need. Because I've just been abandoned in front of an entire congregation. And I'm not ready to unpack why I'm more upset about the guests being cheated out of dinner and a party…than I am about my newly forced singledom.

Addison's nonchalance gives me an excuse not to think. To leave the mile markers of my life hanging in the air.

Just for today.

When we reach the door and Addison turns the key, it sticks, so she jiggles it, black hair falling into her face. She must belong to Naomi's side of the family, since I don't recognize her. There's no doubt I would remember Addison. Dressed in leather and scuffed boots with a permanent sulk to her mouth, she's the polar opposite of my fiancée. *Ex*-fiancée. Not to mention, this neighborhood and her car don't suggest a high income. Whereas Naomi will never have to work a day in her life, thanks to family money.

"Where did you come from?"

"Huh?" Addison finally gets the door open, but pauses in the doorframe at my unrehearsed question. "New York. I've been there about six years, but before that I—"

"No, I mean today. Where did you come from today?" The last hour is a blur, but I try and recall the timing. "If you were in the church to see what happened, you only had about a minute to go get your car. Before I walked out."

"Anyone lucky enough to be near an exit would have fled, too." She rolls her lips inward and lets them go with a pop. "It was painful."

I find myself fighting a smile. This girl is kind of mean. Have I ever met a girl who doesn't hide a mean streak behind back-handed compliments and *bless your hearts*? "Yet you picked me up. If it was so painful, why bring me along as a reminder?"

"Do you always question basic human decency?" She gives an annoyed flick of her hair. "So, before we go inside, I have to prepare you. The place is decorated for Christmas. You will lose count of Santas and Frostys. It can be jarring at first."

"You seem like more of a Halloween girl."

Addison pats her head. "Is it the devil horns? I thought I hid them better." A twist of her lips, then she's pushing into the apartment, flipping on a ceiling light. "This place belonged to my grandmother. She passed away a few weeks ago and left it. To me."

Just as promptly as she makes that pronouncement, she's gone from the room, vanished down a back hallway. My sympathy sits on the tip of my tongue, waiting for her to come back so I can express it. But the longer she stays away, the more I start to think she doesn't want it—and left the room for that very reason.

Shaking my head over Addison's unique nature, I turn and get my first glimpse of the open-plan living and dining area. Well I'll be damned, she wasn't lying. There's fake snow on every surface, Christmas lights—although not plugged in—are strung from every corner of the ceiling. There are no less than eight Christmas trees, some floor-sized, some perched on brightly skirted tabletops. Suspended from the middle of the living room ceiling is a giant plastic sleigh...and eight reindeer being lead by Rudolph.

When Addison returns, she's mid-sentence by the time she clears the hallway. "There's a master switch to all the Christmas stuff. When I flip it on, this place turns into Kevin McAllister's house in *Home Alone* when he's trying to convince the robbers his parents aren't in France. That they're actually home having a party?" She wiggles her fingers. "It's like having the nuclear codes, except I drop fake snow instead of bombs."

"I like it." I turn in a circle, noticing a mural depicting a trio of carolers. "Think of all the time you'll save on decorating in December."

Her shock of laughter brings me up short. It's nothing like the husky purr I would have expected from her. No, it's bright and clear and appreciative. "Exactly." She scratches her eyebrow. "You want to see?"

"Dying to."

"Well...if you feel like getting comfortable..." Her indifference is back in place as she struts to the kitchen. "No one is stopping you."

There was a moment in Addison's car where I thought she was propositioning me. Clearly I was way off. Although, she's nothing like the women I've dated, so reading her in that regard is something of a challenge. Everything about her is bold. Her clothing, the long, black hair that moves with her, the spontaneity. The way she looks me in the eye like we're adversaries even when she's smiling. Like I said, nothing like the polite, often predictable—God forgive me for saying so—women of my experience. Considering her lack of interest in me, I'm probably nothing like the men she sees, either.

Searching the room for signs of a man, I'm not sure why I relax upon finding nothing since I'm only here to check out for a while. When I try to pinpoint where everything went wrong, though, a throb starts behind my right eye. Dating. Couplehood. Based on today's events, I've been doing them wrong. For two years, I've been telling Naomi I love her. I've been her plus-one to parties, we've gone skiing together, double dated, posed for engagement photos. Wasn't that love? Weren't the two of us in love?

Yeah. Yeah...I think we were. When I came back from my three tours overseas, our parents began putting us in the same place often enough that it seemed natural to start dating. We talked about having children and picked out china patterns. She smiled and waved at my campaign events. People don't do those kinds of things for one another unless they're in love. For some reason, though, I missed the signals telling me she wasn't going to show up to the church today. I missed whatever was wrong—and I missed it hard. Last night at the rehearsal dinner, Naomi seemed like her usual smiling self. Not a hair out of place. But someone doesn't just skip town to avoid their own wedding if they're happy. And I had no clue.

"Ready?"

Addison's voice calling from the kitchen snaps me to attention. "Yes, ma'am."

She groans. "Ma'am *this*."

The apartment roars to life. Roars. "Carol of the Bells" clangs from several reanimated toys. Rudolph's nose turns a bright red and the sleigh begins to travel in a circle around the living room. Monkeys slap cymbals together, at least ten different versions of Frosty begin to dance and millions of Christmas lights twinkle, giving the space an ethereal golden glow. It's like standing in one of the department store windows on Fifth Avenue in New York City. Just overwhelming and comforting and...a little terrifying all at once.

"Wow."

"Yeah." Not having heard Addison approach, I turn to find her standing beside me, her head only reaching my shoulder. "Do you get to the City Market very often?"

"I used to." Thinking of the stack of paperwork and emails and invitations waiting for me at City Hall, I sigh, knowing the sound will get swallowed by the abundance of noise. "Used to sneak in for free praline samples when I was young. Haven't been in a while, though."

"Running for mayor is time consuming. That's why I've

never done it."

My laugh sneaks up on me. "Oh, is that why?"

Her lips twitch. "My grandmother had a coveted vendor permit at the market. She's been selling Christmas ornaments there since I can remember. The booth is aptly named Jingle Balls." The floorboards move under our feet as she shifts. "She left me that, too. Added my name to the license and never told me."

"Are you going to run from the room again before I can offer condolences?"

Her arms drop, mouth opening and closing. "I don't know what you're talking about—"

"No explanation needed. But I am very sorry, Addison." I take pity on her by changing the subject. "Are you going to work at the booth?"

It takes her a few beats to answer. "I wasn't going to. I was going back to New York as soon as I tied up her loose ends," she says, sounding somewhat dazed. "But when I went to collect her things...I figured, maybe one more day? And now I've been selling Christmas ornaments for two weeks. In freaking March."

"You like it."

"Yeah. I like it." She turns to me with a far-off expression. "My grandmother raised me. She was really good to me, even when things got hard. It doesn't seem right to abandon her life's work quite so fast."

Underneath the glow of Christmas lights, something is becoming very hard to ignore, though I've been doing a good job until now. Addison is a beautiful woman. That's an understatement, actually. When I was a young boy, I overheard my grandfather describe a woman, saying, "That one could end friendships, start wars and make a glutton suck in his gut."

Seems to me a woman shouldn't be blamed for wars, simply because of her appearance, but I understand the sentiment. Long story short, Addison is a complete knockout.

What the hell am I doing here? My relationship just ended without preamble. Tomorrow morning, I'll be headline fodder. What happened today might even affect the campaign. I've probably got a search party looking for me by now. Hell, I've somehow offended my fiancé enough that she jilted me. The last thing I should be doing is standing in another woman's apartment, noticing she's gorgeous.

"You're freaking out on me," Addison says. "Is it the dancing Frostys?"

"No." I press two fingers to my eye socket. "I'm sorry. Impulsive decisions aren't like me. I should be back at the church saying goodbye to everyone. Denying southerners their chance to give condolences is a sin. They'll want to hear me say I'm fine."

Maybe I should be trying to find Naomi. Weird how I'm only thinking of that now.

"*Are* you fine?"

"I don't know," I say on an exhale. "That's why I got in your car. I needed somewhere to go figure that out."

She hesitates before asking her next question. "What did the note say?"

I dig it out of my pocket, unfolding the pink, scented stationary, complete with a glitter border. "I'm sorry, Elijah. I couldn't do it." Just like the first time I read the note, I'm somewhat alarmed by my reaction. There's surprise. Confusion. But not the kind of pain I would expect from a man being stood up by his bride. "I didn't want to end it this way, but it's for the best."

There's only a flash of sympathy on Addison's face, before she nods and leaves the room. A second later, Christmas powers down and I'm back to standing in the cool, hazy apartment in the muted afternoon light. Before and after. Full speed straight into stagnancy, just like my day leading up to the note being delivered mid-aisle. Bootsteps signal Addison's return and I put the note back in my pocket.

She takes my arm as she passes through the living room. "Come on."

"Now, hold on, Goose…"

We come to a halt halfway down the hallway. "*Goose?*"

"You greeted me with a bottle of the stuff."

"Thank God you won't be around long enough to make that stick." With a decisive nod, she keeps going, leading me into a bedroom. It's big, sparse and clean, not much more than a queen-sized bed and an antique bureau. Any suspicion I have that she's going to invite me to join her in the bed fades with the wide berth she gives me. "If you don't want to go home right away, you can stay here for the night. But I'm not cooking for you."

A reprieve from the responsibilities that face me sounds like heaven. My father is probably dying to strategize a way to spin today's events into getting votes. Reporters are more than likely already camped outside my…my what?

"I don't have a choice," I say slowly. "We were leaving for the Bahamas tonight. When we returned in two weeks, the house was going to be ready."

"What house?" I rattle off an address and her jaw drops. "That corner mansion on the Battery? The one right across from the park?"

"That's the one." I lower myself to the bed and drop my head into my waiting hands, the reality of my situation finally registering. "The lease on my apartment ended and I moved out. Been staying at the Dewberry Hotel until the wedding, but I checked out of there this morning. Most of my things are in storage, waiting to be moved into the new house."

Addison sits down on the bed next to me. "Do you have a friend you can call?"

"Yes, but…" I shake my head. "He has a family. I can't bring a bunch of press down on their heads by showing up there. And they *would* show up. They always do."

"Parents?"

I tuck my tongue into my cheek and don't answer.

"I'll get you some sheets so you can make the bed." She rises and starts to leave the room, but stops with a hand on the frame. Without looking at me, she sighs and asks, "Grilled cheese and tomato soup sound okay?"

"Better than okay."

"Don't get used to it."

CHAPTER THREE

Addison

Who was the mysterious Getaway Girl?
And what has she done with Captain Du Pont?
—TheTea.com

M Y APARTMENT HAS shrunk ten sizes since Elijah walked in the door.

Now the future mayor of Charleston, South Carolina and his smooth southern gentleman's drawl is sitting across from me eating a grilled cheese. He's still wearing his tuxedo, but it has been deconstructed into pants, a white undershirt and an unbuttoned dress shirt that hangs loose around either side of him. The pendant light hanging over the kitchen table gives his robust body a glowing lining, picking strands of his hair to stroke into the color of new pennies. Not that I'm noticing.

I've never cooked for a man before. At best, I've grudgingly shoved a box of Cocoa Krispies across the counter toward a dude who'd overstayed his welcome. There's no denying the pleasurable little flip in my stomach every time Elijah takes a bite, though, chewing with no self-consciousness. Just a big, healthy man enjoying a meal.

To be fair, I barely cook for *myself*. Ever since returning to Charleston, though, I've found myself falling back into habits formed as a teenager. Stopping at the local market on the way home from work and buying the ingredients for something that will last two or three days. The way my grandmother used to do. Stew, lasagna, meatloaf. *They always taste best on the third day*, she used to say, pouring herself a mug of wine from the Bota Box. Saluting me with it.

These recaptured habits probably have something to do with being surrounded by reminders of the highly efficient and hard-working woman who raised me from childhood, after my mother left. I could almost feel her silent disapproval on the first night of my return as I munched on Lucky Charms on a spread-out blanket in the living room.

Fine, I'd muttered to the lit-up room. *I'll go shopping tomorrow.*

"This is great, Goose."

"Oh, come on."

"No, really. It's great."

"I was talking about the nickname."

He acknowledges my gripe with a teasing wink, leaning back in his chair with half a grilled cheese in his hand. "What is with the shoes?" When I merely raise an eyebrow, he gestures with the sandwich. "Over by the door."

I follow his line of sight to my shoe shelf, which is a glass half-moon affixed to the wall. Except for my bedroom, which I've made my own out of necessity, this is my only personal touch in the main living area of the apartment. Neatly arranged on the shelf sit four pairs of shoes. Black stilettos, green rain boots, flashy pink sneakers and basic brown sandals. "I have a theory that human beings only need four pairs of shoes. Those are mine."

"Why do you keep them on a shelf?"

Not used to explaining myself, I squirm in my chair. "Um.

Putting my shoes on is the last thing I do before leaving the house. It's kind of...I don't know. Symbolic, maybe? Like a final touch to assure myself I'm prepared for whatever I've planned that day. A donning of armor before going into battle." I poke the air with my spoon. "If you laugh, Mr. Mayor, I'll dump the rest of my soup on your head."

"I'm not the mayor yet. I still have an election to win." He tosses the rest of his sandwich into his mouth and I try not to watch the muscles of his throat shift and flex. "My mother has a thousand pairs of shoes."

"I'm willing to bet she only wears four on a regular basis, though."

"This is the part where I prove I'm a man and admit I don't notice her shoes." He narrows an eye at me. Something he does when he's curious or asking questions. I'm registering way too many things about him. Like the fact that he waited for me to pick up my spoon first, before picking up his own. The well-muscled stomach beneath his undershirt that boasts just enough padding to make him human. And the way his chest hair curls over his neckline, black and unruly, so at odds with his perfect gentleman vibe. "So the rain boots are an obvious choice for bad weather, sandals for summer..."

"Sneakers for running." Realizing my voice has dropped to a low rasp, I clear my throat. "Heels for going out to meet men."

Why do I say that? For two reasons, I think. One, I want to see his reaction. Is he really as immune to me as he seems to be? This attraction I'm battling for him is wrapped around me so tight, it's hard to believe it doesn't run both ways. Two—and this is most troubling—I'm trying to reassure him I'm only interested in friendship. Because I don't think he'll stay otherwise.

And God, that makes total sense after what he went through

today. He's probably—no, *definitely*—still in love with Naomi and only putting on a brave face, because that's what war veteran politicians with blue blood flowing through their veins do. If I'd been stood up at the alter, I wouldn't appreciate a man trying to get into my pants *the same day,* either. I would knee his balls up into his neck for good measure. Friendship is what he's offering me. So I say the thing about going out to meet men. I say it so he'll feel comfortable being my friend.

"Right." Elijah coughs into his fist. "Well, I'm sure they do the trick."

Is that it, then? The line is drawn? I've never been in this kind of situation. Wanting a man I don't think I can ever have. If sexual attraction was the only reason I was drawn to him, I would go stand in front of his chair and disrobe slowly, drag my nails through his hair and whisper bad things beside his ear.

Sex is rare for me, but when I let myself indulge, it's like going on vacation. It's a free pass to let my thoughts blur and physical instinct to take over. I love sex. The idea of it, mostly. Two people moving like violin and bow until the strings snap. I don't get close enough to men to get bogged down by emotion, though. Or let insecurities prickle under my skin. It's just me there in the darkness. Would it be that way with Elijah? Something tells me no. I'd be very aware of him there with me in the dark. So very aware.

If I turned on the sexy, he might resist, but he'd ultimately follow me to the bedroom. That would be it, though. He would leave. And I don't think I'd see him again. At least not in this capacity, where it's just the two of us and there's no social protocol. Every minute that passes with him in this apartment— which felt so lonely until now—makes me hate the idea of losing the possibility we could spend time together again. God, it might not be possible either way.

"My grandmother only had one pair of shoes. Galoshes. They were army green and she wore them year round." I scrub at a spot on the table with my fingernail. "She would say I'm being very extravagant with four pairs of shoes."

When I look up, his eyes are so bottomless and compassionate, I could fall into them and sink for decades. "You miss her."

I shrug in an attempt to shake free the knot in my chest. "I should have visited more."

"How long had it been?"

Six years. I can't even bring myself to say it out loud. "New York is hard. First you're scrambling just to get a stable situation. A job, a place to live. And then it's a non-stop grind to maintain." My mouth edges up. "Every time we spoke on the phone, she would tell me she didn't have time for visitors, anyway."

Elijah's laugh lines appear on either side of his mouth, carved into his strong, stubbled jaw. "You two sound nothing alike."

I wrinkle my nose at his sarcasm. "What are you going to do tomorrow, Elijah?"

The smile flattens. "I don't know."

"What do you *want* to do?"

His surprise lets me know how often he acts selfishly, doing only what he wants and not what's expected. Never, probably. But he takes a moment to think now, his fingers tapping on the table. "I want to walk into my office like nothing happened. I want to ignore questions. Just walk in and get back to work. I don't want advice or sympathy or greeting cards."

"You're going to need a suit." I stand up and start to collect plates and bowls, pushing Elijah back down into his chair when he gets up to help. "If you want to pretend like nothing ever happened, you can't show up wearing your wedding tux."

"I'm in the public eye. I can't pretend at all, Goose."

Just like every other time he's called me that, warmth expands in my chest, but I go cold as ice when something occurs to me. Something I'd completely forgotten in my haste to play Elijah's getaway driver and my subsequent—and misplaced—mooning over him. How could I have forgotten such an important detail? "I have to tell you something."

A groove appears between his eyebrows. "Yeah?"

"Yeah." I sit down again, the plates and bowls forgotten in a stack. "I didn't think very hard about this today. I just...I figured you would want to get away. So I went to get my car."

"I'm grateful for that." He leans forward. "Whatever it is, Addison, it can't be worse than me being left at the altar."

"Hold that thought." My pulse is ticking in my ears. "Elijah, Naomi is my cousin. Our grandmothers were sisters."

That brings his eyebrows up. "Really." It's almost imperceptible, the way his gaze roams over me, very likely making note of the dark hair and lack of upper-crust polish. "And we've never met because you've been in New York?"

A nervous laugh breaks free of my lips. "Partly. But mostly because my mother didn't get along with Naomi's mother. At all. My mother did some things that didn't exactly endear her to the family." I meet his eyes and find only curiosity there. But the other shoe hasn't dropped yet, has it? When it does, how long until he's out the door? "When my mother was young—around my age—she made some bad decisions. She...slept with Naomi's mother's fiancé." I laugh without humor. "Hold on, it gets worse. There was never a paternity test taken and the possibility was never acknowledged by anyone except my mother, but...there's a good chance I'm the product of their affair. Naomi and I are cousins, yes, but we might be half-sisters, too. Trust me, I have no plans to prove we share a father, but there it is. Bottom line, we're related."

Elijah remains silent.

"Even though my mother was pregnant, Naomi's parents went ahead with the wedding. They got married and my mother never really got over it. Asshole or not, she loved him." I swallow a handful of gravel. "My mother left when I was a child. I stayed with my grandmother."

His frown intensifies. "Addison."

"Someone recognized me at the wedding. By now, they all know who you left with and being with the black sheep is *not* a good look for you." My laughter is strained as I stand up again, collecting the dishes with clumsy hands. "It's been real, Elijah. But you should probably cut your losses and go."

Before meeting Elijah, I would have cackled and patted myself on the back knowing I'd hijacked the groom. I would have thought it perfectly poetic. A middle finger to the past. But the possibility that I might have hurt his reputation bothers me. A lot. I've never felt more like my mother than I do at this moment. Without realizing it, I've become the one woman he shouldn't be caught with.

I'm startled when big hands appear to take the dishes from me. We play tug of war for a few seconds, before I give up and cross my arms, glaring as Elijah sets everything down in the sink. "First off," he says, wheeling around. "I'll admit this does not look good."

"No," I whisper, dropping my arms. "It doesn't."

"Charleston loves to live in the past."

"They do."

"But I don't. Every time we erect another monument or memorial downtown, I wonder why we're not building a school. Or continuing to revitalize North Charleston. I'm more interested in the present. Are you still reserving judgment on us being friends?"

Caught off guard, I sputter. "I—what?" Why is my chest aching? "No."

"No, you're not reserving judgment or no we're not friends?"

"No, I'm not reserving judgment anymore. We're...good."

"All right, then." His head dips and I catch the ghost of a smile. "I'm a grown man and I'll spend time with whomever I choose. I don't know what a black sheep is, but I'm sure they don't go out of their way to offer getaway rides and guest bedrooms without asking for anything in return."

It takes me a few beats to get a breath. "I didn't mention I've been running a tab? That grilled cheese cost you twenty bucks."

His hearty laugh, I swear to God, it makes me want to sob. This is bad. I almost wish he would curse me for being so thoughtless and compromising his political future. That way, I could lock the door behind him and go back to business as usual. Forget I ever met this unique and interesting man.

But I can't shake the feeling that from this moment forward, my existence is never going back to normal.

"Well." I back away from the giant, magnetic force field of Elijah Montgomery Du Pont. "If you do the dishes, it might put me in a good enough mood to drive you to your storage locker in the morning. Unless you want me to loan you a dress. It would definitely distract everyone from your fall from grace."

His mouth curves. "True, but I doubt it would fit."

An image of Elijah pressing up between my legs and growling those same words into my neck gets me moving. *I'm so much bigger than you, Addison. I doubt it's going to fit, but stay still so I can try like hell.* Lord, who knew I was a masochist? Before he can catch my definite flush, I pivot and head for my bedroom. "Your ride leaves at eight o'clock sharp, freeloader," I call over my shoulder.

The water in the sink turns on. "I'll be ready."

"Night, Captain."

"Night, Goose."

I groan at the nickname, but when I close my bedroom door, I lean back against it and smile.

CHAPTER FOUR

Elijah

Captain Du Pont: Suffering? Or suffering no fools?
—Southern Insider News

I TAKE A moment to brace myself before leaving the driver's side of my truck. My smile is brittle as bark, but it stays in place as reporters swarm. *Captain Du Pont, how are you feeling this morning? Any idea why Miss Clemons didn't show for the wedding? Who is the woman you left the church with yesterday? Were you seeing the driver before the wedding? Is that why Miss Clemons chose not to marry you?*

Holding up my briefcase in front of me like a mock shield, I push ahead through the humid morning air. "Am I damaged goods now? Don't I get a good morning?"

A chorus of laughs rings out among the reporters. "Good morning, Captain Du Pont," one familiar female reporter chimes. "The public is just concerned. Could you give us some idea of what happened? Do you think this will have a negative impact on the campaign?"

"No, I don't expect it will." A microphone blocks my view of City Hall ahead and I bypass the aggressive journalist, trying my best not to step on anyone. "I might have been dumped, but I haven't lost my desire to improve Charleston for the better."

"You think you can do better than your father?"

"Yes, but don't tell him I said that."

More laughter. I'm almost to the door and I know from experience at least one of the cameras is pointing directly at my ass. Goddammit. My backside has become something of a fascination with the Charleston press ever since a female journalist—and I use the term "journalist" loosely—pointed out on live television that I'm carrying some extra "junk in the trunk." Now my butt is a local celebrity with its own Twitter account.

@DuPontBadonk. Whatever that means.

I'd never scrutinized my posterior before, but hell if I haven't been checking it more often in the mirror lately. It's not *large*, per se. It doesn't move or shake. The damn thing is hard as a rock, if I do say so myself. But it's...thick, I'd suppose one would say. And the squats I squeeze in at the gym four times a week only seem to make it worse.

Why am I thinking about my ass? My thoughts should be on the questions they continue to fire at me, but I find my mind drifting back to Addison's apartment. To the reprieve those four walls represented. Those over-the-top, Christmas-covered walls. My mouth lifts into a smile—genuine this time—thinking about the tree I discovered this morning. From far away, the ornaments looked innocent enough. Up close, though, they have little phrases painted on the blown glass spheres. *I came to Charleston and got a pair.*

Basically, lots of balls jokes. Turns out Addison's grandmother had a risqué sense of humor. My smile fades when I remember Addison talking about her grandmother last night. How she briefly dropped that mask of *I don't give two shits*. Also known as, the same look she had on her face when she dropped me off at my car this morning after taking me to the storage locker to get a box of clothes.

"See you when I see you, Captain."

I climb out of the Honda, leaving my forearms propped on the hood as I lean in to speak with Addison. "When do you reckon that will be?"

She gives me a sweet smile. "Probably on the news this morning."

"You'll be watching, will you?"

"Might take a glance."

An all-around sassy delivery, but I swear I catch the tremble of her chin. "Thanks for everything, Goose."

She stares straight ahead through the windshield. "Listen, I...I hope this doesn't cause you any trouble."

There it is. Not so sassy after all. "Even if it does cause me trouble, I'd still have taken that ride from you."

I'd closed the door before she could say something smart, earning myself a frown. For some strange reason, I'm still carrying that frown with me like a good luck charm as I open the door of City Hall. But something—maybe the fact that I know Addison is watching—compels me to stop and face the cameras. A move I definitely didn't plan. Based on the way the reporters go silent, they don't expect it, either. I might be a politician, but I'm not the kind that uses every opportunity in front of the camera to manufacture sound bites.

"I just wanted to say that I have no hard feelings toward Miss Clemons. She had to make a very tough decision and I hope she can be happy. Lord knows marriage to me probably would have exhausted a saint." I wait for the scribbling, chuckling and camera flashes to die down. "The woman who picked me up outside the church yesterday is a good Samaritan and friend. But just a friend. Yesterday was the first time I met her and I'm...well, I'm very glad I did. Thank you. You all have a fine day."

Questions go off behind me like bomb blasts as I climb the

curved, white stone steps and push through the double doors of City Hall. I intend to cut through the lobby and go straight upstairs, but that notion bounces like a bad check when I'm greeted by *everyone*. Every damn person who works in the building is standing in a big semi-circle, some of them holding flowers and stuffed animals.

"Bless your heart, Captain Du Pont. How are you feeling today?"

"You're going to be just fine, you hear me?"

"You've got no use for a wishy-washy woman. I say you dodged a bullet!"

"Can I have everyone's attention, please?" When mouths snap shut around me, I realize I'm using my captain's tone, but maybe it's for the best. If I don't handle this correctly right now, I'm going to be living with the fallout of yesterday forever. "I appreciate everyone's concern. Truly, I do. But where do you think I'm going to get enough vases to hold all these flowers?"

"My wedding gift was a vase. A nice, crystal one," someone offers, before promptly turning pink and ducking behind a co-worker. "Never mind. Sorry."

"I'm sure it was very nice." I clear my throat. "Now, please. Take those stuffed animals home to your children and grandchildren. I wouldn't know what to do with one."

"They're meant to comfort."

"Yes. I understand. But I'm doing just fine, everyone. Just fine." I put myself back in Addison's kitchen last night when she asked me what *I* want. How I thought returning to work, muscling down and pretending the last twenty-four hours never happened would be impossible. Somehow it feels possible right now.

Last night was the first time I've ever shut off the noise

around me and let myself think. Be. Maybe I can do it again right now, though. I can focus on what I need to do to move forward, instead of dwelling on the fact that I've essentially been abandoned in front of my entire address book. Weirdly, though, I don't...feel abandoned. Standing there in the middle of my campaign staff and employees, I realize half of me stayed behind in the glow of Christmas lights. In the quiet buzz of silence when they shut off. "The election is in two months. We have a lot of work to do between now and then. Can't afford any distractions, can we?"

"No, Captain."

"That's right. Now if you'll excuse me, I have to meet with the current mayor. He gets cranky when kept waiting." I move through the sea of bodies, smiling at some of the older women who look utterly heartbroken on my behalf. "There's a lot of unopened liquor that didn't get used yesterday. If we win the election, we'll break it out at the afterparty. How does that sound?"

A cheer goes up and I use that opportunity to leave the main lobby, taking the stairs up two flights and rounding the corner into my father's corner office.

After returning from overseas, I ran for city council and I've been holding a position ever since. But I've been performing mayoral duties in an unofficial capacity for over a year now. More or less, my father just comes to the office to fundraise and reminisce about days gone by with the older councilmembers. His corner office has been offered to me on more than one occasion, but I refuse to take it until I win the seat.

The faint smell of cinnamon and coffee greets me first, letting me know my father has just finished his usual breakfast of steel-cut oatmeal. On his office television, the footage rolls of me walking into the building, just minutes ago, my voice mingling with laughter. My father is turned to the side with both feet propped on his desk, hand poised on his glasses as he views the screen. Ten years ago, the optometrist informed him he needed assistance to see, but he still keeps those fingers locked around one side, as if he'll rip them off at any minute and transform into Superman. As the longest-sitting mayor in Charleston history, a lot of this town believes him to be a caped hero. I do, too, some of the time. But it takes a shrewd man to hold any political office for so long—and my father is no exception.

Standing near the television with hands clasped behind his back is Preston. He's been working with my father for the last four years, starting as a part-time consultant before being promoted to full-time advisor. With the upcoming transition taking place of late, he's become more of a glorified errand boy for my parents...and there's something about him that makes me exercise caution. There's an assumption on my father's part that I'm going to hire Preston after the election, but I don't think Preston has made that same assumption. There's an unaddressed tension between him and me, and he's clearly aware of it. Seems to even enjoy it somewhat.

My theory is partly confirmed when Preston seems poised to comment on the television footage, but notices me in the doorway first and shuts his mouth. "I'll leave you to it, Mr. Mayor," he says to my father, passing me with a nod. "Captain Du Pont."

"Preston."

The advisor closes the door on his way out and I continue into the office. "Well played, son," my father says, using the remote to turn off the television. "A little more grief in front of the cameras wouldn't have gone amiss, but the public will want a resilient mayor. Not someone who takes to bed over some woman."

"She wasn't some woman. She was going to be my wife." Even as I defend Naomi, I can't even remember our last conversation. Or if I kissed her last night after the rehearsal dinner. None of it. I'm sure once I have some time and perspective, those things will come back to me, but right now, I'm coming up blank. I clear my throat. "How is Mom?"

"Miffed as hell. You know how she likes playing hostess." My father lets his feet drop from the desk and sends me a smirk. "I suppose she's a little worried about you, too."

Guilt turns over in my chest. "I'll give her a call to let her know I'm fine."

He drops his chin, sending his voice down into a lower register. "We'll give this a month to settle, then we'll find you someone else. A new love interest that plays well with voters." Two fingers lift to massage the bridge of his nose. "People care less and less about the issues these days. A blossoming romance will keep their interest."

This suggestion does not come as a shock to me. Some of my first memories are of being thrown up on my father's shoulders for a photo opportunity. Protecting one's persona is the nature of the beast in politics. My father served in the army, like me, and has dedicated his life to what he believes will better this town, though. This city runs in his veins and he's been the face of recovery after storms, perseverance through tragedy. To a casual observer of this conversation, he comes across as callous and self-serving—and maybe he is, on occasion. After all, he's a politician. But he's a man who is passionate about public service. And oatmeal.

In two month's time, I'm the front-runner to take his place in this very office. At sixty-five, he could probably go on serving for another decade, but my mother is tired of the long hours he works and wants to travel. She also wants grandbabies, which is on hold for a while, since I'm an only child and freshly jilted. My father expects me to pick up exactly where he leaves off. To lead Charleston the way he's done, without deviating.

Part of me wonders if it's worth the inevitable battle and disappointment if I do things my own way. My father is a member of the proverbial old boys' club. There's a spot waiting for me there, too. Do I want to take it, though? Taking it means favors, funding, deals made at the country club. Traditions as old as time, but not ones that make a real difference.

Addison's frown creeps back into my head. If I told her I had fresh new ideas that I was on the fence about introducing, what would she say? More than likely, she would probably threaten to dump soup on my head. Again. For just a couple seconds, I let myself remember the glow of the Christmas lights and Addison's voice at my shoulder. If I'd gotten married yesterday, I never would have known such a unique person and place existed. That thought causes an uncomfortable flattening in my stomach.

"You're on board with the new love interest idea?"

"I think you know I'm not," I respond, unable to keep the weariness out of my tone. "You didn't marry my mother for appearances' sake."

"*I* got lucky." He picks up the remote control and taps it on the desk. "We can't all find a diamond in the rough, though. You'll meet another girl like Naomi. Good upbringing, looks, class. She'll give you a comfortable life and respectability." A pregnant pause starts a tingle at the back of my neck. "That girl you left with yesterday will give you none of those things, so I hope you scratched the itch."

Black edges into my vision. "Excuse me?"

"If you were seeing Addison Potts while you were engaged to Naomi, I don't want to know about it. Didn't get a good look at her yesterday, but some of your mother's friends did. Urges are a powerful thing, son. Especially if she grew up to look anything like her mother." He sets down the remote with a firm clunk. "But seeing a woman like her again will lead to political ruin. If the press is suspicious now, just wait until they dig up the past. They'll pounce on the fact that she's a relation to the Clemons family. Eventually there will be uncomfortable questions about who fathered her. It could go national."

"First of all, I'm not living my life for the press. Second, don't refer to Addison as a woman *like her*." My hands curl around the chair arms and squeeze. "What the hell does that even mean?"

"Careful, Elijah. You were less offended when I called Naomi *some woman*."

The truth of that is like a bucket of cold water to the face. Jesus. My father is trying to be helpful and I'm ready to go a round over a perceived insult. Over a girl I've known for one day. Letting go of the chair, I stand up and pace to the window, looking out over the church-steepled skyline. "Yesterday was the first time I met her. I didn't know she was Naomi's…cousin."

My father sits back. "All right, that's good. There's probably some way to prove that."

"She was in New York until a couple of weeks ago."

"Already have someone working on gathering dates and details."

I grit my teeth to keep from demanding he call off his efforts. Addison just lost her grandmother and had her life transplanted in a new town. Any kind of investigation or media interest could disrupt it even more. "I want them off her trail. I want her left alone."

"Then you better do the same."

CHAPTER FIVE

Addison

Look at me. So firm, juicy & mayoral. You want this.
A vote for Du Pont is a vote for this sweet, sweet junk, girl.
—Twitter @DuPontBadonk

I HEFT THE sack of puff paints and ribbons onto my shoulder and lumber up the stairs, attempting to slip my apartment key out of my shorts. There is one thing I didn't consider when I took over Jingle Balls from my grandmother. Eventually we would run out of merchandise. Including myself, there are two employees. I take the weekday shifts. Darlene, a college student transplant from Virginia, does nights. And an elderly gent named Terry with a fondness for mesh tank tops handles weekends.

When the supplies started to run low, I called everyone in for a meeting, only to be informed my grandmother did all of the designing herself. *Where?* I'd asked, in a hysterical, high-pitched voice. To which I was greeted by identical shrugs. I returned home that same evening to find the guest room closet packed to the rafters with tubs of glitter, hooks, bulbs, paint, ceramic statues and price tags. An entire vocation crammed inside an advertisement for the Container Store. Of course this is the *one* closet I hadn't opened yet.

As I sat in the wobbly metal chair in Jingle Balls, inventory thinning around me, I had to make a decision. Do I shut the operation down and bail? Go back to Brooklyn and hope my stabilized apartment hasn't been rented out yet (keep dreaming)? Or do I get my ass in gear and start making some fucking decorations?

Sitting on the floor of my bedroom learning how to operate a hot glue gun on that first night, I started thinking. My grandmother was an ambitious woman. A woman who wanted the whole wide world decorated for the happiest time of the year twelve months out of twelve. It surprised me that she was happy confining those dreams to Jingle Balls. What if she *hadn't* been happy with it, though? What if she'd wanted to expand and never got the chance?

That question has remained with me all week and the more I create, the more I'm infected by the holiday spirit I used to have—in grudging teenage fashion—when my grandmother was still alive. I've even started having these crazy, ridiculous daydreams about a decorating business. Store windows, residential houses, municipal buildings. December would be a mad rush, but wouldn't it be satisfying to decorate an entire town?

Whoa there, I'd told myself. *Learn to operate a glue gun first.*

Once I did that, the rest came easier, until creating the decorations became fun. And before I knew it, there was enough inventory to last another two or three weeks at the market. Meaning...*I* would be staying at least another two or three weeks.

But my decision to stay in Charleston had nothing to do with Elijah.

Nothing.

I haven't seen him since the morning I dropped him off at the storage locker, anyway, and the message is loud and clear. We were a one-night stand. Of friendship. Even though I expected nothing from him, his impromptu press conference outside City Hall set loose a little bubble of hope inside me. It floated and floated for days, before popping. It turns out he wasn't that glad he met me, after all.

"Need some help, Goose?"

I lurch to a stop and lose my balance, the heavy bag stealing my center of gravity. Oh God. Trying to compensate for the sudden lack of stability, I drop my purchases, but that doesn't stop me from falling backwards down the stairs.

Wow. That was fast. I'm going to die.

Only I don't, because I land in a pair of strong arms. The man they're attached to doesn't even budge. But when I tip my head back to look at his face, he's white as a ghost. "Ah, Addison. Sugar, you okay?" He throws a glance over his shoulder. "I thought you saw me when you pulled up and you were just ignoring me."

"I didn't," I rasp. "I d-didn't see you."

His mighty exhale blows my hair around. "I'm sorry."

How long am I going to lie here like a stoner watching infomercials? It's just that…he looks so handsome. And tired. There's weight underneath his chocolate eyes I don't remember from before. The circles do nothing to detract from his innate sincerity, though. *Too long. You've been staring too long. Plus you haven't heard from him in a week.* "Um." I wiggle until he sets me down. "No, I don't need any help. Thanks."

I stoop down to pick up the fallen bag, but Elijah beats me to it. "You're cross with me."

"No, I'm not." Ignoring his tilted head and furrowed brow, I turn and stomp up the remainder of the stairs. "In order to be cross with you, you would have to disappoint me in some way. Which implies I had some kind of expectation. And I." Insert apartment key. Jiggle it. Open the door. "Did not."

Elijah follows me inside, setting the bag down on the kitchen table. "Cross."

"Don't smile when I'm frowning at you."

"I can't help it. It confuses me, too."

God, I can smell him on me. Different from his wedding day. Less menthol aftershave, more eucalyptus and masculine bite. Like he's been outside in the sun and his sweat wore off the freshness of his morning shower a little. It's annoyingly amazing. Addictive. They could bottle the aroma, call it *Eau de Elijah* and it would fly off shelves. "What are you doing here?"

"Explaining where I've been."

"I didn't expect you to come back."

"Yes, you did." He pulls a newspaper out of his back pocket and tosses it on the table. "I'm about to be one hundred percent truthful with you. It might make you even angrier—"

"That's a safe bet."

"But I'm not going to lie on top of cutting and running." My throat is too tight to respond, so I just shrug and wait for him to continue. "There was a lot of curiosity about you, Addison. It's not typical behavior from me to jump into a car with a stranger. They wanted to know the timeline of our relationship. And I didn't want them bothering you, so I nudged them in the right direction. New York. My whereabouts since you arrived. They spent a lot of time trying to put us in the same place at the same time, but they couldn't."

For the last week, I've been positive he never thought about me once. I guess I was wrong. This man—one of the most influential, powerful men in Charleston—is standing in my cheesetastic holiday-themed apartment, taking up space with his big personality and bigger shoulders, looking totally contrite.

He's spent the last week tidying up a clusterfuck I sent into motion by playing his getaway driver…and he's worried about *my* anger? A girl whose career path now includes the manufacturing of reindeer testicle ornaments. "I'm waiting for the part where I get upset."

"There's an article in today's newspaper titled 'The Captain's Getaway Girl.' It could have been worse. If they'd found some proof we'd been…"—he clears his throat, hands tucking into his pants—"…messing around, it would have made the front page. As it is, there's only a short interest piece on page three. Somehow they've missed the family connection between you and Naomi— I'm guessing because of the different last names and the fact that your two sides aren't close. Unfortunately, they *do* know you work at the market now."

I snatch up the paper and flip to the correct page. "Oh wow. I should have listened to my teachers. The internet really is forever."

"For what it's worth, Goose, you look very nice."

"Elijah, I'm doing limbo in stripper heels."

"I guess at one time you had more than four pairs of shoes."

I shoot him a look and go back to the article. "This is insane. They even interviewed my landlord in Brooklyn."

"It's a good thing this place is still listed under your grandmother's name or they would have tracked you here. Still could happen, too." He scrubs at the back of his neck. "I'm sorry."

"I'm the one that picked you up," I mumble, setting the newspaper down. "It's fine."

A smile tilts his lips. "I like it when you forget to be mean to me."

My words are horrifyingly breathy when I say, "I never forget. I'm just keeping you on your toes." I swallow a golf ball. "And anyway, since they mentioned Jingle Balls, this whole thing kind of scored me some free advertising. Joke's on them."

He laughs, casting a glance down the front of his body. "Guess I didn't need to wear my protective cup, after all."

"Oh, you were expecting a knee to the nuts?"

"More than one, in fact."

Flipping my hair back and cocking a hip comes as natural as breathing. "That'll teach you to try and predict me next time."

"I want to move in here." When I start to choke on a cough, Elijah raises an eyebrow. "You're not the only one who's unpredictable."

What is happening here? Am I being pranked? Yes. That has to be it. This rich, future mayor of a major city does not want to live in my prehistoric two-bedroom. "Very funny."

He opens his mouth to say more, but closes it and drops into one of the dining room chairs. "I know it could never work, but damn. I've only been here a few minutes and..."

"And what?"

A few beats pass as he regards me across the table. "When I spent the night last week, that's the most normal I've ever felt. No pressure. No campaign talk or reminders of the greatness that came with my father and *must* come after. It was like I shed the job for just a little while and it was easier to concentrate the next day. To see this path in front of me clearly—the way *I* want it to look." His head lifts, dining room light caressing his shoulders, those deep brown eyes holding me hostage. "You're part of it, Addison. You treat me like what I am, not what you think I should be. I appreciate that kind of friendship."

Oh God. I need to tell him. He needs to know being his friend isn't as easy for me. I have a fascination with him that definitely wouldn't go away if he was sleeping across the hallway.

Tell him. Or...I keep my mouth shut. I don't utter the truth, because the prospect of him showering in my bathroom and eating in my kitchen is being paired with your crush in science lab, multiplied by one thousand. What if his laugh was a fixture inside these walls? There wouldn't be any more uncertainty if I'll ever see him again. Or if he'll remember me.

He wants me to be his friend, though. After what he just said, it's obvious he really needs one. I find myself wanting to be that for him. Almost as much as I want him to lay me across this table, unzip his pants and fill me. "It wouldn't be a good idea," I say, skirting around the table to sit down beside him, firmly ignoring the electricity that races over my skin. "If the press lost their minds when I gave you a ride, imagine if you moved in here. There would be a riot. Especially when they find out I'm related to Naomi."

"And you'd be the target. That's what's stopping me."

"That, and I haven't invited you." I look down my nose at him, as if my heart isn't fluttering in my ribcage. Was he this protective of Naomi when they were together? If so, how could she have left him? I shake the thoughts free and focus on the improbable conversation. Elijah wants to *live* here. "What would be in it for me?"

In what seems like an unconscious move, Elijah leans back and loosens the knot of his tie, a smile playing around his mouth. "Hadn't thought about it, but I suppose I could help you carry heavy bags up the stairs. You have to admit, you're a little clumsy."

I gasp. "Only when scary politicians leap out of the shadows."

"I think you mean charming."

My laugh won't stay put. It comes flying right out of me. "It's just as well it could never work, because I'm turning your room into a Christmas ornament assembly line." I gesture to the bag. "Today's haul from the craft store is only the beginning. Turns out, I can't just show up and be a market vendor. I need things to vend."

His attention shifts to the closest Christmas tree. "Your grandmother was making everything by hand?"

"That's the long and short of it."

"Better write that down." He winks at me. "There's a balls joke in there somewhere."

"Oh, just move in," I blurt.

Elijah tilts his head. "What was that?"

This is his fault. He had to go and be smart and gorgeous and funny, all at the same time. I was doing so well, enumerating reasons why him sharing my apartment would never work. But right now, in the perfect ease between us, I can't imagine him leaving. Especially now that I know this place makes him happier. That…*I* make him happier. As a friend. *Only* a friend. "I was just thinking…maybe we could get around the press if you only stay occasionally. When you need a break from everything you have going on." I roll a shoulder. "No one has to know you're here. They don't know you're here now, do they?"

"No."

"There you go."

Wheels crank behind his narrowed eyes. "We shouldn't have to keep a friendship secret, dammit."

His hand is resting on the table and I want to slide mine beneath it, so I tuck it under my thigh. It's symbolic of what our relationship will be like. Hiding. Such a perfect parallel to the past, to my mother, I want to scream.

For the first time in my life, I understand her actions. I understand common sense taking a back seat to literally everything else. Pulse, heart, scents, sight. A week ago, I didn't think there was a person alive on this planet capable of making me humble myself. He more than exists, though. He's telling me he wants to exist *with* me. Not in the way my body and heart are craving, but it's something. It's something where *nothing* was before.

I've been living in the shadow of my mother's poor choices. Men are a novelty to me. With every one I've enjoyed and discarded, I've been proving to myself I'm not her. That I'm better and smarter. My eyes are open. I didn't realize how empty my actions left me until Elijah spent one single night in my apartment. He filled a space I didn't know was available. Maybe it wasn't available at all until I saw him standing at the altar. Whatever the timing, the idea of letting this chance pass leaves me anxious, the specter of emptiness opening a pit in my stomach. This situation is going to hurt no matter what I do, isn't it?

"There *are* reasons you staying here would have to be a secret and you know it. They won't believe we're friends. And I'm not Naomi. I'm already seen as the tipsy girl in the newspaper wearing six-inch heels. Not suitable for the potential mayor. Ergo, potential mayor makes bad decisions."

"No." His jaw is harder than I've ever seen it. "That's hogwash."

"Watch your mouth." We share a flat smile and I stand, throwing my hair back. "You don't have to decide now. But if you're staying tonight, you're cooking. I'm not running a charity."

My heart is in my throat as I leave the room, taking the bag of supplies with me and stowing it under my bed. I stand in the still, dark room for long seconds, listening, listening so carefully I can hear the dull thread of buzz in the silence. I don't realize I've been holding my breath until I hear the clink of pots and pans coming from the kitchen.

I've either just made the best decision of my life or the worst. Only time will tell.

CHAPTER SIX

Elijah

Getaway Girl tight-lipped on her way into the Market.
Association with Captain Du Pont over?
—*Charleston Post*

"PASS THE GLUE gun." Without looking, I pinch the blue handle between my fingers and dangle it in Addison's direction. "There'y'go."

"Hold on." She squints down at the wiggly eyeball she's placing on an abominable snowman ornament. "Now I know why my grandmother always wore a wrist brace. At this rate, I'm going to get carpal tunnel before I turn thirty."

"Art is worthy of the suffering that yields it. Isn't that the saying?"

"It must have been coined before bedazzling was invented." She tilts her head at the placement, nods and takes the glue gun. "How is your St. Bernard Santa coming along?"

I go back to tying a red bow around the figurine's neck, but my fingers don't want to cooperate. "Considering this is my ninth attempt?"

"It's not like fashioning a Windsor knot, huh?"

"No, ma'am. Necessity forced me to get that technique down early."

A smile ghosts across her mouth. "When you get it right once, it'll come easier." She's quiet a moment. "You sound grim. Another fundraiser tonight?"

"Yeah. Glue gun, please."

Addison passes me the hot tool, jerking back when I accidentally brush our fingers together. "You shocked me," she mutters. "I, um. There's a key on the dresser in your room. If it's late and you don't want to crash at the hotel, just let yourself in."

Taken by surprise, my head comes up so I can search Addison's face, but she's busy cutting a swath of black felt to make claws for her evil snowman. "Thanks, Goose. You didn't have to do that."

Addison shrugs. "I was sick of you knocking at all hours and waking me up."

I keep right on smiling at her until she looks up and acknowledges it.

She rolls her eyes.

Not a rare occurrence—her exasperation with me—but I enjoy it every damn time. Since my thwarted wedding, everyone walks around me on broken glass. Or they take the tough love tactic, slapping me on the back and telling me to get back in the saddle. Plenty of fish in the sea, old boy. Make hay while the sun shines. The world is your oyster, son. I've lost track of the bad platitudes and veiled hints to get back on the dating market. I've even been contacted by two national magazines about appearing in their Most Eligible Bachelors issues.

I'd rather lick mud off a pig's behind.

Over the last couple weeks, Addison's place has become where I get my dose of normalcy. I was only supposed to spend the night here once in a while, but it turned out to be more like five nights out of seven. Probably would be the full seven, if the campaign didn't keep me working through the night on occasion. I let reporters follow me home, wait a couple hours, then quietly sneak out the side entrance to meet my Uber driver, Paul. In exchange for pretending I'm just another passenger, Paul now has a fancy permit that allows him to park for free anywhere he pleases within city limits. I'm not proud of myself for being unethical, but I can't find it in me to be sorry, either.

Addison doesn't ask me about poll numbers. Doesn't tiptoe around me or ask me *what's next*. What's next for the future mayor of Charleston? Has heartbreak affected his candidacy? Has he sworn off love forever? It's so easy between us, I wonder where I'd be if she hadn't shown up outside the church. There are times when I look over at this girl who keeps me company—sometimes until the early hours of the morning—and I *can't help* noticing she's incredibly gorgeous. Tonight is the first time I've seen her in these emerald-green pajamas with the pocket and I want to compliment her on them, but she'd probably tell me to shut up.

And that's why I ignore how she looks. How she…smells and smiles and thinks. I don't want to disrupt this flow. I like having this friend who wants nothing from me other than cooking on Tuesdays, Thursdays and Saturdays. I like her telling me to shut up and griping at me for showing up unannounced. No one else treats me the way she does. And…hell, I'm not so sure I *haven't* sworn off love.

That's the truth of it. I haven't heard from Naomi since she left me the note and blew off our wedding. Shouldn't I be more upset about that? Shouldn't I be going over every second of our time together, trying to figure out where things went wrong? Love is supposed to be this powerful, compelling feeling and I'm starting to think I'm useless at it. I *can* be a friend, though. I can be a friend to Addison without disappointing her or blurring the lines of this perfect thing we have.

Yes, Addison is a head turner with a great sense of humor. Yes, sometimes I sniff her hair while she's cooking at the stove. Or find myself swallowing over the smooth lines of her neck. Noticing how incredible she is doesn't preclude me from being her friend, though. This friendship is untouched by the chaos of my life. It's separate and preserved, it makes me happy—and I'm *not* going to mess with it.

"You know what would be crazy?"

I glance up from my task to find Addison biting her lip and mimic her without realizing right away, as if wondering what it would feel like. "If you made us another round of grilled cheeses?" I say, shaking myself. "Sometimes crazy is the way to go."

"Good God. I'm convinced your stomach has a trap door."

"Is that a yes?" She shakes her head and goes back to working. "What were you really going to say, Goose?"

"Never mind."

Something shifts in my gut. "It was important and I just made it about food, didn't I?"

"No." But I can tell by the way her shoulders climb up around her ears that she's downplaying. "Not important."

"Not important, but crazy." I survey the completed projects around us in various stages of drying. "You're thinking of expanding."

She sucks in a breath, the materials falling from her hands. "How did you know?"

My sixth sense dings. I've just stepped in something. Could be a land mine or a stroke of luck. "I was going to say, you're thinking of expanding from ball joke ornaments to incorporate female anatomy jokes, too." She purses her lips. "Okay. That wasn't it."

"I mean, it's not a *bad* idea. Boobies would definitely draw the male clientele to the booth, which has definitely been lacking."

Forget I said anything.

I almost make the confusing comment out loud, but swallow it. "You meant expanding the business, didn't you?"

Addison hesitates a few seconds before nodding once. "Yeah. Like maybe the occasional store window or…for people who don't have time to decorate their homes for Christmas. Maybe even other holidays, like Halloween or Independence Day. I was thinking I could put together a website, put out flyers at Jingle Balls. You know, just to gauge interest."

It's important. And she's been thinking about expanding for a while, but might be afraid to make a big deal out of it. She won't look at me, either. Addison has this way of staring me straight in the eye, like she can't help being challenging and wants to break me. I haven't totally figured it out yet. But it's impossible to ignore the fact that she's self-conscious about this idea. "Is this something you want to do? Or is it more of a way to honor your grandmother?"

I've got her attention on me again—and it's a kick in the ribs, because I've surprised her. "Both." She rubs her palms on her thighs. Not that I'm noticing her thighs. "Before I left for New York, I enjoyed this, too. We enjoyed it together. Year-round Christmas. Somehow I forgot." Her laugh is more high pitched than usual. "Even if it's based on dick jokes."

That kick in my ribs grows more intense. "You should do it. Look how fast you picked up an entire business without letting it skip a beat." My hand lifts to reach out, to touch her in some way, but I force it back down. "It's a great idea, Addison."

She opens her mouth to say something, but snaps it closed. "You have some glitter on your nose," she mumbles, throwing a plastic pouch of baby wipes at me. "Doofus."

I make a show of wiping everywhere but my nose. "Did I get it?"

"Yep," she answers breezily. "You got it."

We laugh and go back to work.

I WALK OUT of the bedroom to find Addison stretching. In leggings and a bra.

A danger siren blares in my head and I turn on a heel, returning to my room like the hounds of hell are after me. Fine, it takes me a few ungentlemanly seconds to get moving—and when I do, I can't see anything but pink, but I manage.

"Elijah?" Her husky voice stops me in my tracks. "You're up early."

I glance down at the front of my pants. *No kidding.*

Morning wood. That's all it is. I'm not turning harder than steel for Addison.

"Yeah." Clearing the rust from my voice, I make sure my shirt is providing coverage and move in a slow, funeral shuffle back toward the hallway. And yup. I didn't imagine it. Addison has one leg pulled up to her butt, causing her back to arch. There's no way to avoid looking at her breasts. They're lifted up and swelling over the neck of her bra, a tiny mole winking back from the right one. "Where are you going?"

"My run. I'm usually back before you get up." She switches to the other leg. "You want to come with me?"

"You go out running like that?"

Her eyebrows draw together. "Like what?"

I sidestep the landmine. "Early."

Suspicious. The lady is suspicious. "So? Do you want to come?"

"Actually, we've got a gym at City Hall. I usually hit it after work or on my lunch break, but you conked out early on me last night, so..."

"You're the one who made me watch *Meet the Press.*" With a saucy wink, she bends forward at the waist and hoists her ass in the air, tight and separated into two perfect buns. A groan climbs my throat, but I swallow it down. Not good. I usually handle my business quickly and quietly in the shower. Or at night while Addison is safely in her own bedroom. I'm not a man who needs to stroke off ten times a day. It's more of a stress reliever and I've managed to keep the object of my fantasies faceless. Hell, I always have. Using a woman's image without her say so makes me feel too guilty afterward. Right now, though, with my cock straining under the waistband of my gray sweatpants, I know I'm doomed to picture Addison winking and bending over for me the next time. There's no help for it.

"You're the one who taped it for me," I rasp.

She straightens, bouncing her tits around in the pink bra. "What?

"*Meet the Press.* You're the one who tapes it." Addison is looking at me funny, so I soldier on. "Anyway, I woke up before my alarm. Figured I'd head to the gym this morning, instead of this afternoon."

"Or you could come running with me."

I could. I *want* to. I don't relish the idea of her out running in that bra alone, looking like she does. I don't like it at all. But I can't very well ask her to wait ten minutes while I jack off, can I? And there isn't a hope in hell of me running with this thing throbbing between my legs.

None of that matters, though, because Addison ducks her head. "Never mind. I...wasn't thinking. Of course you can't come running with me." She laughs under her breath. "I haven't had my coffee yet."

She's right. Being seen together would only start the gossip mill churning. It would put her in the line of fire with the press when they've only begun to lose interest in a possible relationship between us. Right now, it's early in the morning. They would know for certain we'd spent the night in the same place. That being said, I really don't like being responsible for her disappointed half smile as she ties her shoes. "I try not to run in public anyway."

It's out of my mouth before I can stop myself. Addison quirks a brow. "Why not?"

This was a bad idea. I can't operate when half my brain cells have relocated to my groin. "No reason." I cross my arms and look stern. "Do you carry pepper spray?"

"Yes. And a miniature knife disguised like a key." She takes a loose-hipped step in my direction, and the other half of my brain cells join their friends. "What's this about not running in public?"

"Addison, drop it."

"No. It's weird."

"Well now I *really* want to tell you." She watches me and waits with a rare patience. "It's my ass. When I run outdoors, they...for some odd reason...like to photograph it. There might even be a..." I have to sigh. "...a slow-motion GIF floating around somewhere on the internet."

The silence carries for one beat, two, until Addison bursts into laughter. "Holy shit. I was not expecting that." And just like I should have anticipated before opening my idiot mouth, she circles around behind me, hands linked together beneath her chin—a kid on Christmas morning—but I turn in time to evade her.

She gasps and follows. "I just realized you always untuck your dress shirt before walking in my front door. Have you been hiding a GIF-worthy ass from me, Elijah Montgomery Du Pont?"

"Addison Potts, this conversation is indecent."

"I'm an indecent kind of girl."

I frown at her. "You most certainly are not."

She tosses her hair. "How would you know?"

That question distracts me long enough for her to get around the back of me. I'm so distracted, actually, wondering if Addison was referring to her sex life, I don't try to stop her when she lifts the back hem of my T-shirt and…growls. She *growls*.

"Elijah…it's glorious."

"People usually reserve that tone for the Sistine Chapel."

"Not even Michelangelo could have pulled this off."

The press has been fascinated by my ass since I ran for my first government position and my reaction has always been mild annoyance. Confusion. Fine, maybe some self-consciousness. Honestly, it's just a butt. Get over it. Everyone has one and they're all shaped differently. My reaction to Addison essentially whispering in awe over it…that's quite another story. And it shouldn't be. We should have a laugh about this and go our separate ways for the day. Just like usual. Just like friends do.

My cock is heavy and uncomfortable, though, and it has more than a little bit to do with her breath on my back, her fingers brushing my spine. Knowing she likes what she sees is not helping my situation whatsoever, either. Especially not while she's wearing a bra and leggings.

"Addison—"

"May I?"

"May you what?"

"Just a teeny tiny squeeze? It's so thick but it looks *rock hard.*"

I grit my teeth and breathe through my nose. "Christ."

"Your ears are red." A floorboard creaks as she steps closer, her voice softening. "You're actually insecure about it, aren't you?"

Maybe. But not right now. I can't think of anything but my immortal erection and how she'd be confused about what's between us if she saw it. She'd think I want more. Right now in this moment, more is obviously what my body wants, too. But we'd regret it afterward.

"Is that a hard no on the squeezing?"

She starts to lower my shirt and hear myself rasp, "No. Go ahead."

Big mistake. Her palms slide down over both curves, fingers splayed and my balls tighten. Hard. "Oh my God," she breathes, gripping me, fingertips digging in deep. "I'm your friend, Elijah. I wouldn't lie to you, all right?" Her hands slide down, down and she lifts me, warm breath casting over the middle of my back— and are those her breasts brushing me ever so slightly? *Jesus.* I'm still as a statue but I'm chaos on the inside. *She's your friend. Pull your shit together.* "When people stare at you here? They either want to sink their teeth into it. Or they're just jealous. Own it."

I'm in the process of turning around with no idea of my game plan—I'm not going to kiss her, am I? I can't—when Addison drops my shirt and breezes past me with a bright smile, her own backside twitching side to side in the black, shiny material. "Catch you later, Captain."

I'm relieved when the door closes behind her. Right?

Yes. No. Not sure. I'm not sure of anything as I stride to my bedroom and kick the door closed behind me. It's rattling on the hinges when I shove a hand into my sweatpants and wrap a fist around my hard-on. "*Ohhhhh fuck,*" I grit out, my body hunched over the bed, left hand planted there to keep me standing, my right fist pumping in a blur. I only make it about two seconds before I think of Addison turning around to present her ass, asking me in her smoky voice to return the favor and squeeze her back. "Bad girl *bad girl,*" I pant, biting down on my lip and drawing blood as fantasy Addison tugs down those leggings and presses the side of her face to the mattress. "Ah God, looks so tight."

Touching you made me all wet, Captain. Use it to slide inside.

Guilt trickles in, but in the unbelievably worked up state I'm in, my cock only swells under my heavy conscience. *Shouldn't be doing this. Shouldn't be thinking of her like this.*

No amount of self-loathing can keep me from coming, though, and I give a close-mouthed roar as white liquid fountains up into my hand and rolls down my knuckles, wrist and fingers. And still I keep going, falling to my left elbow while my right one works my flesh in rough jerks. It's like my insides are relocating, my muscles snapping and growing under the strain. Easily the best orgasm I've had in…years. Longer. I can't ever remember coming this fucking *hard.*

Moments later, I turn and sit on the bed, breathing like I just ran a marathon. "God, you're a bastard."

I'm late for work, because I have no choice but to launder the comforter, not to mention make a call to the head of security at City Hall. I wasn't aware of Addison's morning runs and I don't like her out there alone. And when I go shopping for our dinner that night, I practically buy out the whole cereal aisle and stock her cabinets full of them before she knows I've arrived. Not the best sorry-I-jerked-off-while-thinking-of-you in the world, but a verbal one? In this case, it's not an option. How would I begin to explain anyway?

I have a friend. A completely platonic, non-romantic one.

But occasionally I rub one out to her.

Cereal it is.

CHAPTER SEVEN

Addison

Want the secret to getting your dream booty?
Captain Du Pont inspires new all-cereal diet craze.
Click for details.
—TheTea.com

HUMMING ALONG TO the Muzak version of "Take a Chance on Me," I toss a box of ziti into my shopping cart, allowing myself to smile since I'm alone in the aisle. I prefer fusilli over ziti, so Elijah and I switch our noodle every week. Thursdays we do pasta. I buy the ingredients, he does the cooking. It's my favorite night, because he overeats when we do Italian. While I clear the table, he lies on the couch and bemoans his lack of control, while loosening his belt. It's all so…domestic.

I'm domestic. Look at me. I'm in the supermarket with a purse full of coupons, excited about adding fresh basil to the mix. I used to get excited about dressing up or adding a pink streak to my hair. Now I have Pasta Thursdays.

Should it terrify me that I wouldn't trade it for the world?

Yeah. It should.

It has been a little over a month since Elijah became my nightly house guest, ducking in through my front door every evening wearing a low baseball cap and street clothes. Watching

the tension leak from his huge shoulders, his sigh mingling with
the sounds of Laura Marling...it has become an addiction. I'm
his safe place. Or my apartment is, rather. But I'm a part of it,
too.

We're friends. Best friends, even.

A best friend he hides away.

Ignoring the snarky voice in my head, I throw a hunk of
Parmesan cheese into my cart and leave the refrigerated aisle—

And I run smack into Elijah with my cart. "*Oh.*"

The moment is crackling with clarity, the edges of my surroundings sharp. I watch dread pass over Elijah's features, notice
the look he tosses over his shoulder. Girl. He's with a girl. My
stomach turns into a boiling pit of acid, inviting all of my organs
to drop down into the brew and get destroyed along with the rest
of me. I'm going to be sick. I'm going to be *sick*.

"Addison?" He tugs at the knot of his tie. "You shop here?"

"Not usually. I wanted to..." My hands flop around like
caught fish. How am I even saying words? "The other place
didn't h-have fresh basil..."

"Fresh, huh?" Surely I'm imagining the hint of a smile that
tugs at his mouth. "That's new."

"Yeah." Oh God, I've never felt like more of an idiot in my
life. When we're inside my apartment, talking about mundane
things like basil and favorite movies and childhood memories it
isn't strange at all. But under the bright lights of the supermarket,
talking about the new recipe I'm trying—for him—makes me feel
like a teenager sending a love letter to Theo James. Pathetic.
Especially if he's with a girl. "Maybe we should take a rain
check," I mutter, circling my cart full of food, fully prepared to
abandon it. "See you around."

He takes hold of my arm. "Wait a second, Goose."

I tug my limb free just in time to see the reporter following him. The man is older, wearing a bright blue windbreaker with a local news station logo over the breast. He's trying to be inconspicuous, even going so far as to scrutinize the back of a pretzel bag. But he's watching Elijah and me out of the corner of his eye. There's no doubt.

So...there's no girl. Elijah is on edge because there's a journalist following him.

And he doesn't want to be seen in the same place as me.

It was so easy to pretend we were keeping our friendship a secret because that's how we wanted it. Like it was our choice. But it's not. I'm a liability to this man's career. Worse, my mother's past and my lack of blue blood make me a liability to his respectability and standing in the community.

My pulse pounds in my temples. "Oh, right," I push past numb lips. The reporter lifts his cell phone and I turn away fast, already walking in the opposite direction. "You know what? I'll just go out the back. Make your own pasta."

Elijah's sigh of my name follows me up the aisle, but I don't look back.

He doesn't come over tonight, either.

Elijah

I'VE KNOWN MY friend Chris since we went through the Citadel together. Sophomore year, he started dating his now-wife, Lydia, so I've known her almost as long. Chris supported me when I returned from overseas and everything seemed unfamiliar, because he'd gone through the same thing after his own two tours of duty.

Because I grew up as the mayor's son, I had an easy inroad to popularity. When I was very young, I took that road, only to realize quickly there are two types of friends in this world. Those who become your friend thinking you'll give them an advantage. And friends who expect nothing but your honesty. For you to show up and have their back.

Chris and Lydia are good, solid friends and I don't have many, besides them and Addison. In my position, it's better to have acquaintances that don't expect me to compromise myself in the name of a favor and I'm more than good with that.

Chris, now a Charleston police officer, stood up as my best man at the wedding, their six-year-old daughter, Sonia—my goddaughter—all dressed up to be the flower girl. He's been suspicious as hell over me turning down dinner invitations, but he's been letting me slide on the excuse that I'm busy with the campaign. Lydia, not so much.

This afternoon she marched into my office and informed me I was coming over for dinner. All morning, I'd been too distracted to work, the words *make your own pasta*, ringing in my head like hourly church bells. But that's when the idea hit me.

I'll bring them to Addison's.

"Here we go, Sonia," I say, taking hold of the little girl's hand to guide her up the stairs. "I seem to recall your daddy telling me you love Christmas. Is that right?"

"Yes. I'm asking for a phone this year."

I glance back at Chris where's he's guiding his wife up the stairs. He shakes his head.

"Now why would you need a phone? Who are you going to call?"

"My friends' moms." She blinks up at me. "To set up play dates."

"I see. You're cutting out the middle man." I bite back a laugh. "Maybe I should give you a job in my office. You'd be able to afford your own phone."

"Mommy, can I?"

"Someday, maybe." Lydia catches up and flicks my ear. "Stop encouraging her."

"Sorry, ma'am," I say absently, noticing a shadow move beneath the door of the apartment. I'll be lucky if she didn't change the locks after last night. Until that moment in the supermarket, I'd managed to keep Addison stashed away in a box only I get to open. Then there she was. Standing right in front of me with her fresh basil, glitter-covered clothes and running sneakers. I'd been more panicked over sharing Addison with the world than I was about exposing a relationship between us, friendship or otherwise. She's my respite.

Christ. I've been a selfish prick to my best friend. A *worthy* friend would have escorted her to the checkout and paid for the groceries, compromising photos be damned. But I don't have the freedom to do that. I'm ten points ahead in the polls and my competitor continues to schedule press conferences and campaign door to door, neither of which are my strong suit. I'm focused on plans—big ones. Ones I think can bring change to a broader number of people in Charleston, instead of directing taxpayer money toward programs that have more than enough. I *want* to win this race. If I don't, necessary actions won't be taken to redirect resources where more people stand to benefit.

In addition to keeping the wheels moving on my campaign, my father is breathing down my neck, the press never leaves me alone—and I'm *not* dragging Addison into the storm.

I'm not losing her, either, though. By bringing my friends to meet her, I'm making her a part of my life. As much as I can without distracting or possibly jeopardizing the upcoming election. Or more importantly, bringing her every move under scrutiny.

"Now where exactly are you taking us, Elijah?"

I stop on the landing, waiting for the three of them to join me. "It's a little complicated." I take the keys out of my pocket, singling out the newest, shiniest one. "This is my friend Addison's place. You might remember her from—"

"The Getaway Girl?" Lydia asks, tucking a bottle of wine she brought underneath her arm. "From the newspaper?"

"Yes, she's…both of those things and none of them." I search for the words to explain who Addison is to me. And politician or not, I can't really find them. "Just meet her."

"Sure, man." Chris lays a hand on his wife's shoulder. "We trust you."

"Thanks." Until I slide my key into the lock, I don't consider that Addison could very well bash me over the head with a skillet for bringing company over without any notice. There's no time to change my mind, now, though. Frankly, I don't think I could leave and spend another night in my hotel room, either. This is where I want to be.

I open the door, just enough to make sure she's decent—and there she is. Standing in the doorway to the kitchen, the arch of one foot propped on the opposite knee, drinking a can of Diet Coke and looking bored. Wearing jeans and—thank God—not a sports bra and leggings. "Can I help you?"

"Hi, Goose." Already the strain of the day is melting off me. "Can this be one of those times you forget to be mean to me?"

"Yea'nope."

"Are you sure? It would make a little girl's Christmas."

Her frown makes me smile. "Are you drunk, Captain?"

"No, but I got that way last night. I had to."

She looks away, but not before I catch the softening around her eyes. "So whose Christmas am I ruining?"

I urge Sonia to peek through the door. "Hello," she says.

"Ah!" Addison jumps a good foot in the air. "What—you were serious? Whose kid is this?"

"Ours," answers Chris with a polite smile, pushing the rest of the door open and stepping past me to get inside. "Sorry for dropping in on you like this, Addison. The captain kidnapped us under the pretense he'd be buying us dinner."

Lydia steps forward and offers her hand. "Turns out he wanted to introduce you instead. I'm Lydia, this is my husband Chris. And you already met Sonia."

Appearing dumbfounded, Addison shakes her hand. "Nice to meet you." I watch in fascination as Addison shoves stray hairs into her ponytail and turns in a circle, bumping her hip off the wall. Oh…wow. I don't think I've ever seen her nervous. Not once. Something about it makes my throat ache. "I didn't go shopping. I was just going to eat Honey Bunches of Oats."

"Well, I'm in the mood for takeout anyway—" Lydia cuts herself off, her attention clearly arrested by the apartment's décor. "Oh. This is…eerily festive."

"Mom! Look!" Sonia skids to a halt near a row of freshly painted mailboxes, all of which say Letters to Santa in red and white stripes. "I can ask for my phone!"

"Um. Wait." Addison retreats into the kitchen and two seconds later, the apartment explodes with Christmas, lights flashing, "Carol of the Bells" playing, statues dancing. Chris and Lydia take a hasty step toward each other, as if under attack. When Addison comes back into view, she's waving a magnetic notepad I recognize from the fridge. On top, it says, "Dear Santa.

Here are my demands..." and each letter looks like it has been clipped from a different magazine or newspaper. One of Addison's biggest sellers these days—and an idea she came up with herself. "You can use this to write your wish list." She hands the notebook to Sonia. "I'm basically one of Santa's elves, so I'll make sure he gets it."

Sonia turns to her parents wide-eyed, then launches herself at Addison.

Addison's arms lift slowly to return the hug.

As quickly as the moment starts, it ends, Sonia running circles around the apartment to take everything in. Addison rubs hands down the sides of her jeans, shifting on the balls of her feet. She looks over at me and I'm caught. There's a sheen to her eyes and just like seeing her nervous, it throws me off, because it's so unlike her.

"I'm sorry," I mouth over the music, relief swamping me when she nods once.

I'm just beginning to wonder if there's something seriously wrong with my throat when Addison lifts her chin and waltzes past me, rolling me a look down her nose. "Well? You know where the takeout menus are, Captain. Make yourself useful."

Smiling like an idiot, I head for the living room side table, but I'm brought up short by Chris and Lydia's identical expressions. They're looking at me like I've just announced I'll be running for mayor of the moon.

"I'll go help Addison with plates," murmurs Lydia.

Chris jolts. "Yeah. I'll...make sure Sonia doesn't break anything."

Their sly smiles tell me what they're thinking. That only one bedroom in this apartment gets occupied at night. I can't even blame them for making that assumption. But I've been in love—

and I know what I have with Addison is even better. No one understands this thing between Addison and me. No one but us. And I'm just fine with that.

CHAPTER EIGHT

Addison

The all-cereal diet ruined my life: one woman's claim.
—Southern Insider News

I HOP OFF THE bus at the Meeting Street stop, picking up the pace once the disembarking passengers thin, everyone heading in their own direction, me zipping toward the market. It's a gorgeous April day—but it's a hot one. Businessmen amble past, fanning themselves with newspapers. Sidewalk vendors can't sell cold bottles of water fast enough—and it's only the morning. Still, I can't find it in me to complain. Not after last night.

Elijah brought his friends to meet me. I got angry with him and he...came through. Fixed it. Apparently he missed the memo that men are only supposed to make things worse.

Not only did he make this gesture and apologize, but I really liked his friends. Sonia with her adorable rambling and Lydia with her soothing wisdom voice. Chris watching them both like he's the luckiest man alive. And most of the time...I'm pretty sure I watched Elijah. It's hard not to on a regular basis, but throw in people he feels comfortable around and he's even more incredible. Halfway through our meal of Chinese takeout, I had to lock myself in the bathroom for a reality check. It was not a double date. No matter how much it felt like one, with Chris trying to embarrass Elijah by telling stories from their days at the Citadel. The way a friend might try to do in front of his friend's love interest.

I turn the corner and take a deep whiff of the boiled peanuts scent hanging in the air. Smelling them is almost as good as eating them, which is a good thing, because I'm too stuffed full of cereal to fit even one little peanut. For some reason, more and more boxes keep appearing in my cabinets and I can't resist that second bowl in the mornings.

Maybe the faux-date scenario is the reason I had a sex dream about Elijah last night.

In the dream, he blew into my apartment and didn't say a word, barely bothering to close the front door before shedding his tie. His eyes were hard, hungry. All of him was. I stood in the living room—naked as the day I was born. Exposed. Unable to breathe. He looked at me and knew everything. The feelings I've been suppressing with no success. How much I want him inside me, pinning me down, using me. One sweep of his eyes and he knew.

Dream Elijah reached me, now shirtless. So aggressively male and muscular and big all over. "Are you ready for your fuck?"

"Yes."

He ran a hand down his stomach. "Come and get it, sugar."

Even in sleep, I could feel my tether snap and I wasted no time unfastening his pants with shaking fingers and taking out his waiting erection. I climbed him, whimpering and sobbing, sinking down onto his rigid inches while he watched me, his lips curled in a cocky way. For a while, he let me struggle around on him, bouncing and trying to get an advantageous angle. And then he laughed. Laughed, turned, slammed me against the wall and fucked me like a man who'd chosen me as his last meal.

God, I can still feel him thrusting in and out of me as I turn the corner toward the market, sidestepping a woman pushing a stroller as I go. When I woke up from the dream in the dim morning light, I was already halfway to an orgasm, a pillow stuffed between my legs. I've never been desperate enough to hump a pillow, but yes I did turn over and ride it like a rodeo bull, peaking less than ten seconds later. Yes, I did.

I stop at the corner and take a deep breath, not wanting to walk past a bunch of vendors with flushed cheeks. I'm already wondering how I'm going to manage the feat later when I see Elijah. Will I ever be able to look him in the eye again and not think of him in beast mode, taking me up against a wall?

Oh who are you kidding? You've been imagining that for a month.

"True facts," I mutter, stepping into the street—

—just in time for three reporters with cameras and microphones to rush me.

"Getaway Girl!"

"Miss Potts!"

"Is it true you're related to Naomi Clemons?"

I drop my purse and stoop down to pick it up, my pulse going bananas in my ears. Okay. Okay, they made the connection finally. To be honest, I'm a little surprised it took them this long, but I was enjoying the delusion they'd lost all interest in me. At least it doesn't seem like they're speculating about Naomi and I sharing a father—that's a huge plus. "Um…" Doing my best to gather my thoughts, I stand, put my head down and look for a way through the reporters. "Excuse me, please. I have to get to work."

"Are you dating Captain Du Pont? Have you seen him *at all?*"

"Where is your mother now, Miss Potts?"

The wind is knocked out of me, but I rally. "If you find out, let me know," I say on a humorless laugh, making another move to get around the group. "Let me pass."

"You're not close to Miss Clemons. Why were you at the wedding?" One of them persists, pushing a microphone in front of my face. "Were you there for Captain Du Pont?"

Yes, I just didn't know it at the time.

Feeling a lot like I did in my dream last night—naked and exposed—I pause with my hand on the market door. "Look, I'm not dating anyone, but I'm partial to blonds with strong chins and dimples. I don't know where my mother is, and I went to the wedding because I was in the neighborhood." I blow a kiss at the camera. "More importantly, we're having a flash sale on ornaments today at Jingle Balls. Buy one, get one half off. And I'm taking fall appointments for commercial and residential decoration services, starting with Halloween and ending with Christmas." I rattle off my newly designed website, give a pinky wave and leave the reporters with their jaws on the floor.

As soon as I'm out of their line of vision—and thank God they don't follow me into the market—I drop down and stick my head in between my knees, breathing like a racehorse.

"Oh my God. Oh my God. I just started a business." My cell phone rings in my purse and I fish it out with a trembling hand, already knowing who it is. "Hey."

Elijah's exhale blows down the line. "I didn't catch you in time."

"Nope."

"How bad was it?"

Thankfully, the market isn't open yet, because I fall into a cross-legged position, right in the center of the main aisle. "Eh."

"Eh?"

"I didn't answer their questions. But they asked about my mother." I tilt my head back and focus on the ceiling. "That sucked a little."

A pause. "You haven't talked to me very much about her."

"There's nothing to say. She left when I was in first grade."

Elijah curses under his breath. "I'm sorry. Didn't realize you were so young."

I swallow. "I had my grandmother. That's more than some kids have." Refusing to wallow in something that happened a decade ago, I push to my feet and head down the aisle toward my booth, where it's nestled in between a hot sauce vendor and a fancy hat saleswoman. "In other news, I just plugged the expanded business on the air. Website and everything. So I guess there's no turning back now."

"No shit?" His boom-crack of laughter makes me smile. "You found a way to make them work for you. That's my Goose."

My heart lifts up like a balloon, lodging in my throat. "Yeah." I turn into Jingle Balls and drop my purse on the closest table. "I don't think...I probably wouldn't have done that unless you'd told me I could do it."

Did I just admit that out loud, sounding like a starry-eyed schoolgirl? I can almost feel his breath against my ear. Slow and steady. "Aw, sugar. Just telling the truth."

Everything about the confession and the moment makes me way too vulnerable, so I rush to put it behind us. "Also, we might have to postpone our dinners for a while. I have a feeling a lot of blond dudes with dimples are going to be knocking on my door."

"What?"

The jealousy I think I hear in his voice is *definitely* just wishful thinking. "Bye, Captain."

"Hold on, now. Wait. What did you mean—"

"Smooches and butt squeezes. Byeeeee."

"Addison, I'm coming over tonight."

This is fun. "I'll *probably* be there."

"Don't give me a probably."

"Do you know anything about the cereal that keeps appearing in my cabinet?"

"I have to go," Elijah says, clearing his throat. "See you tonight."

When he disconnects, I frown down at the phone. "Huh. That was weird."

I THOUGHT DEATH would be more dramatic. Storm waters rising up and carrying me off or ex-husbands surrounding my bed, demanding to know where I buried the gold. One thing I did not expect was to perish surrounded by blinking Christmas lights and tourists. But here I am. I am most definitely meeting my maker within the hour.

There's a layer of clammy sweat under my clothes, I'm short of breath and I can't seem to focus. Everything is dull, moving in a confusing kaleidoscope. Sick. Common sense tells me I'm sick, probably with the flu, but I don't have the energy to do anything about it. My head tilts right and I stumble, ramming into a display of glass shepherd figurines.

"Miss, are you okay?"

"Yes, thank you." My words boom in my skull, rattling everything. "Ow."

"I'm a nurse, miss." Hands guide me into my folding metal chair. "You're not well. Is there someone I can call for you?"

It's on the tip of my tongue to say Elijah, but I don't and it makes my ribs ache even more. We're two weeks away from the election. He can't just waltz into the City Market. If the abundance of tourists didn't recognize him, the other vendors and smattering of locals would. "There's no one. I'm fine. There's only an hour left until we close."

"You need to go home, sweetie," says the disembodied voice. Vaguely, I register hands digging in my apron and more talking. I see my cell phone in someone else's hand and make a grab for it, but the effort costs me and I slump back in my chair. "Is this Elijah? Yes, my name is Francine and I'm a nurse. No—no, sir. Calm down. She's *fine*. She's right here, but she's very sick. You were the last number she called and I just…"

The next thing I remember is being carried like a limp doll. I recognize these arms. They caught me once when I almost fell down the stairs outside my apartment. The one and only time they were around me. I curl toward the warmth of my savior, then immediately begin to burn up and squirm to be put down so I can cool off. The arms don't let me.

"You were just fine last night, Goose. Just *fine*." Elijah's voice makes me slump, because surely the familiar, hearty timbre of it will heal me. It's much angrier than usual, but it'll work. "You think you can be mean? Just wait. I'm going to give you *hell* once you're better."

His heavy tread jostles my face against his chest and I take a huge gulp of his scent, tugging his coat close, rubbing against it like a cat. "You don't have a mean bone in your body."

He's quiet so long I wonder if I imagined him and I'm just floating down the street. "I can be mean when a nurse calls me from your phone. I can be mean then."

"Are you going to lose the election now?"

A hand ghosts over my hair. "No. And you don't worry about things like that."

"I worry about it all the time," I whisper.

I can sense him leaning down, can smell his shampoo. Malin + Goetz. He keeps the simple white bottle of it in my shower and I allow myself to sniff it every third day. "Why don't you talk to me about it?"

"Because that's not why you keep coming back."

"Addison..."

My subconscious is screaming at me to shut up, but I barely have the strength to acknowledge it, let alone follow instructions. "I don't have time to be sick. Requests have been coming in all week from the website. Everyone in this town wants a nativity in their front yard on Christmas. I'm the *ball* joke salesgirl, Elijah. Now I have to add mangers to my wheelhouse."

"I'll help you when the time comes. Right now, just stop being sick, please."

"Blond men, too. I'm getting a lot of website requests from blond men." My laugh is semi-hysterical. "They're definitely not interested in mangers."

"What are they..." Elijah growls. "Never mind. I don't even want to know. You're not really planning on accepting dates from these idiots, are you?"

"No. I'd just spend the whole time missing you."

There's a break in his step. "I'd miss you, too, Goose."

A few seconds later another voice, calm and familiar joins the haze. "Okay, Captain. Put her in the back seat with me." Being upended causes me to groan and Elijah to curse, but I'm quickly leaned up against something soft. "It's Lydia, Addison. We're taking you home now, sound good? We'll fix you right up. Have you taken any medicine or..."

Everything is upside down. Lydia's words turn into sounds and eventually fade into nothing. I think I hear Elijah yelling at me, but I'm too tired to answer. And then I can't, because sleep claims me and I'm more than happy to allow it.

CHAPTER NINE

Elijah

Captain Du Pont to the Rescue?
Witnesses claim to have seen Charleston's favorite mayoral
candidate
swooping in to rescue Getaway Girl. Romance revived? Or did it
never die?
—TheTea.com

MY FATHER TAUGHT me a very important lesson when I was a young boy. When a man doesn't know how to fix a situation with a woman, he best get himself to a florist. I've made three trips in as many hours while Addison sleeps, filling the living room and kitchen with sunflowers and roses. Lydia is in the bedroom with Goose, doing important things like trying to bring the fever down and I'm out here, digging for more vases. Eventually, I run out and start to use drinking glasses, which I'm sure Addison will yell at me about once she's feeling better. If that doesn't happen sooner rather than later, I'm going to clean out the damn florist.

Something is bothering me. I can't find the source of the itch under my collar.

Am I annoyed that Addison went to work with the flu, instead of finding a replacement?

Bet your ass.

It's more than that, though. The woman who called me had to walk Addison out of the market to meet me outside, because I couldn't go in and get her myself. And that's not sitting right. I don't like these *limitations*. I'm starting to think I've put limitations on more than one area of our relationship, too. Like when she was half delirious and confessed she worries all the time about me losing the election.

Why don't you talk to me about it?

Because that's not why you keep coming back.

I'd just miss you the whole time.

That was the first time Addison has ever admitted to really wanting me here. I mean, I reckoned she did, since a woman like Addison wouldn't agree to something that made her unhappy. But why would she hide it?

The way she clung to me as I carried her...

I realize I've had the scissors poised over a rose stem for at least fifteen minutes. Giving myself a shake, I keep cutting, even though I don't know what the hell I'm doing. Of course she was clinging to me, the poor thing must have been scared half to death. Not to mention, I'm her only friend in this town and she'd been too afraid to call me herself. Relief probably caused her to act out of character. That's all.

"Elijah?"

I drop the scissors and turn to find Lydia entering the kitchen. "Hey. Is she awake?"

"She was. Briefly. I got her to take some more medicine." She arches an eyebrow at the piles of leaves and cellophane wrap. "Her temperature has come down, but she needs a lot of sleep. The girl is exhausted."

"Yeah." I scrub both hands over my face. "This is my fault. I've been keeping her up."

"Oh?"

"Not like that," I growl, dropping my hands. "I just don't come over until late and she stays up with me talking, cooking, making ornaments."

Lydia stares at me with a blank expression.

That same itch under my collar is back. "What?"

"Elijah…" She takes her time leaning against the counter. "Don't you think this relationship between you and Addison is a little odd?"

"Yeah, I do." That seems to surprise her—maybe it even surprises me, too, and it takes me a few moments to gather an explanation. There is no patented description for what's going on here. Addison started as my escape from the political grind and quickly became more than that. Her face is the one I want to see at the end of the day. Yes, she takes my mind off things, but her unique perspective on even the most mundane topics has made me think differently, too. Made me want to do my job better. She's blunt and honest and lives life according to her own rules. I've found myself taking pages from her book while in the office and its been…amazing. Being around her makes me a better man. A better man for this city.

Sure, there are some definite complications. Namely the fact that I can't stop picturing her incredible body while I'm jerking off, which has gone from an occasional indulgence to a frequent one. It's her eyes, her mouth, her hands, too, that invade my head while I stroke toward release. Her *voice*. It was only meant to be once, but now that the barn door is open, I *can't* get it closed. I've tried and failed over and over again. Hence her increasing supply of guilt cereal. She could feed an army at this point.

So is our relationship odd? Yeah. There's probably never been another one like it, while my relationship with Naomi could have been predicted to the letter.

I can still remember the real estate agent walking us through the house where we'd planned to live. Until she'd pointed out a room meant to be the nursery, children had never been discussed between Naomi and me. But my fiancé never batted an eyelash, continuing the tour while I lagged behind. *This is what's expected. This is what we do*, I'd thought.

Every single requirement had been ticked off the neat, carefully constructed list, but I somehow got it wrong nonetheless. Among other things I'd never spoken about with Naomi was my job. And she'd been perfectly content without knowing the details.

I'd been fine with it, too. Addison, though…I'm not so sure she wants to be kept in the dark. And I'm *not* fine with Addison wanting something and not giving it to her.

Lydia clears her throat and I struggle to remember where the conversation left off.

Don't you think this relationship between you and Addison is a little odd?

Right. "Here's the thing. I spent two years in a relationship that was considered totally normal. Every plan was set in stone, right down to our plans to buy a golden retriever and the slightly kooky wedding announcement. It blew up in my face." I pick up a thorny rose stem and tap it on the counter. "I'm happy with the way things are with Addison."

"Are you really?"

For some reason, I think of the way she rubbed her face on my coat as I carried her, but I set the image aside. "Yeah, I am. She's the one thing in my life that hasn't been planned." *If there are no plans, none of them can backfire, right?* "I'm happy when she's around and…I don't want to force this into something conventional." I slide my finger beneath my collar, searching once again for that itch. "What's the other option? Start dating her? I'm not going to force her into a pattern. My whole life is made of patterns."

Lydia shakes her head. "Who says it would be the same with Addison?"

A weight presses down on my lungs, but I laugh my way through it. "Why are we talking about this? We're just friends."

Ignoring how hollow those words sound, I go back to inexpertly cutting flowers.

$$\sim$$

Addison

I PRESS THE yellow rose between the pages of *The Remains of the Day* and close the book tightly. It belonged to my grandmother and it was on her bedside table when I arrived, on top of a stack of other depressing classic literature. For some reason I've never moved the books from their place, enjoying the vision of my grandmother reaching for one in the morning. Catching a few pages before hitting the shower and picking it back up at night.

Now every time I wake up, I'll think of one of Elijah's roses locked inside, flattening and drying, so I can keep it around longer. Maybe it's a bad idea—a self-destructive one—but I find myself returning the book to the nightstand, arranging it carefully and remembering the veritable greenhouse I'd glimpsed through the doorway before Lydia left this morning. At my request, she'd handed me one yellow rose and I've been staring at it in kind of a half-delirious state since then, trying to envision Elijah's giant hands handling something so delicate.

By all accounts, I should probably be dead. Half of me still feels that way, my ribs sore from coughing, my head light and foggy from spending a full day trapped in a fever, another one coming down from the boiling height of it. I didn't die, but something about me feels different. Restless. In a moment of clarity during the fever, I remember experiencing this immense grief over never having kissed Elijah. Now I'm being prodded by some weird urgency that wasn't there before. I either have to squash it or do something about it.

Squash it. Definitely squash it.

And speaking of prodding, my bladder has been complaining for an hour. I really need to get up. When I push aside the covers, though, my eyes are drawn back to *The Remains of the Day* and I notice the edge of something peeking out among the worn pages. I pick the book back up and set it on my lap, sliding out a...visitor's guide to kayaking in Charleston.

Say what?

A local phone number is circled at the bottom of the brochure, along with a man's name and a date in July. But July hasn't happened yet...unless this is in reference to a previous July? It's possible, since there's no year. Did my grandmother have plans to go kayaking? Or did she already go? Sure, she was fearless and adventurous once upon a time, before my mother was born. I can't exactly picture her paddling down a river, though.

Resolved to investigate once I'm done peeing, I put the book and brochure back on the nightstand. I've only set one shaky leg on the ground when my bedroom door bursts open.

I scream at the top of my lungs.

"Just me." Elijah holds up his free hand, since the other is holding a glass of orange juice. "Are you decent?"

"*Jesus.*" In a series of hasty movements, I belt my robe and make sure my breasts aren't showing. Normally I'm not so self-conscious, but I've been in bed for two days and feel like I've been rolled in shit. "You're supposed to ask *before* you walk in."

His smile belongs on the cover of *Esquire*. "Ah, Goose. If you can snap at me, you must be feeling better."

Over the last couple days, Lydia told me Elijah carried me from the market to his truck, made sure I got home and even called my employees to cover my shifts. Pretending to be someone else, of course. I'm poised to say thank you for everything, but I'm too wrecked and raw from being sick. I'd probably make a fool out of myself and start listing the reasons he's so wonderful. "What are you still doing here? Go to work."

"I'm on my lunch break."

Cold crackles in my belly. "You shouldn't be coming here when it's light out."

His smile dims. "And I told you not to worry about things like that."

"When?"

For several beats, he says nothing. Did I miss him telling me not to worry about his career? I've been waiting for that day he'll come home and finally unload on me about election pressure or hint that he needs encouragement. Anything. But the longer its taken for him to share, the more I've begun to assume Naomi must have been his sounding board. Maybe they traded anecdotes about his politics and her pageant days or charity work as an end-of-the-day ritual. It's possible he's just not ready for a new confidant.

I'm distracted from my useless thoughts when Elijah moves closer to offer me the orange juice. My stomach—chilled only moments before—heats the closer he comes. In his tailored suit and rolled up sleeves, his strong forearms are on display. God, he's so tall and smells incredible. My gaze is level with his lap and I think of what it would be like to have him climb into bed with me, demanding I touch him everywhere. Lifting the hem of my robe as we're spooning so he could slip inside me for a lazy afternoon stress reliever.

"Seriously, you should go. I can take care of myself."

Elijah ignores me, tipping the glass of orange juice to my lips. "I have a meeting not too far from here in half an hour." He scrutinizes me, appearing thoughtful. "There are vacant parcels of land along Montague Street and I'm speaking with developers about using the land for housing in some places, commercial growth in others." His thumb swipes a drop of orange juice away from below my bottom lip and my skin zings. "The governor is more interested in putting a sports arena smack dab in the center of the community and doesn't give a damn that the residents don't want more traffic congestion and even lower property values. Not when they've made so much progress revitalizing."

I don't realize until my lungs start to burn that I've been holding my breath. Elijah never talks to me about work. Why now? "S-so you're trying to change his mind?"

"That's the plan. I'm putting together an initiative, but that'll only be the beginning of the battle. In the event he agrees to use the land to benefit North Charleston residents, I want to hire local." He shakes his head. "No big-name outside developers. If we're trying to benefit a community, we should put the money in the pockets of the people who live there."

If I wasn't already out of my head for this man, his passion and conviction as he speaks would have sealed it. "Do you have a lot of support behind you?"

"No." He laughs, setting aside the orange juice. "Not yet, anyway. My father's supporters want the arena. It'll be a feather in the city's cap."

"Better housing and shopping districts won't give them that."

"No again." Elijah sighs. "There's support out there for the plans, but it'll come from people who are still reserving judgment on me. They think I'm planning to carry on a legacy for my father. And I am. I *will*. But it'll come with changes."

Remembering Elijah's conviction when he told me I could expand the Christmas business, I reach out to lay a hand on his arm, but draw it back at the last second. He frowns at the action. "You're worthy of people's trust, Captain. If they haven't figured that out yet, it'll only be a matter of time. Some might say politicians are all words, no action. But you're proving the opposite. You're fighting." I pick imaginary lint off my bed-spread. "You have my support."

His devastating smile almost sends me back into the pillows.

"Okay," I manage. "Time to go. You're going to be late."

The smile dims to concern. "Is this the first time you've gotten out of bed alone? You might be a little shaky."

I shrug.

"That's what I thought. Do you need the ladies' room?"

A laugh catches me off guard. "So formal."

"Not formal. Professional." He winks at me. "It's my way of trying to make it easier for you to rely on me. I know you probably hate it."

Earlier this morning, I tried to stand and my legs collapsed like jelly, so my choices are limited. With an eye roll, I lift my arms. "I just need you to get me started."

He stoops down, wrapping an arm around my waist and lifting me with ease into the heat of his body…and I have no idea if it's the perfect giving warmth of his solid body or my weak legs, but I sway. I sway hard, land against him and stay there, inhaling eucalyptus and Elijah. "Now," he murmurs. "There you are."

"Thank you for coming to get me." I push my gratitude past

the twinge in my throat. "I don't remember a thing, but I'm assuming you swooped down in a mask and cape." I drop my voice several octaves. "Mayor Man. Able to conquer anything, except his impulse control on Italian night."

His rumble of laughter is heaven against my ear. "Thanks for leaving out the superhero tights." He holds me tighter. "You scared the shit out of me."

"Sorry." I could stay like this forever, just sagged in the hold of a hero, pretending he never wants to let me go, either. But reluctantly, I tap him on the shoulder. "Okay, I think I can walk now that I'm up."

"Sure?"

"Yeah."

He's right behind me as I pad across the hallway, my legs feeling a little more capable with each step. Right before I close myself in the bathroom, Elijah inserts a hand to stop the door from closing. "Goose?"

I grip the sink for balance before turning to face him. "What?"

"Election night is less than two weeks away." He pauses just enough to make me worry—worry that it all ends right here. He needs to cut off contact now that the day is drawing close. But I'm caught off guard when he says, "Will you come?"

"Me?" I blurt the word, immediately shaking my head. Who else would he be talking to? Still... "That doesn't seem wise."

"I've asked for no cameras or press while the results come in. We'll be in City Hall, after hours. It's just going to be me, my parents. Chris and Lydia. Maybe one or two trusted staff members. And I want you there." His expression is usually so open and relaxed, but right now, he seems...determined. Maybe even a little ragged around the edges. "Will you come?"

"Yes."

"Good." His head tips forward, a relieved smile on his mouth when he comes back up. "I'll wait out here until you're done."

I flip on the water as soon as the door closes, but don't get anything accomplished for a good five minutes, because all I can do is smile like a goof at my own reflection. I have no delusions that Elijah will magically start thinking of me as more than a friend. I can't. Whenever I start to let hope run away with me where Elijah is concerned, I think of the vacancy in my mother's eyes as she sat, day in and day out, waiting for her ex-lover to come back. Until the light completely went out and she broke, running away as far and fast as she could. Hope can be the devil for women when it comes to men. Especially men who've already pledged their love to someone else. To an ideal that a Potts girl could never fit.

As long as I continue to reality check myself, though, a tiny pinprick of hope won't hurt, will it? Carefully, I let myself feel it, exhilaration filling my lungs with air.

Maybe, just maybe, Elijah isn't going to hide me away forever.

CHAPTER TEN

Elijah

Exclusive
Dewberry Hotel staff claims Captain Du Pont's bed never needs to be made!
So exactly whose sheets has he been messing up?
Unrelated: Getaway Girl positively glowing on her way into the market on Election Day.
—Charleston Post

"CONGRATULATIONS, SON." MY father slides a tumbler of bourbon into my hands, sending a nod toward the television and the series of pie charts on the screen. "Your performance in last week's town hall put you over the mark. The son of a bitch has no chance."

My throat burns under the slide of liquor. I want to correct his use of the word *performance* but decide to let it slide for tonight. It's rare for my father to be in a good enough mood to stop plotting and laugh, plus we're not the only people filling the downstairs conference room. My father thinks the development plans I outlined in last week's event were just lip service to secure votes. That I intend to maintain business as usual once I'm elected. How well does he really know me, if he thinks I'm not a man of my word?

Not for the first time tonight, I glance at the door, willing

Addison to walk through. Her encouragement, her belief in me, provided the boost I needed before last week's town hall. And I want her here now. I want someone in my corner who has no doubts about who I am.

Taking another sip of my bourbon—my third of the night—I nod at Chris's thumbs up, Lydia's encouraging smile from where they sit speaking with my mother. My oldest friends believe in me, too, but something about it doesn't feel the same as Addison giving me her confidence. Not as...satisfying.

My thoughts are interrupted when the conference room door opens and Addison slides inside, closing it behind her without making a sound. I'm not sure why I stand there like a moron, my drink caught in midair. Something about seeing Addison outside the confines of the apartment is almost surreal. It has only happened a few times. Once after I was jilted, another time in the supermarket. And the final time was outside the market when she looked like she had a reservation with death. All moments when I was more than a little distracted.

It's election night, so I'm the epitome of distracted. Right? But not enough to notice she's gone shopping. I've been in her closet to hunt down ornament supplies at least a hundred times— and I'm certain I've never seen the dress she's wearing. It's ruby red with some kind of silvery flower print and it's very...fluttery around her legs. Her hair—did she get it trimmed today?—is down and brushing her arms, her back. *God*, she's pretty.

She's wearing new silver sandals. Did she replace the brown ones?

My father does a half turn to follow my line of sight. "What in God's name—"

"Addison. Thanks for coming." I smile at her across the room, holding up a finger to let her know I'll be right over, although Chris and Lydia have already jumped up to greet her. Giving them my back, I send my father a look of warning. "I asked her to be here."

Wheels turn behind his eyes. "You've been seeing her all this time, haven't you?"

"Not in the way you think. But if I had, that would be my business. Not yours—and not the people of Charleston's, either."

"Then why've you been keeping her all to yourself, son?" My father laughs at my silence. "You know what kind of women to trot out in front of the media. And you know which ones to keep under lock and key. Don't play the saint." He takes a long swig of his drink. "When it comes down to it, you'll do what's best for the office you hold. Same as me."

"You're wrong on both scores. I've only kept her out of the public eye because they poison everything they touch. They'd hound her—and they'd never understand what we have is a friendship." I finish my drink and set the empty glass down on the conference room table. "Second, there are a lot of things I won't do. Pretending some decades-old feud has any relevance is one of them."

"Feuds never die in the south."

"This one dies with me."

My father rolls his glass between two hands. "What are you going to do about this *friendship* when there's another woman in your life? You think Naomi would have appreciated you making time with some—"

"Be very careful."

"With another woman. A damned attractive one, at that."

Maybe I've been distracted with the campaign or flat out haven't given another romantic relationship a single thought since the wedding that wasn't. But the point my father makes hasn't occurred to me even once. If I started dating someone, I would have to sever ties with Addison, wouldn't I? In no world could I continue to spend time with her. "She's important to me," I say, past the discomfort in my throat. "You'll treat her with respect."

His eyes are shrewd and I know this isn't over. "Very well."

My father follows me to where Addison is laughing with Lydia and Chris. "Hey, Goose." I lean down and kiss her on the cheek, noticing a dash of glitter behind her ear. "Were you decorating without me?"

"Well, you were kind of busy," she murmurs, an uncharacteristic blush painting her cheeks. "But I saved you the snowman buttons to glue on next time you're over."

"You know they're the only thing I can't mess up." I can feel everyone in the room watching us, but I'm not ready to pull away from Addison yet. Election day has been nothing but one stressful interview and update after another. Having her close by now has the same calming effect of walking into her apartment every night. "Did you get a haircut?"

"No." In my periphery, I see her dimple pop. "I got *all* of them cut. Are you, um…going to introduce me?"

"Yes." I straighten and pretend I'm not greeted with curious expressions. "Roy Du Pont, I'd like you to meet Addison Potts."

"Getaway Girl," my father says smoothly, taking her offered hand and bowing over it. "You're something of a mystery in this town. No one can get to the bottom of you."

She smiles and takes her hand back. "I'm just a girl who sells ornaments in the market."

"Now, if that were the case, my son wouldn't be sneaking off to see you."

"Roy," I warn, stiffening. "That's—"

"I'm probably the only one who'll put up with his annoying

habits," Addison cuts in, smiling. "He talks to the television during the eleven o'clock news, he never wraps the cheese back up properly. And he leaves his jacket draped everywhere but the coat rack. Honestly, I don't know why I hang out with him. If I hadn't just shaken your hand, I would swear he was raised by wolves."

A couple seconds pass in total silence, nothing but the television noise to fill the void. Then my father drops his chin and laughs, along with Chris and Lydia. "Hold on, my wife needs to hear this. Honey…" I'm still standing there in shock as he waves over my mother before elbowing me in the side. "Go get Miss Potts a drink, son. Where are your manners?"

"See? What did I tell you?" Addison wrinkles her nose at me. "Wolves."

It takes me a beat to get moving toward the makeshift bar we've set up near the windows—and I can't put my finger on why. Maybe I'm shocked over how well the introductions went and kicking myself for not making it happen sooner. Or more likely, I'm watching my father and wondering if his easy acceptance of Addison is too good to be true.

While I'm making Addison her drink, my father and I trade a long look over her shoulder. And I can't help but recall how many times I've seen that same guileless expression before during debates and press conferences. He might be playing the charmer, but his opinion of my relationship with Addison isn't going to change. An opinion that could sour further now that I'm slowly bringing her out into the open. Was it a mistake to bring her here?

No. It wasn't. Two weeks ago, when I was forced to wait outside the market for someone else to help Addison out, the secrecy became a burden. It weighed on my nerves, reminding me hourly that if something happened to her again, I'd have to watch from the sidelines—and that wasn't going to fly. There's no reason for secrets and I'm not going to be half a friend to Addison when she's been a whole one to me. Inviting her to meet my parents is my way of letting everyone know she's not going anywhere.

And she *isn't*.

I hand Addison her tumbler of bourbon just in time for my mother to approach.

"Miss Potts," she says smoothly, inclining her head at Addison. "The papers haven't done you justice. Aren't you just the *spitting image* of your mother?"

For the first time since walking into the room, Addison's smile falters and there's an answering jab in my chest. "You knew Addison's mother?"

"Of course." She takes a leisurely sip of champagne. "Why, we were all schoolmates as young girls. She was Della's cousin, after all. They were inseparable. Until…"

Until Della's fiancé slept with Addison's mother and possibly got her pregnant.

I'm not clear on my mother's intentions, but those stinging words hang in the air unspoken and I take a step toward Addison, laying a hand on the small of her back. "Since we're recalling the past," I say slowly, "You'll remember Addison didn't have a hand in any of it."

"Of course not." My mother flattens a hand on her chest. "Forgive me, Addison, for bringing up something ugly. They've been feeding me champagne. It's lovely to meet you."

Addison recovers and holds out her hand, shaking my mother's. "It's lovely to meet you, too, Mrs. Du Pont."

"Please. Call me Virginia." Her shoulders pop up to her ears.

"Ooh. Addison, have you met Roy's adviser, Preston?" She cups a fragile hand to her mouth and calls to the young man across the room who's pacing the floor, phone in hand. The only one in the room who *isn't* friends or family. My father has been at City Hall less and less over the last few weeks, and in turn Preston hasn't darkened the hallway much, either. His name remains on the tip of my parents' tongue, though, so I know he's still on the payroll, probably arranging speaking engagements for my father and ferrying my mother to charity functions.

As I've been poring over Preston's work in the last four years, I've noticed the patterns of a yes-man. He never tells my father he's wrong or submits alternate ideas, he simply runs with the play, likely leaving my father in the dark about the particulars— or setting aside of ethics—it takes to accomplish the task. When I'm mayor, I don't want people like that around me. I want people who aren't afraid to tell me I'm damn well wrong. This late in the game, there's no question about my lack of interest in hiring Preston to my team, so the atmosphere between him and me has gone from mildly uncomfortable to glacial.

So when he approaches us to be introduced to Addison, I don't like it.

I don't like it *at all*.

"Preston," my mother says smoothly, guiding him closer. Too close. "This is Elijah's friend, Addison Potts. She's new in town."

"Uh…" I feel Addison's quick glance up at me, before she extends her hand toward Preston for a shake. "Yes. I grew up here, but it's been a while since I was home."

"There are probably a lot of new things to see," Preston says, hitting his S's hard enough to abuse my eardrums. "Has anyone showed you around?"

Is Preston considered good looking? I guess so. Addison did

say she prefers blond men. I'm not blond, though. Which *doesn't* matter. And *doesn't* bother me at all. Except to say I'm highly aware of not being her type...and if he doesn't take his hand back soon, I'm going to snap it off his body. I don't necessarily blame my mother for this, but Preston's question makes it painfully obvious she'd been discussing my relationship with Addison within earshot of Preston. No, someone hasn't shown her around. Because I've been keeping her stashed away like a hidden treasure. He knows it, too. They all know it. "I've seen enough to know it hasn't changed too much," Addison murmurs, pulling her hand out of Preston's and tucking it under the opposite arm. "Still beautiful as always."

"Charleston isn't the only thing that's beautiful." Preston does a weird bobble head move as the skin draws tight all over my body. "And if you'd like a tour, I'm your man."

"If she needs a tour," I snap off. "I'll be the one to give it."

Silence falls over the group, but I don't break eye contact with Preston. Maybe I don't have any right to send this message, but I'm sending it nonetheless. *Back the hell off. You're not good enough for her.*

"Elijah, look." I'm still trying to stare a hole through Preston when Chris gets my attention, pointing toward the television. "Your opponent is conceding the race."

Pride replaces my anger. The spell breaks for now, the conference room filling with cheers. Preston fades away and my mother puts her arms around me for a hug, my father shaking my hand over her shoulder.

But I can't help it...I look for Addison. It doesn't feel like a victory until she smiles at me.

"Congratulations," she mouths. "You're still cooking tomorrow."

Addison

LORD. I DESERVE an Oscar.

My stomach has been in knots since I arrived earlier tonight, but I don't think anyone was the wiser. Hopefully I succeeded in fooling Elijah, too, something I have ample experience in doing. It was naïve not to anticipate having my mother's decisions thrown in my face at some point. I didn't expect it to be Elijah's mother. Nor did I expect to have him standing beside me when it happened. Watching me. Trying to read me. But I was determined not to let anything ruin his election night. I'm glad I brazened tonight out.

The past came up. It happened. And I'm still standing.

I even made it through Virginia's obvious attempted set-up between me and Preston. Elijah's body language made it clear right away that he didn't like the younger man and I don't blame him. Later on, after the election results were announced, I caught Preston watching me from the back of the room in a way that made me feel yucky and unclothed. A far cry from the polite charmer he pretended to be in front of Elijah's parents.

Now, Elijah and I stand in the dark lobby of City Hall, waving off Lydia and Chris as they climb into their Uber. Elijah's parents and Preston have already left, although I think the mayor would have stayed all night celebrating and reminiscing about his thirty-five years in office if his wife hadn't overdone it with the champagne. He definitely didn't want to leave Elijah and me here alone, which is laughable considering we're alone almost every night of the week.

Rest easy, mayor. Your son pretty much only touches me if I'm ill or falling to my death.

I lean against the receptionist's desk, smiling at the faded collection of Cathy cartoons taped to her work station. But as usual, my attention drifts to Elijah, where he leans against the wall, all casual male power, his tie loose around his neck. Big, beautiful Elijah. "Um. Are you coming over tonight or heading to the hotel?"

"Coming over. I can pick up my truck in the morning."

"I can drop you off on my way to work."

"Thanks, Goose." Elijah takes out his cell phone. "I'll call the driver."

Now that we're on the verge of leaving City Hall, I remember my secret mission with a jolt. "Oh! I…can you hold off? I have to use the ladies' room."

He drops onto a leather bench and manspreads like a pro, the picture of a guy who runs shit but isn't immune to the effects of bourbon. "Take your time," he drawls, squinting at me through one eye. "You were something tonight, you know that?"

"So were you," I breathe, my face flushing. Oh God, I've had too much bourbon, too, haven't I? "Be right back."

Ducking into the hallway, I bypass the ladies' room and creep up the stairs, rounding the turn and stopping outside Elijah's soon-to-be office. I had to look it up on the hallway directory when I arrived tonight. The mayor's corner office has belonged to his father for over three decades, but Elijah let it slip recently that he'd be occupying it the morning after election day, providing he won. And he has.

Now, I retrieve the shopping bag I left sitting outside the door. Careful not to make any noise, I let myself inside and begin to remove the bag's contents. One by one, I place picture frames on the desk, angling them so they can be seen by whoever sits in the chair. There's a photograph of Elijah in his army uniform shaking his father's hand. One of Elijah, Chris and Lydia posing beside a cannon at the Citadel. Another one of—

"I knew you were up to something."

I trap a shriek inside my throat at the sound of Elijah's voice. "Why couldn't you just leave me to it?" He only smiles in the face of my deadliest glare, which really takes the fun out of it. "This was supposed to be a surprise."

Elijah rounds the desk with loose steps, picking up the first frame and studying it in the darkness. "Where did you get these?"

Pleasure steals through my blood at the awe in his voice. "I stole the key to your storage locker." *You sound like a pathetic lovesick goober monkey.* "They were right on top. I didn't even have to dig."

"You lying little Goose. I didn't have time to label boxes or categorize when I packed everything up. These must have been spread out and buried." He sets down the frame and begins to sift through the bag, taking out a few more framed photos. *Don't notice how his lip tugs at the right corner. Don't notice how sexy and rumpled and huge he is.* My lungs are starting to ache from holding my breath when Elijah looks up. "You weren't going to take credit for this, were you? If I hadn't caught you."

I don't answer.

"Thought so." With a frown, he leaves the framed photos in a stack on the desk and roots through the remaining ones. "There are none of us."

My heart is trying to beat inside a jar of honey. It's all slow and sugary and thick. I shouldn't have had so much to drink. The last time I drank liquor...I was probably imbibing from the same bottle of Grey Goose I offered Elijah outside the church. My thoughts all have a pining quality to them. Is he staring at me? Is he laughing at my jokes? And holy hell, I just want to be touched.

Ever since he whispered in my ear back in the conference room about hair cuts and snowman buttons, my thighs have felt restless beneath my dress. I'm unsatisfied.

I'm *unsatisfied*.

Months of existing around this sexy, earthy, heroic, *sexy* man have rendered me useless where I stand. I'm bust. I can feel the bad decision manifesting before I've even made it. The alternative to not following my impulse is more suffering, though. More brushing against Elijah in the kitchen and mentally begging him to drop the spatula and kiss me to no avail.

If I can make it through tonight, there's a good chance I'll be fine in the morning. Well, not *fine*. But more capable of withstanding this never-ending yearning. The need.

Right now, though? With him frowning over having no pictures of us? The hunger is rampant and the bourbon is giving me permission to do something I would never consider in the light of day. Never. Not when the potential consequence is losing Elijah.

Don't think of that, whispers the liquor heating my blood.

"Well…" I stop to clear the rasp from my voice. "If there's no picture of us together, we should take one."

"Good idea." He crooks his finger at me, unwittingly sealing his fate. "Come here."

I put my jacket on downstairs when I thought we were leaving, but I take it off now, simply letting it fall. "I want you in the mayor's chair."

His eyes stray to my pooled jacket, then tick to mine. "You what?"

"In the picture. I want you sitting in the chair."

"Oh. Right." He slides out the brown leather, high-back executive chair and drops into it. "What about you?"

My bravery slips. Whose wouldn't? This powerful, gorgeous

man sits before me, outlined by the city he's been elected to run. His thighs are thicker than my waist, his sleeves caught up around his elbows. A strong man. A man of conviction who will not be seduced unless he really wants to be.

Or is driven out of his mind and can't resist.

Before I can second-guess myself, I move between his outstretched thighs and ease myself onto his lap. "*Addison*."

I send him an innocent look over my shoulder. "Yes, Captain?"

His chest rises and falls. Once. Twice. "Take the picture."

The fact that I'm playing with fire stops psyching me out...and begins to excite me. Maybe it's the gravel in his tone...or the big fists that come to rest on the desk. No...it's definitely the way he presses his nose to my hair and inhales. As if I'm not going to notice. But I do. I do and it makes me braver. Makes me throb between my legs.

"The picture, Addison."

"Sorry." I lean across the desk where I set my purse, taking my time digging through to find my cell before pulling it out, searching for the camera app. All the while, his muscles bunch beneath me, harder and harder...and that's when I feel it. His erection lifts under my backside, so thick and glorious, I bite my lip to stop from crying out. I want to, though. I want to sob at the proof that he's physically attracted to me and at least I have that much.

My hands are shaking as I lift the camera, my instincts screaming at me to grind down. Elijah's breath is pelting the back of my neck. Other than that he's completely still, though. But when I flip the camera around to selfie mode and get my first look at his face, there isn't a jury on the planet that would rule him unaffected. His eyes are closed, nostrils flared, mouth open against my hair. "You've got five seconds," he says. "Take it, or—"

"Or what?" Elijah stands up and takes me with him, my ass pressed to his lap, feet dangling off the ground. As if I weigh nothing more than a child. It only lasts for a couple mind-blowing seconds, though, before he settles me on the ground behind his desk. His heat begins to leave me and I sense my chance slipping away, so I twist around to face him. Still mere inches away from me, he pauses with his head tipped forward, hands flexing at his sides. "We could be more than friends." After easing myself backwards onto the desk, I snag his necktie and tug him closer, guiding his hips between my open thighs. "Just for tonight."

His laugh is more like a rough expulsion of air, the scent of bourbon hitting me. "That's not how things work," he says, his palms scraping up my thighs, twisting in the hem of my dress. "Goddammit, Addison. You're not supposed to tempt me like this."

Tempted. He's tempted. My blood cells crash together. "I don't always do what I'm supposed to," I murmur, leaning up to bring our mouths close, a breath separating them. "If I wasn't your friend, would you kiss me right now?"

His eyes fasten on my mouth, seeming darker than usual. Predatory. "You felt what you did to my cock, sugar. You know the answer to that."

Elijah's uncharacteristic use of filth sends moisture rushing to the apex of my thighs. Prickles crawl in every direction on my skin, leaving goosebumps behind. "Aren't you curious what you did to me?" I rest my fingers on his belt buckle a second, before letting them travel down, closing them around his huge, heavy flesh, massaging him there and feeling him swell. "You own this city now, Mr. Mayor. Right now, that includes what's under my dress."

"Ahhh, fuck. That's *enough*." His mouth drops to my cleavage, his tongue skating over the right slope, the left, turning my nerve endings to zapping little spark plugs. "We have to stop this. You're my—"

"Friend. Believe me, I know."

I squeeze his hips between my thighs and he yanks my bottom closer on the desk, hesitating for two breaths, before pressing his arousal up against my wet panties. "*Fuuuck*," he roars, bucking against me, snarling into my neck. "*We can't.*"

"Yes, we can." My teeth rattle at another drive of his hips. "If we weren't friends, you'd already be inside me. So deep. Your pants would be unzipped and my thong would be hanging out of your pocket."

"*Stop.*"

"What if we're not friends for the night?" I whine a little in my throat when he goes still, his fevered eyes lifting to mine. "I'm just your shiny new secretary and I want to give you everything you need."

"A couple problems with that. I don't have some ridiculous secretary fetish." He kneads my bottom in a rough massage. "And I have eyes, Addison. I'll know exactly who I'm inside of."

My fingers draw his attention as they lift to my neckline and tug the material down, low enough for my breasts to pop free. "Would that be so bad?"

CHAPTER ELEVEN

Elijah

The public has spoken.
This booty is reporting for duty.
—Twitter @DuPontBadonk

W OULD THAT BE *so bad?*

No. The problem is it could be so good. *Too* good.

I've been a bad friend. Ever since the morning I walked in on Addison getting ready for her run and she treated my butt like molding clay, I've been thinking things I shouldn't. Dreaming up fantasies that I was wrong to have. My favorite one is Addison climbing into my bed at night and telling me she's cold, asking me to warm her up...until things get out of control. It's my favorite fantasy because I get to take care of her, using my body heat to stop her shivering. If that's where it ended, maybe my conscience could have remained in the clear. But it always ends with me tugging her panties down to her knees, my cock rifling in and out of her as she cries out *"Elijah"* into my pillow.

Now I've got her ass in my hands, and Christ, the fantasies were nothing compared to this. She's *seducing* me. Everything about her is turned up to full volume. The persuasive purr in her voice, her body language, the words coming out of her mouth. And it hits me hard that she's been holding so much of herself back. I don't know *this* Addison. I don't know this girl who looks almost shy while she's spreading her thighs, then says things that make my cock throb.

Possessiveness crackles in my middle, before starting to burn. I'm supposed to know everything about her. Are there people out there who know Addison as this bedroom-eyed temptation? It doesn't help my jealousy that she was almost set up with Preston tonight. No. The memory is like throwing gasoline on a fire. "Is this how you behave with men?" I grind her against my lap, darkly satisfied when her mouth opens on a gasp. "Have you been out with any men since you came to Charleston?"

Sparks plume in her gaze. "How can I date, when you take up all my free time?"

"That's not an answer." I thrust into the notch of her thighs, the desk creaking underneath her. "Have you worn the black high heels?"

Until the question scrapes out of me, I don't realize it has been on my mind. That every time I pass her shoe shelf, I check to make sure those heels aren't in use. What would I do if they were? Is it any of my business? For a moment, she simply stares, letting my words hang in the air. "No, I haven't worn the heels. No men, either." She leans up and in, so close I can feel her breath on my mouth as she whispers. "Although, there's always a possibility that I'm lying. Why don't you taste my mouth and see if you can tell?"

My growl ends abruptly when our lips meet.

Oh. Jesus.

Her mouth has been close so many times and this? *This* was waiting for me? How have I managed not to fucking *maul* her? Our lips haven't even parted yet and I'm in trouble. She whimpers a little and a devastating current passes through me, my tongue tracing her lower lip, rubbing more fully, our noses, chins, cheeks touching.

And the second she opens up for my tongue, I have no choice but to fuck her tonight. My best friend, my roommate, my conscience. The lines around our relationship blur immediately and fade into nothing. *God.* She's nothing I've ever experienced.

There's no resistance or pretense. She's my sexy little offering with open thighs and an eager body—and she wants me to know it. *Wants* me to take. Her head falls all the way back, a gasp leaving her throat when my hands close over her tits. Hard nipples press into the center of my palms, plump flesh fitting and begging to be molded. I want to suck them, but I can't get enough of her smooth bourbon and cool mint flavor. Her mouth corresponds to mine, meeting my movements as if maybe we've done this before but have been deprived of it for a very long time. *Too goddamn long.* Every time our tongues stroke together, she shifts around on the desk, like she's hurting as much as I am.

And Jesus, am I hurting. I've *never* needed this badly. There's a voice in the back of my head telling me I will regret jeopardizing what I have with Addison, but for the first time in my life, I can't set aside the hunger of my body. It's always been healthy, but it has never reared up before and stolen my common sense. In the past, sex has been a necessary exchange. Polite, even. There's nothing polite about the way Addison pushes her tits into my hands, her hips rolling under the friction of mine. So the hell with it. If I'm giving in, I'm giving in hard. Is there even a choice?

Dropping my hands from her breasts, I shove Addison's thighs wider and break our kiss, ready to unzip and ride out this lust. But when I see her dazed expression and puffy lips, affection catches me like a fastball to the chest. "Lord, you're beautiful." I run my thumb across her shiny mouth. "Aren't you, sugar?"

Her gaze lifts to mine. "I wasn't lying about the shoes," she murmurs. "Or the men."

"I know you weren't." I reach under her dress, snagging the side waistband of her panties and peeling them down her legs. "You tasted nothing but sweet."

That seems to shake her out of her fog, although I'm not sure why. All I know is she sits forward and begins to unfasten my belt, her lower lip caught between her teeth. My zipper comes down a moment later, followed by Addison pushing my pants and briefs down, down, until they stop, bunched at my knees. Our mouths meet as she removes my jacket, my own hands fighting to lift her skirt at the same time. But everything—my blood flow, my coherent thoughts, time itself—stops when she begins to stroke me off.

"You're so big," she rasps against my mouth, a shuddering passing through her body. "And I'm not sweet, Elijah. You don't have to be sweet with me, either."

So many things demand my attention. The sight of Addison's hand traveling up and down my cock, the bare flesh I've revealed by lifting her skirt, the sound of us struggling to breathe. My hands beg to touch and I don't deny them, my fingers parting the folds of her wet pussy, a finger sliding into the heat. "Don't you dare tell me this isn't sweet," I groan, twisting my finger to get it deeper into the tight space. "Same way you forget to be mean to me sometimes, this wet little pussy can't hide its sweetness, either, can it? Yeah, it's letting me know exactly how nice it's going to be to me."

Addison moans, her walls clenching around my single digit. "Please. I can't wait."

"Me either," I mutter, adding a second finger between her legs and listening to her cry out. "Tight girl wants a hard fuck, doesn't she?"

"Yes. *Yes.*"

"Wants to get it on my desk so I won't be able to work without thinking about her spread thighs and little pout, isn't that right?"

Her only response is a shaky exhale.

I've never spoken to a woman like this before—never even been compelled to—but it's instinct telling me Addison will respond to it. Hell, that *I'll* respond to it. Nothing has ever felt more natural than releasing filth into her ear, while pressing my fingers up inside her, finding the spot that makes her jolt and tickling it, tickling it, harassing it until she screams. Alcohol. It's the alcohol, right? I ignore the voice reminding me this isn't the first time I've been tipsy during sex, but it is the first time I haven't been restricted. Held to my daytime standard of respectful son and future mayor. Here and now, I don't have to be a gentleman with Addison.

"*Elijah,*" Addison whines, biting at my ear, her strokes of my cock losing rhythm. "I want you inside me. I need you inside me."

"Condom." The single word scrapes out of me. "I don't have a condom."

"Pill. I'm on the pill," she breathes, thumbing the head of my dick. "You can come inside me so deep, I—"

"*Enough.*" I can't hold off any longer and there's no need because my fingers are slippery and warm from her body. *You can come inside me. You don't have to be sweet with me.* Those words ring in my ears as we guide my cock home and I punch my hips—once, twice—sinking my inches into heaven and hell. Her scream rattles my eardrums and my own growl joins in, flaying my throat raw. She's too tight to move right away, but I can't physically keep myself from holding her in place while I grind into her heat. "Go ahead," I rasp, my lust deafening enough to drown out any remaining reservations about sleeping with my best friend. Starvation takes the wheel and I'm all animal need. "Complain some more about how I take up all your time. Complain even though you wait up for me. Made me the key yourself."

"I love it. I love it," she pushes through her teeth, her eyes blind. "M-move. *Please.*"

I wrap an arm around the back of her hips and start to thrust, my muscles ready to snap in half over the need for release. Already. Slowing down is impossible, though, with Addison's bare backside squeaking up and back on the desk, her tits lifted by the neckline of her dress and jiggling enough to drive me insane. "You're not to go jogging anymore in that outfit," I say, baring my teeth against her ear. "You know the one I'm talking about."

"No, I don't," she gasps. "Which one?"

"The one with the pink bra." I lift my head to find her face flushed, excited. "The one that makes me think of every matching pink part of your body."

Her eyelids flutter, remaining at half-mast. "You think of me in my bra, Elijah?" She leans closers, takes hold of my shirt and rips it down the middle, sending buttons pinging in every direction. "Do you think of me wearing it while you touch your—"

"*Yes.*" I bring my thumb between us to tease her clit, my pumps growing more forceful out of necessity. Because I'm talking about things that I've never spoken about out loud and I'm so close to coming, it's like I'm being choked. "I'm sorry. *Fuck.* I couldn't help it."

"You're sorry?" She sinks her fingernails into my ass. *Hard.* "What you were doing was a little wrong. Did the wrong make you bigger and harder?"

The pressure in my balls becomes so unbearable, I can't respond, but in my head I'm answering *yes, yes, yes.* How does she know?

"You felt guilty looking, didn't you, Elijah? Wanting to push up my flimsy little bra and put your mouth where you shouldn't." Her finger slides down the split of my ass, stopping over the back entrance, but pushing, pushing. "What else did you think about?"

"Keeping you warm in my bed." I sense her breath catching, but my focus is deadlocked on the pressure she's placing on me...there. "Pushing down your panties and..."

"Fucking me?" she whispers in my ear. "Show me how hard you've wanted to do that."

I'm sucking in gulpfuls of air now, my mouth buried at the crook of her neck. What the hell is happening here? It's like she reached into a part of my brain I wasn't aware of and now she's exploiting what she found. At this point, I'm battering into her like a beast during mating season, my cock so sensitive I can feel it rubbing her clitoris, can feel that nub growing plump as her breath grows shorter. And that finger of hers. What is she going to do with it? "*Addison.*"

That's what pushes her over the cliff. Me saying her name. "Elijah, oh my God. *Oh my God.*" Her head falls back on a choppy moan and she tightens around me like a bolt, her hips twisting as she rides it out, feet bashing off the desk. No way I can hold on with her pussy spasming around me, so tight. So fucking tight. I drive deep just as Addison sinks that finger into me and light slashes across my vision, guttural curses ripping from my throat.

Need and pressure leave my body so fast and with such force, I go lightheaded, no recourse but to pound into Addison harder. Light up top. Heavy, heavy, heavy between my thighs. It's an unusual sensation, but she wraps her legs around my hips and breathes into my ear, grounding me. I'm guilty for liking it, this thing I never considered, and maybe that's what makes me shake under the force of the good. It just keeps going and going. And even while the storm keeps raging and my body depletes itself on an endless round of climaxing, I'm hit with the sudden certainty that I'm right where I'm supposed to be.

That certainty tells me I've made a huge mistake.

Addison

I'VE NEVER BEEN more thankful to already be dressed. It only takes me a split second to locate my thong on the ground and drag it up my legs. Shoving my feet into my sandals almost simultaneously leads to some balance issues and I have to catch myself on the desk—thank you, bourbon-bolstered orgasm—but I'm fine. I'm fine. *I'm fine.*

The guy I'm nuts about—hello, understatement—could not be making it any clearer that he would rather be on a melting ice cap in the middle of the fucking ocean, but hey, it's cool. You win some, you lose some, right? And I've definitely lost this one.

Knowing my complexion must be tomato red, I keep my face down and turned away, while I search for my coat. The coat I shed like a lame version of a Bond Girl intent on seduction. What was I thinking? Elijah is well-mannered gentleman who dates female versions of himself. He has probably never had a woman beg so brazenly for sex, let alone dirty talk him and stick their finger up his ass. Oh God. I just stuck my finger up *my best friend's ass.*

I mean, I loved it. A lot. But he obviously didn't. He's got that thousand-mile stare he usually gets after a terrible day at work. Or when someone brings up his wedding.

He's still in love with Naomi. He probably doesn't even realize it, but he is. Ever since he moved in with me, I've suspected the change of scenery meant he wouldn't have to think about her or the incident. But I've just forced him to think of it. Her. Haven't I? How differently things could have been. How great of a match they were, especially compared to him and me.

There is no him and me.

And I've probably just lost him as a friend, too.

My legs are still doing a post-orgasm shake and I've never been more satisfied on a physical level, but mentally I'm breaking. I have to get out of here.

When I try to leave the room, Elijah blocks my exit. "Wait. Let me straighten myself up and I'll see you home."

My heart plummets into my stomach. "You're…not staying at the apartment now?"

He's looking down at the belt buckle he's fastening, so I can't read him. "The hotel is closer and I have an early morning."

"Right," I manage. "That makes sense."

Finished with his task, Elijah props both hands on his hips. "Addison, I take full responsibility for this. We've both been drinking—"

I interrupt him with a laugh. Producing the noise when I want to scream loud enough to shatter the sound barrier hurts. But I do it. "It's fine. I really don't need to hear this."

His brows draw together, like I just suggested we train to

become gymnasts. "We need to talk about what just happened."

"Fully disagree." Smiling, I pat him on the chest. "I know you haven't gotten lucky in a while, but you're making a big deal out of nothing."

"It's not nothing." I try to bypass him again, but he snags my wrist and draws me to a halt. "Listen to me very carefully," he says in that deep, southern big daddy drawl. "I'm not going to let this come between us."

"Oh, really? You've already changed your plans for the night." The words are out before I can stop them and I hate the guilt that creeps into his expression. "You know what? Don't bother coming over tomorrow, either. I have early workdays, too."

"I know you do." He steps back with a laugh lacking all humor, seeming to gather his thoughts. "What we have is honest, Goose. I don't think I've had an honest relationship in my goddamn life until you. Know why? Because once sex and expectations and future plans distort everything, that's when people get disappointed. That's when lies are told and promises get broken. I don't want that to happen to us."

It's killing me not to shout *it won't, it won't*. My throat aches from the effort of keeping those words trapped. And my stupid heart is singing and dancing because he just called what we have a relationship, which is pitiful. Completely wretched, since he's just trying to let me down easy. I've gone from his cool girl pal to the girl who will want more things from him—and he doesn't have more to give. Another woman has his more already. "I get it. Sex is a huge no no, but it's cool that you've been picturing me in the pink bra to rub one out."

Have to admit, his chagrin gives me a measure of satisfaction. "I've felt like shit about it, too. That's why I can't pass a supermarket without buying out the damn cereal aisle for you."

"You've been buying me *guilt cereal?*"

A corner of his mouth ticks up. "That's what I've been calling it, too."

Idiot. Adorable, well-raised, gesture-making gentleman *idiot.*

I hold up my hands. "What do you want from *me*, Elijah?"

He moves closer and I can't help it, I suck in a lungful of eucalyptus and sweat and our scents mingled together. It's better than I could have imagined. I want to bury my face in his chest and feel his arms around me, but he wouldn't interpret it right. Or he *would*, rather, and he wouldn't want my adoration. "I want the same thing I've always wanted." He sends a glance toward the window. "Your place feels like home to me. It's where I want to be."

"Then take it," I say, Elijah staring back at me in utter confusion. "Since you love my place so much, you can have it for now. In the meantime, *I'll* take *your* colossal mansion on the Battery. Sound good?"

"What are you talking about?"

Honestly? I have no idea. Until I make the suggestion out loud, my brain doesn't quite process it. Here is what I know. I can't—I can't—go back to domestic non-bliss with Elijah. Not yet. Not when I know what he feels like inside me. Perfect, huge, hot. Not when I know he likes to act possessive when he's turned on. Oh, I know those rough demands were all an illusion in the cold post-coital glow, but my God, how will I sleep knowing the man who issued them with such authority is across the hall? My lips still feel molded to the shape of his. The sound he made when I used my finger on him echoes in the dark recesses of my head. Agonized ecstasy.

No, I can't go back to greeting him with a high five when he walks into my apartment. Or sitting on the opposite end of the couch when we watch Kimmel. Not yet. But while I get my heart back under control, I don't want to lose him completely. The very idea fills me with a terrible, excruciating panic. Moving into his house means our connection won't be severed. It might even allow me to feel close to him, in a way, without having him close.

"You've been staying with me for months. Return the favor." I gesture to his pocket, silently urging him to give up the key. "It's a shame to leave it sitting there unused and I think…maybe after tonight, we should just take some time apart—"

"This is ridiculous." He drags a hand through his hair. "What is this really about, Addison? Wounded feminine pride?"

I narrow my eyes. "Tread very carefully."

"Duly noted." As I watch, his gaze trails down to my neckline, before lifting again. His throat works in a long swallow. "The sex was fucking incredible. Is that what you need to hear? Are you marching out of here with a temper because I didn't say so?"

"Okay, now I want the key just so I can stab you with it." I take a giant step closer to him, tilting my head back to keep eye contact. "I don't need you to tell me it was incredible. I was there. Key, please." A thought hits me out of nowhere and I don't quite manage to keep my bravado intact. "Unless you think people won't approve of Addison *Potts* inhabiting those four fancy walls."

His anger is so raw and brilliant, I forget to breathe. With jerky movements, he reaches into his pocket and removes the key, folding my hand around it. "For the record, I think taking this ridiculous break is only going to make things worse. Fuck the hotel. I'll own that mistake. I'd come home with you right now, if I didn't know you so damn well. If I didn't know you aren't finished being stubborn."

"Shut up."

"In a minute." He shifts closer and I can't tell in the shadows, but my lips are tingling. Is that where he's looking? "If anyone says a damn thing to you about being there, they'll be picking their teeth up off the floor."

"You can't do things like that," I whisper, commanding myself not to levitate. "You're the mayor now."

"Watch me."

Elijah might not have a single romantic notion about me, but he's a good friend. God, why can't that be enough? Why can't I be satisfied? "Can I go now?"

After a long hesitation, he nods and I'm out the door a second later, focusing on putting one foot in front of the other. As soon as I hit the bottom of the stairs, I'm calling the closest Uber, not wanting to have another encounter with Elijah outside the building. Maybe he's right about romance ruining everything. I'm already trying to avoid him, aren't I? My best friend. My other option is being in his company and pretending I don't want to make out with him, though, so this is where I'm at right now. Out of choices.

Thankfully, my Uber pulls up within three minutes and I slink down in the backseat, letting out a shaky breath when we begin heading in the opposite direction of my apartment. In no time at all, the houses get bigger, more opulent. The parked cars turn expensive. I lower the back window of the car and salt air lands on my tongue. I've never been to Elijah's mansion before and didn't know the exact address, so I used the park across the street as my destination when I called the Uber. The driver lets me off outside now without a word and I stare at the three-story—home?—across the street. It sits on the corner, looking more important than any other mansion along the Battery. It's white with a balcony on each level, decorated with black wrought-iron rails and pillars. Wind sweeps off the Ashley River and rustles the palm trees in quiet welcome.

I swallow and cross the road. The gate groans when I let myself into the courtyard, but I bury my wince. If the neighbors look out their windows at me, so be it. I've been putting up the owner of this house for months and he's given me the damn key. I have a right to be here.

Briefly, I wonder what my mother would think. Or my grandmother. To know I'm about to walk into the Du Point mansion, pretty as I please, considering neither of them were allowed inside after what my mother did. Maybe it's the eerily still night or the old-fashioned style of the house, but I'm hit with a sense of nostalgia. A sense that I'm righting a wrong done to the women of my family. That feeling keeps my chin held high as I unlock the door, cross the threshold and flip on the light—

My mouth drops open, heart going wild in my ears.

Light from an overhead chandelier sets the floors gleaming, like a lake of cherry wood fire. Staircases hold out their arms to me on either side of the massive foyer, an architectural welcome. The musky smell of disuse hangs in the air, but there's an undercurrent of wealth. Professionally cleaned carpets and oiled wood and pine.

It's extraordinary. No, it's…more than that. Exquisite. Timeless.

I want to run back outside and slam the door.

Who has Elijah been kidding? He preferred my dusty, cluttered Christmas-themed apartment to this place? This…millionaire family man's respite on the water?

No. No, he's been avoiding his life. Back in his office, I had the fleeting realization that Elijah had been staying with me—in year-round Christmas—to avoid reality. And what happened with Naomi. That theory cements itself now. Hard. He's been hiding away with me. I've been giving him an *excuse* to hide. A place to do it.

This is where he belongs. Not with me.

I'm holding him back.

My vision blurs as I close the door behind me. With the click still hanging in the air, I slump into a cross-legged position on the floor. Beneath my fingertips, the floor is smooth and rich, even through a layer of dust. This place is unfamiliar to me, yet I don't feel like a stranger. Because it's so Elijah, right down to the masculine class and robust ceiling beams. It's a false sense of comfort, though, because he can't have this place *and* me as a friend. It was easy to pretend in my out-of-the-way two-bedroom, but *this*? This is a life to be embraced.

There *will be* a wife and kids in this place one day. There might even be a chance for Elijah to win back Naomi. But not as long as I'm spending time with him. Causing people to whisper about us and speculate. Allowing him to avoid his future.

I'm hurting him. I have to let him go.

But not before I fix everything.

CHAPTER TWELVE

Elijah

Du Pont victorious in mayoral election despite Getaway Girl scandal.
Gets busy at his desk without delay!
—Southern Insider News

I PULL UP behind the moving truck and shift into park. In front of me, men are already hopping out of the front cab, putting on gloves and taking one final pull of their morning coffee. A man in coveralls throws me a salute, then rolls up the back hatch, probably waking up half the neighborhood. At least someone will be awake. I'm more zombie than human this morning.

Last night, I didn't go back to Addison's apartment. Didn't go to the hotel, either. In fact, I sat on the couch in my office so long, the sun started to come up before I knew a minute had passed. What the hell happened? In the space of an evening, I was elected mayor of Charleston, had the hottest—filthiest—sex of my life. And I think I lost my best friend.

That last one is what has a wrench stuck in my throat.

Somehow this is my fault, but I can't for the life of me figure out where I took a misstep. Yes, I was an active participant in fucking Addison on my desk. There are consequences for what happened. But I'm not seeing the full picture. Something is hanging out right in the periphery of my consciousness and it won't become clear. No matter how much bourbon I drink. No matter how many times I replay Addison's mouth under mine…her breasts in my hands. How uninhibited she was. Those satisfied whimpers.

"Not helping," I mutter, taking a swig of my own lukewarm coffee. "Idiot."

A whole night of thinking and here is what I came up with: Addison can't just stay in my home without furniture. As well as I can remember, there's nothing but a couple twin beds in some of the guest rooms and a handful of rolled up carpets. I'm the owner of the home where she's staying and in the south, there are laws against guests being uncomfortable. Which is why I've moved my furniture out of storage at the crack of dawn and delivered it here, instead of showing up at City Hall the day after the election. There's probably a cake and a banner in the lobby, all manner of folks waiting to slap me on the back, but I'm in last night's clothes trying to see the outline of Addison through the windows. Has she already left for work?

"Hey, boss." That muffled greeting is followed by a knock on the window. "You have the key to the front door?"

"No. We'll have to knock." I open the driver's side door and climb out, my mouth tasting like sludge. "Let's go find out if the lady of the house is present, shall we?"

"Yes, sir." A trio of men follow me up the steps, two of them carrying bubble-wrapped side tables. "I'm glad to hear everything worked out."

My hand pauses in the act of knocking. "I'm sorry?"

"With your fiancée." He taps the side of his head. "I'm glad she came to her senses."

Is he talking about…Naomi? The notion of her coming back and moving into this house, like nothing ever happened, is so absurd, I can't help but laugh. During last night's Epic Evening of Thought, Naomi made an appearance once or twice, but only in the capacity of what came after the wedding. Walking out of the church and feeling like an abject failure. A disappointment to someone who'd once believed in me enough to accept a marriage proposal. It's something I try not to think about, but last night it continued to jump out and bite me. I'm not sure why. "No, this is a different woman who came to her senses."

The mover's face falls. "I'm sorry, boss, I didn't realize."

"Don't worry about it." Everyone still seems uncomfortable, so I give them each a nod. "I appreciate you coming out so early. Lunch is on me later."

"Can I help you?"

Addison's voice comes from the bottom of the stairs and I sidestep the men to get a look. Ignoring the odd ripple in my gut, I see that she's sweating from a run, one earbud dangling from her right ear. Her cheeks are chapped from the wind and wispy black hairs are coming loose from her ponytail. I'm usually at work by the time she returns from her run, so it's rare that I see her like this. But it feels like the first time. Probably because we're miles away from her apartment and nothing looks or sounds or feels the same.

Also probably because I came inside her last night.

"Elijah?" she says, tilting her head and prompting me. "What's up?"

"Come unlock the door. You're getting furniture."

She's just as surprised by my irritated tone of voice as I am. "I...*no*. I don't need it. There's running water and a bed. A couple pots and pans. I was going to go grab sheets and towels at my place later."

"What about a couch, television, dining table..."

"I'm not planning on staying forever."

Why that rushed statement is a right cross to my face, I can't say. But it serves to make me even more determined to deck out the house like a palace. "Unlock the door or I'll call a locksmith. You're going to be comfortable in my home, goddammit."

Her mouth wobbles and she breaks into a laugh. "What is this? Aggressive southerning?"

Realizing I sounded like a moron, I can't help but laugh, too. Unfortunately, that's when I realize the movers are staring at her like she's a siren straight out of Greek mythology, so my mirth is short lived. "Gentlemen." I cut them a look, then send Addison the exact same one. "Goose."

"Look out, boys." Addison sways up the steps, removing the house key from a tiny, zippered compartment hidden in her running pants. "He's flexing that mayor muscle now."

"The inauguration isn't for weeks," I say, when she's even with me on the porch. A sweaty strand of hair sticks to her neck and vaguely I wonder who saw her running. Men? Did they exchange words or a smile? The possibility makes me feel seasick, but I chalk it up to the hangover. "I'm just getting warmed up."

"You're going to be unbearable when it's official." She unlocks the door and pokes it open with a finger, throwing me a wink. "I take that back. You're unbearable now."

Relief settles in my stomach. Things are back to normal. Apart from the fact that she's living in my house without me, that is. But if she was still out of shape over last night, she wouldn't be poking fun at me just like always, would she? Truth be told, though…I'm not as relieved as I would have expected.

I follow her into the house, but come to a stop when I see a collection of cleaning supplies gathered just inside the foyer. "Lord almighty. Tell me you didn't clean."

"I didn't clean?"

"You did." I pinch the bridge of my nose. "This is an outrage."

She wrinkles her nose as the movers lumber past with a couch. "I know this is going to come as a shock, but most people don't have cleaning ladies. Don't be dramatic."

"*I'm* being dramatic? You changed residences in the middle of the night."

"Now you're stuck with a squatter." She studies her nails. "This is why you never get in cars with strangers."

"Now that's dramatic," I say, pointing at her. "And you're not a squatter. You're a guest."

"Well, then." She drops her hand and looks around. "The hospitable thing to do would be to give me a tour."

"Haven't you already taken an unguided one?"

"In the dark, yes. But I only poked my head into a couple rooms until I found a bed." She smiles. "And before you ask, yes, I slept on a mattress with no sheets."

"The hits just keep on coming," I mutter. "All right, then, Miss Potts. Let's start with the kitchen."

"Aye aye, captain." She clicks her heels together and salutes me. "Lead the way."

When I pass her on the way to the room in question, I have the insane urge to pick her up and tickle her until she screams. But since day one, there has been an unspoken no-touching rule between us. Until last night. I'm determined to put this friendship back on solid ground, so the rule is back in effect, starting now. Ignoring my strangely itchy hands, I hold the swinging door open for her, my eyes straying back to that sweaty hair stuck to her neck as she passes. "Have you been in here yet?"

"No," she whispers, coming to a stop. "I can't believe you

wanted to cook in my dinky little kitchen when you had this waiting for you."

Frowning at her words, I regard the sun-drenched kitchen. Cream-colored cabinets, vintage fixtures, tiled backsplash. Marble-topped island, dark wood floors, stainless steel appliances. No denying it's huge and almost over-the-top glamorous. Big enough to hold the members of a large catering company comfortably when we entertained. We. Naomi and I. Although, we never really spoke about entertaining, did we? It was just a given. Something our parents did and we would be expected to do. "Don't be alarmed when you come home and the pantries and refrigerator are stocked. I'm appointing an intern as soon as I get to the office."

She turns to me with an open mouth. "Elijah, no."

"Addison, yes."

"I'm moving back out."

"Oh no. You're staying put." I escort her back out of the room. "This is what happens when you offer getaway rides to big, bossy southerners."

"Don't steal my jokes."

My mouth twitches. "Downstairs would have been the billiard room. I'm guessing some kind of wine cellar that I never would have set foot in—"

"Why are you talking about everything like it's past tense?" She stops me from climbing the stairs with a hand on my arm, but pulls back like she's been shocked. "This is your home. All these plans you made don't have to be thrown out like yesterday's bath water."

Discomfort climbs the back of my neck. "Are you saying you want a roommate?"

Her cheeks go pink, but she scoffs. "God, no. I came here to get a break from you."

The impulse to pick her up is now twice as strong as before. Only instead of tickling her, I'd like to throw her down on these stairs and call her bluff. After her admissions last night, I know she likes having me around just fine. *Loves it*, if I recall correctly. The only thing that saves her is the movers. And that's a scary thought. It's scary that after last night, I'm noticing how the light makes her skin glow, how she says my name like a sigh. How tight her running pants are in the posterior. Pull it together. That's what I tell myself, even as I search for a way to call her bluff without putting my hands on her. "If you want me to go, just say the word."

Her eyes go wide and vulnerable, but she recovers fast. "Look who's back to being dramatic." She waves her hand at the staircase. "Finish the tour."

My chest tightens with satisfaction. Sort of. Just like last night, I'm still unsettled and it's more than what happened between Addison and me. There's something out of reach and it's driving me crazy. With a tight nod, I head upstairs and turn right down the south hallway. "Guest rooms, mostly, down this way. Although that door at the end…"

"What?"

"I think she…"

"You can say her name to me," Addison says, her voice bright as she glides past. "This was going to be her house."

"Right." I follow Addison, wondering why my ex-fiancée's name sounds so foreign on my tongue. "I think it was going to be a meditation room."

"Oh."

A crack of laughter leaves me. "How do you pack so much judgment into a single word?"

"Practice." She seems to brace her shoulders before walking into the small room that overlooks the bay. "I can't get over the view. I spent most of the night sitting on the third-floor balcony watching the boats."

Don't sing to them or they'll crash on the rocks. The thought catches me off guard, but it sticks. I can picture her up there, dark hair flying around in the wind, beckoning to passing sailors. Will I ever get to see her up there? "You like the house?" I rasp.

She shrugs one shoulder. And coming from Addison, that's a resounding yes. "It reminds me of you."

Why am I holding my breath? "Does it?"

"Mmmhmm. Old-fashioned and charming..." She squints at my backside. "With a big old kitchen."

The heat that weaves up my neck is humiliating, but I cough my way through it. I'm not sure if my usual embarrassment is at play, or if I'm remembering for the thousandth time how hard I came when she used that damn finger on me. Was it supposed to make me shake like a damn teenager? "It's not polite to make ass jokes about your tour guide."

"Oh come on. You know I love that thing."

When she crosses to the window and looks down, I ask, "What are you looking at?"

"Just checking to see if your milkshake brought all the boys to the yard."

I sigh.

She rolls her lips together to flatten a smile.

"Since meditation isn't your thing, what would you use this room for?"

The smile drops completely. "That hardly matters."

"I want to know."

Her hands slide into her pockets as she turns in a slow circle.

"Probably...an ornament assembly room. I don't know." I barely have time to picture her materials and ribbons strewn all over the floor before she shoots out of the room. "Okay, Captain. I got up early and swung by my place to pack some clothes and get my car, because I have plans. Let's wrap this hospitality mission up."

Plans. I want to know them. Badly. But her tone tells me it'll be a cold day in hell before she tells me a single one.

"Hospitality doesn't have a time limit," I say, following her while trying to ignore the tight side-to-side sway of her backside. Not so easy, now that my hands are acquainted with its shape and texture. "You should know, you've been generous with yours for months."

She slows to a stop and pivots to face me, a line between her brows.

I've gone from wanting to tickle her, to getting her under me...and now I just want to shake her. "Why do you look surprised?" I step closer, pressing a finger to my chest. "I'm grateful, Addison. For all the times you stayed up and kept me company, made me dinner, let me be in a bad mood. Let me have the remote." We both laugh quietly. "Now it's my turn."

"I liked having you there," she whispers, turning her face away. "It was okay."

A thud starts in my chest. "I was an asshole last night. I'm sorry. I shouldn't have disappeared into my own head like that. We should have gone home together and talked once we'd gotten some sleep." She says nothing. "We were good, just as we were. We can go back to that right now."

She opens her mouth to respond, but the movers choose that moment to breach the top step with a headboard. It takes me a second to place it—hell, I barely had a hand in picking any of the furniture—but the rich wood finally rings a bell. The master bed.

Addison and I stand there and watch as one of the movers nudges open a door with his foot, guiding his partners back through the entrance. It's obvious she didn't include the master bedroom as part of her nighttime tour, because she gasps at the size of it, the domed ceiling, the view of Charleston's wealthiest neighborhood beyond.

"We can't go back, Elijah," she murmurs. "We should never have been living together to begin with. It put all this on hold."

What? "No. *I* put it on hold."

"And I helped make it okay."

The half-defeated, half-determined tone of her voice is making me nervous. "Addison—"

She's already moving. "I have to go."

"*Wait.*" Halfway down the stairs, she turns, framed by the foyer, chandelier above and a hand poised on the railing. I get this odd déjà vu feeling, like I've seen this image before. Or maybe I've dreamed it. "Yes?"

"When am I going to see you?" I'm shouting and I don't care who hears me. "Or are you just cutting me off."

"Even best friends don't see each other every single day." She laughs, but it falls flat. "Just…can I have a little time?"

Time to do what? After a dead string of seconds, I nod, no choice but to agree. When the door closes behind her, the energy in the house drops and scatters…and I can't shake the certainty that nothing will be the same next time I see her.

CHAPTER THIRTEEN

Addison

As we live and breathe.
Was that Getaway Girl getting cozy in the mayor's
house...without the mayor?
Looks like someone dug for gold and struck pay dirt.
—TheTea.com

I SNAG THE canvas rope looped around the front of the kayak and tug it down the beach, toward the water of the Cooper River. With the oar in my other hand, I definitely look like a bowlegged penguin, but so does everyone else launching into the river today. So at least I'm in good company.

"You sure you know what you're doing, now, ma'am?" calls the fortyish rental guy behind me. "I can take you out the first time, if you're not sure."

"That's not necessary," I say over my shoulder. "I've done this before."

Okay, so I watched a YouTube tutorial, but it was really detailed.

I stop at the edge of the river and take a deep breath, trying to remember when kayaking went from potential future activity to my current situation. Probably around the four-day mark of not seeing Elijah. Sounds about right.

Upon calling the phone number written on the kayaking

brochure I discovered in my grandmother's copy of the *The Remains of the Day*, I found out it belonged to a rental hut at Remley's Point. It took a little convincing to make them go through their records, but it had been worth it. I found out my grandmother had indeed rented from them frequently.

Check you out, woman. A secret kayaker.

The Christmas apartment makes me feel close to her. But it's enclosed by walls and crammed so full of distractions and noise, I wondered if thinking of her would feel different in a wide open space, seeing the same sights she passed, listening to the water ripple.

It was the perfect chance to remember my grandmother and do something different, at the same time. Something that doesn't involve my job, my old apartment or my new—*temporary*—mansion. All those things remind me of Elijah, though. And if I'm going to reclaim at least some of my heart from the man, I need new. I need exciting.

I need to risk injury or death.

Today, I'm marking a full week since I left Elijah standing on the staircase of his home, furniture that another woman picked out being positioned around him. There have been traces of him, of course. Such as my favorite foods showing up in the pantry. And my shoe shelf, which I hadn't had a chance to detach and lug to the mansion yet, appearing beside the entry door.

Do I miss him?

No. No, I just feel like a field that hasn't soaked in any rain or sunshine in a month. That's all. I thought some time and distance might dull the effect of him, but it's not helping. My mind keeps inventing excuses to show up with groceries at the apartment, cook dinner and pretend like nothing ever happened. Like I can't still feel his mouth moving on mine, his hands all over my body. Or hear his warm voice, his wry jokes, the way he sometimes calls me *sugar* when he's feeling sweet. *Goose* when he's teasing me.

I place my backpack in the kayak, careful not to jostle the contents. I remove my shoes and socks, stowing them in the hull, as well. Then I push it out into knee-deep water and step inside, muttering a thank you when the rental guy appears beside me to study the vessel while I climb in. He gives me a push and...I'm off. I'm actually moving, cutting through the faint chop of blue. There's hardly any wind today, but here and there, a breath will lift the hair off my neck. I'm just grateful it's not enough to knock me off balance, because my body is already straining under the effort of not tilting the kayak too far in one direction. The sun beats down, occasionally blocked by puffy white clouds. And when I start to lose myself in the stroking rhythm of the paddle, I remind myself why I'm here.

Up ahead, Drum Island draws closer. None of the other people who launched at Remley's Point are stopping there, continuing down the river in the direction of downtown Charleston. Which makes it perfect for me, because my plans definitely don't need an audience. In fact, they're probably illegal and that's the main reason I refused the guide's help. With the Arthur Ravenel Jr. Bridge traffic rumbling in the distance, I paddle up onto the shore and climb out, grumbling when my bare feet sink down into mud. Tugging the kayak behind me, I continue to walk until I find more solid, grassy ground. I take my backpack with me and sit down, legs outstretched, the river spreading out in front of me.

"Shit, that's pretty," I breathe, unzipping my backpack. A second later, the "urn" holding my grandmother's ashes is in my hand. A nifty little zap tickles up my arm and I huff a disbelieving laugh, setting the statue of Mrs. Claus down between my legs. "So…" I swallow the lump that builds in my throat. "Come here often?"

If possible, the empty island grows even more silent around me.

"You don't have to answer me. Actually, I'd prefer if you didn't. I'm not a huge fan of ghosts." I bury my heels in the earth. "Not that I don't want to see you or anything. Although would you recognize me now? Not so sure. It's been a pretty long time. I'm *sorry* it's been such a long time."

A gentle wind passes me, ruffling the grass, so I run my fingers through the fine green threads. "I just…I don't know. I came to tell you something. Or maybe I just needed to tell someone out loud, so I don't back out." I search for the right words to say to my grandmother, who may or may not be listening. "So I fell into the same trap as…Mama." God, I haven't called her that— haven't called her anything in so long—the word tastes acidic on my lips. "I fell for a man who I can't have. But I want you to know something. I'm going to make things right. Instead of just running away, I'm going to weave everything back together, the way it's supposed to be. At least, I'm going to try. When he's around me, I don't seem capable of anything but praying he can't hear my heartbeat.

"I understand Mama now. I'm not mad at her anymore, but I'm…I want to be better than her. I don't want to be someone's regret."

I'm not sure how long I sit there, laying my path out in front of me, brick by brick, but when it's solid and I can see the finish line out in the distance, I just kind of slump back into the grass and stare up at the sky. Oh God. This is going to hurt.

"You know, I was going to scatter your ashes here today, but I don't feel ready yet. Is it okay with you if I wait for another day? Don't answer."

Using the ground as leverage, I stand and shake life back into my legs, surprised when I check my cell phone to find out two hours has passed. I only have one bar of reception, but today has given me a buzzing sense of adventure. So I don't think. I just use my measly cell coverage to pull up my contact for Lydia and dial her number.

"Hey," she answers on the second ring. "I thought you joined the circus."

Her voice is warm and familiar against my ear. It also makes me think of Elijah, but I shake off his image. "Um. I tried, but they've already filled their freak quota."

Lydia's laugh tumbles down the line, static intercepting some of it. "What's up?"

I square my shoulders. "I was wondering if you wanted to go grab a drink tonight?"

Elijah

I STAND OUTSIDE the apartment, turning the key over and over in my hand. The tip sticks in my palm and I let it bite deep, trying to get rid of the queasiness in my stomach. It has been there all week, simmering, reminding me of the week before Basic. Being stuck in limbo while anticipating the unknown. I've never been the guy who collected friends—I'm more of a few and fierce kind of man—but hell if I haven't been...lonely, even while surrounded by reporters, staffers, a transition team, constituents and interns.

I've been living in the Dewberry for a week and haven't set

foot inside Addison's place, except that time I used my lunch break to steal her shoe shelf. There was that. But no significant amount of time has been spent here. Not like usual, when my whole day is working toward the moment I can walk through her door.

There have been droves of interviews and meetings and appearances since election day and I've needed the comfort of this apartment more than ever. Just a place where I can check out and not be prodded every ten seconds for solutions. My kind of solutions don't happen over night. They're not quick fixes and they're built to last, but that's not what the press wants to hear. So I smile at their impatience and work twice as hard. Plowing through paperwork until I'm exhausted has suited me just fine this week, because getting stuck in a quiet moment like this is when I think too much of other things.

Every time I climb into my truck to come here, I get back out and say I'll make the drive tomorrow, instead. When I'm not so busy. When I'm free to shut down my phone and zone out.

So here I am. Standing here, my whole body experiencing a weird lethargy, trying to stare a hole in the door.

"What is wrong with you?" I mutter, sliding the key into the lock and jiggling. "Standing out here like a goon…"

I know the second I step inside the apartment and don't feel the usual crackle of rightness. I know why I haven't come here. Or why it just feels like four overly decorated walls and nothing like it used to.

Addison isn't here.

Feeling like I'm in a daze, I close the door behind me and leave my briefcase sitting on the dining table. I go into the kitchen and flip on the master switch for all the decorations, hoping to revive that sense of calm I used to get. But everything sounds tinny and kind of terrifying, like a haunted carnival.

"Dammit." I turn off the cacophony of sounds and the place goes silent. So silent, I can hear the television next door, a cat meowing behind the building. "I'm a jackass."

Deep down, I know I've been coming to this place only because of my best friend, haven't I? It's why I let a week pass without making the short journey. She's the only reason this goddamn two-bedroom in Eastside ever felt like home. Now it's got that same cold, expectant air as the mansion. Before Addison moved in, anyway. Last week, nothing about it struck me the same way it did when Naomi and I met the realtor.

No, it was better. Brighter. I could see possibilities that weren't there before.

Because of her.

I lean back against the kitchen cabinets and drag my hands down my face. When did I grow a beard? I have a vague recollection of my father telling me to shave, but it went in one ear and out the other, like everything else this week.

What the hell am I going to do? I miss my best friend. I can admit that much to myself. Now that I've stopped drowning myself in work, it's finally becoming apparent how much. A slice was cut in my stomach when she walked out of the mansion last week and it yawns wider every time I breathe. Her mean remarks and grudging smile are what make me happy. Sitting beside her on the couch, making ornaments, cooking—activities we never did in my home growing up. Addison gave those to me and I don't want to give them up. I don't want to give them up *with her*, because I'd be fooling myself if I said cooking with Chris and Lydia would be just as satisfying.

Even best friends don't see each other every single day.

Addison was right about that. Yet I can't deny having somewhat of a...preoccupation with her. Questions that travel through my head on an hourly basis include: Which bedroom is she sleeping in? What if she twists her ankle while jogging? Is she still sitting on the third-floor balcony at night?

The answer to that last question is yes. She is. I gave in on the second night and drove past the house. Twice. That's what a man does when he misses his friend, right?

Wrong.

I can't keep pretending that there isn't *more* to my relationship with Addison. There's attraction. Jesus *Christ*, is there attraction. Ignoring it stopped being possible at some point before the election and now it's what keeps me awake at night. The way her body arched on my desk, her eyes teasing me. Her frown. And god*damn*. Her wet little pussy keeps me tossing and turning more than anything. How her body could welcome me so sweetly while barely fitting what I've got...I can't stop thinking of how incredible every thrust felt. How she encouraged me to be rough, in a way I've never been with a woman.

The way I miss her is so much more than sex, though. It's everything that came before we went there, right down to that thing she does with the glue gun, drawing it like a Wild West outlaw and quoting Dirty Harry.

Before I can think better of it, I'm on my feet and moving toward her bedroom. My hand pauses on the knob, though. "This is an invasion of privacy. You should not be doing this." My hand drops, but immediately returns. "I'll confess and apologize someday when she's in a good mood."

That's if I get to see her again.

The abrasive thought is what pushes me into the room, the scent of her lighting me up like a thousand-watt bulb. There are no sheets on the bed, which I'm surprised to find disappoints me.

What was I going to do? Sniff them? I wonder what the people of Charleston would think to know they elected a secret sheet fetishist.

I move to the pile of books on her nightstand, taking note of the titles. *The Girl Who Kicked the Hornets' Nest*, some smaller, paperback romance novels. A few classics. Noticing there's a gap in the middle of *The Remains of the Day*, I pick it up and flip to the center page. There in the crease, still somewhat fresh and fragrant, is a flattened yellow rose. One of the yellow roses I brought her when she was sick? It has to be. It can't have been inside the book longer than two or three weeks, matching the timing.

Something shifts in my chest and I sit down on the edge of the bed, holding up the yellow rose to the window light. Preserving a flower doesn't seem like an Addison move. At all. She's not the whimsical type. At least that I know of. I wasn't aware she could dirty talk me into another dimension, either, was I? Didn't know she liked to look out over the water for hours on end. Or that she could gasp over things like master bedrooms and gourmet kitchens, while looking kind of sad at the same time.

Do I know the whole Addison or just pieces?

Not liking that second possibility at all, I carefully place the yellow rose back inside the book. After staring at it for a moment, I enclose it within the pages once more and place the book back on the nightstand.

My cell phone vibrates in my pocket and I groan, already resolved not to answer. But when I tug the object out of my pocket and see Chris's name, I hit talk. "Hey, man."

"Hey." A short pause. "You don't sound like the guy I just watched charm Charleston on the evening news."

Did I charm people? In every one of those interviews, I'm

positive they're getting sick of my voice laying down the same facts again and again. "Listen." I mash my index finger and thumb into my eyes. "You feel like a beer?"

"That's why I was calling," Chris says. "Bring your ass over with a six-pack. I'm on babysitting duty tonight."

"Sounds like a plan." I take one last look around Addison's room and get up from the bed. "Where's Lydia?"

"Out."

Something about the way he says it so fast piques my interest. "Out where?" My pulse starts to kick in my wrist. "With who?"

No answer.

"Is she with Addison?"

I'm ready to jump down the phone by the time he gets around to answering. "Come to think of it, that rings a bell."

Jesus. Is there a pickaxe stuck in my belly? I glance down to double-check, but nothing is there. Addison is out on a Saturday night? Just…looking the way she does around a bunch of hounds? When we stayed inside the apartment together every night, her attractiveness was safe. This is not safe. An image of her laughing with another man tightens my hand around the phone. No. *Nope*. This isn't going to work. Addison is my best friend. And she's now the woman I crave on an hourly basis. Ignoring how badly I want her is insane. Especially when someone could take her from me. I don't even like the idea of her *in the company* of someone else. "I'm going to need to know where they went."

Chris sighs. "Are you going to pass this off as a protective big brother act?"

"No. I'm not."

"About time." He says something muffled to his daughter, before coming back on the line. "Listen, she's out with my wife. They're not prowling for a hookup."

"You don't know that. Lydia could be playing Addison's wingman."

"Wingwoman. And I can see no amount of reason is going to convince you they're just having tapas and going dancing."

My head almost explodes off my shoulders. "*Dancing?*"

"Girls dance with each other, Elijah. This isn't the army ball." He laughs and I can visualize him shaking his head. "How old *are* you?"

Done waiting, I collect my briefcase and stride toward the door. "Text me the name of the place."

"You're not going to do yourself any favors storming in like Kool-Aid Man. You're the future mayor. Or did you forget?"

I pause in that act of locking the door, because he's right. I'm not thinking clearly. My past relationships didn't have all this…what is this? Angst? How undignified for a thirty-four year old. "I owe you a six pack," I grumble, disconnecting before Chris can respond. Knowing I'm acting out of jealousy doesn't stem the tide. It seems to churn hotter in my gut on the drive to Off the Wagon, where Addison and Lydia have gone dancing in downtown Charleston, a place I've never been, but know is only a fifteen-minute walk from my house. Or…our house. I'm not sure whom it belongs to at present.

One thing I *do* know?

I miss Addison. Like hell.

I also want to fuck her until she's speaking in tongues.

Romantic relationships have begun with far less, haven't they? We started as friends and now we can graduate to more. That's all. There's no pressure. It can be something of our own making. Not quite friends with benefits, because that title cheapens how much I care about her. But I've already been down the "promised couple in love" road and it doesn't work out. Naomi and I loved each other, but once expectations and duty weigh a relationship down, someone gets left behind while the other plows ahead. I can't let that happen to Addison and me.

What we have is friendship. And heat.

It's perfect and it's all we need.

CHAPTER FOURTEEN

Addison

Why the dark circles, Mr. Mayor?
We've got the homemade remedy on page six...
—*Avant-Charleston*

Just where did Miss Naomi Clemons disappear to?
Experts speculate.
—*Charleston Courier*

I F I SQUEEZE my eyes shut really tight and concentrate on the music, I can feel like my old self. The girl who, sure, had some mommy issues, but was mostly a good time. A *great* time, even. When I lived in Brooklyn, just a short while ago, this is who I was. I was low stress dancing girl who wasn't looking for a one-night stand, but if someone impressed her enough, she'd consider it. No attachments, no insomnia, no yearning for some elusive contentment. Just this. Arms above my head on the dance floor. A body in the darkness.

Lights change colors and crawl over unfamiliar faces, until Lydia's comes briefly into view, before she twirls away. Bass tickles my blood. It feels amazing to be making an effort. Just knowing that I can put on a skirt and *move*. There's no cure available for the injured heart that ails me, but the act of seeking one is enough for this minute. Maybe this hour, if I keep dancing.

Calling Lydia was the best decision I could have made. I've been in Charleston for months, but it's still such a mystery to me, apart from the market and the immediate area surrounding my apartment. This place, this vibe and the music, is right down the street from where I'm living. I'm going to take advantage while I can. Yes, my main motive is distracting myself from thoughts of Elijah. He's literally *everywhere.* On the news, in the papers, on the deed to the mansion where I lay my head at night.

But being out tonight is more than a distraction. It's reclaiming my time. Reminding myself that I make choices for Addison. Locking myself away and narrowing my world down to Elijah got me nothing but this giant burden of unrequited love. Something tells me I would still love him even if I'd only given him a ride to the corner on his wedding day, but that hurts too much to think about.

Bottom line is, this is a big step. It's proof I'll be able to survive when this is all over.

"Addison." Lydia slides in front of me, no longer moving. But I get the impression she's battling a smile. "Do you believe in coincidences?"

"No."

"Me either." She sips from her cocktail, which has melted down to a few ice cubes and their runoff. "Elijah is here."

The floor vanishes from under my feet and I'm free falling. At least that's what my stomach feels like. An elevator with snapped cables racing to the bottom of the shaft. Thank God the loss of equilibrium has stopped me from swiveling around like a barber chair to find him in the bar area. Am I really having a mild stroke over seeing my best friend? A man I used to eat dinner with on a nightly basis?

Lydia's hum draws my attention. "Well, you just filled in all my blanks."

"I-I just wasn't expecting him," I rasp. "Should he be in a bar? Isn't that bad PR?"

"He doesn't seem to care."

Finally, I allow my gaze to travel across the dance floor and find Elijah. Oh, sweet mother of God. If I thought my stomach was free falling before, it's broken through the bottom floor now and is hurtling toward the Earth's core. No one in the packed bar is taller than his shoulders. He's like a living legend, receiving applause, shaking hands and taking pictures. His tie is a little loose and he has...grown a beard? Making him look kind of disheveled. A man of the people. Someone presses a pint of beer into his hand and he hefts it up to a round of cheers.

And then his eyes cut through the darkness and land on me. They stay there, drinking me in as sure as he drains a portion of his beer. Black-tarred need scrapes along the lowest part of my belly, sticky and a little bitter. My back straightens to lift my breasts, as if I have no choice in the matter. It's all about chemicals and masochism. Because Elijah's set jaw and hooded eyes tell me he came here for a reason. It had nothing to do with nickel wing night.

"Should we go over and say hello?"

Lydia's voice jolts me from my fog. "I guess so," I say unevenly. "He's making it pretty obvious he knows us."

"Us," she snorts. "Sure."

I'm unprepared for Lydia to take my elbow and drag me across the dance floor, but my heart sings with rapture the closer I get to Elijah. One week has passed since I've seen him and all my senses are making up for lost time. My nose searches the air for eucalyptus, my fingers curl in on themselves wanting to remove that tie. I don't know what I'm expecting when I reach him, but it's definitely not what happens. When I'm a few feet away, Elijah drops his beer on the bar and sweeps me up in a bear hug. I barely gulp down my pitiful sob of pleasure in time.

"Your nose is sunburned, Goose," he says gruffly, into my hair. "It's cute."

My eyelids flutter. Is it possible to stay locked in these arms forever? It's the safest and warmest I've ever felt in my life. "I went kayaking today."

"Did you?" He pulls back to peer down at me. "You're full of surprises."

"Better than just being full of shit, like you." His laugh shakes my whole body—and that's when I remember we're in public and everyone is watching us. "You shouldn't be hugging me this long. It looks…"

"Maybe it looks like what it is." I'm reeling from those seven stupefying words when he says, "Hey, Lydia. Where are you headed?"

"I have to be mommy bright and early tomorrow. My Uber is already waiting outside."

Elijah still hasn't taken his eyes off me. What is happening here? Heat is like an anchor in my belly, pressing down and turning my panties sodden. "I'm going to make sure she gets into the car safely." His attention dips to my mouth and the vibration of his growl wreaks havoc on my lady parts. "When I come back, we're going to have a drink."

I nod dumbly—a first for me—disengaging myself to hug Lydia goodbye with a promise to hang out again soon. Elijah leads Lydia from the bar and I watch through the front window as he stoops down to shake the driver's hand before sending them off with a tap on the roof. Realizing I'm still standing in the same exact spot like a nincompoop, I hop onto the closest available barstool and command myself to woman up.

Although…what is happening here? Has the week apart made a difference? Does he…want me? As a—gulp—girlfriend?

Even as my heart trips all over itself, panic sets in. This is not the plan. I'm not the one that ends up in the mansion with Elijah, floating down the staircase in a silk robe every morning. Or hosting galas like Scarlett O'Hara. I've come to terms with that. Haven't I?

"Bourbon, please. Neat." Elijah takes the seat beside me with a tug of his tie, such classic male charisma, I want to smash a glass. "What are you drinking, Addison?"

"Hold on," the bartender says, stabbing the bar with his index finger. "You're the Getaway Girl, ain't you? You've been dancing over there for an hour and I didn't place you."

Elijah turns to me with a tight smile. "Dancing only with Lydia, I hope."

I'm a hot second away from letting him know I can dance with Lucifer, if I so choose. But the words melt on my tongue like sugar. Later. Later, I'll tell him. When I'm not giddy over him being possessive of me—at all—let alone in front of a stranger. "That's me," I manage smoothly. "Still haven't gotten the imprint of his backside out of my passenger seat."

That sets the bartender off howling and even Elijah can't keep a straight face. "I'd be honored to buy this round, folks," the bartender says. "What are you having, miss?"

"A gin and tonic, please."

The man moves away and Elijah looks me over, starting with my shoes, working his way up my bare thighs. "I guess I should be grateful you're not wearing the high heels."

I lift a shoulder, let it drop. "I'm not looking for a man."

He takes a slow drink of his bourbon when the bartender sets it down. "Maybe you'd be willing to reconsider for me?" Humor tugs on his lips, but his eyes watch me closely. "Even though you prefer blonds."

That earlier panic rears up again, in the midst of my joy. Is he asking to be *my* man? In what capacity? And where did this decision come from? It's not like Elijah to be vague. Not at all. It's as if he doesn't even know what he's asking me. "Why don't we talk for a while?" I thank the bartender for my drink, then take a deep breath. "Have you made any progress with the governor about developing Montague Street?"

Elijah is clearly amused by my sudden professional tone, but there's an overriding pleasure that I remembered the details of our conversation. "Yes, I have. I spoke publicly on air this week about my vision for that plot of land and the governor was asked to comment. Caught him off guard, but we've got the attention of community organizers now—and support is building, along with pressure. He can't ignore that. And I don't think you're as bored with politics as you sometimes pretend to be."

"Maybe. Maybe not." I hum and stir my drink. "Mark is the best message taker at the governor's office, though. If Jessica answers, I hang up and call back."

His drink hits the bar with the clunk. "You phoned in your support."

"No big deal." I shrug. "I was bored."

Elijah's laugh heats me all the way down to my toes. "Damn. You're something else, Goose. Thank you." My shoulders and cheeks flush everywhere his gaze lands until it's a struggle not to squirm in my seat. Finally, he finishes his leisurely scrutiny, his voice tender when he asks his question. "Kayaking. Want to explain?"

"Yeah," I laugh and tuck loose hair behind my ear, like a girl on her first date. "Turns out my grandmother was even more badass than I thought. She used to launch from Remley's Point and kayak down the Cooper River. So I went out today and did the same. I...wanted to see it through her eyes."

He reaches out and rubs his knuckles on my knee—eyes full of comfort—before taking his hand back. "Did you wear a life jacket?"

I keep my features guileless. "What's a life jacket?"

"Not funny. I've never been convinced kayaking around Charleston is safe. Not when there are speed boats ripping past you going ninety miles an hour." He frowns into his drink. "I'm going to look into it on Monday."

"This is when you stomp your cane." I give him a teasing look. "You're not going to pass a law to prevent me from kayaking, are you?"

"I might." His eases off his chair and moves close. Close enough that his belt buckle brushes my knees. "I'd do that and more to keep you safe."

Lungs. They don't make them like they used to. Mine are clearly malfunctioning. "Why did you come here, Elijah?"

His body is angled in such a way that the room can't see his hand settle on my thigh. Or the way his thumb creeps high along the inside. "I was in your apartment today. Didn't relax me as much as it usually does." He shakes his head. "Didn't feel like home at all without you there."

I'm completely helpless while he's touching me. That fact has never been more obvious. Listening to Elijah tell me I'm the reason he kept coming back, my breaths are rattling in and out, my heart stuck in my throat. "Really?"

"Yeah."

My words are almost slurred from hope and happiness when I speak. "S-so what are you going to do about it?"

He wets his mouth, his fingers twisting in the hem of my skirt. "I don't know where this can go, Addison," he says in a low voice, resonant. "I need us to stay friends, because I don't like my days passing without you. But I want your nights, too. Goddamn." His laughter is pained. "Goddamn. I need to get underneath this skirt so bad, I'm not fit to be in public."

Pain cuts my lust down the middle so fast I get dizzy. On some level, I think I might have been expecting this, though. Our sex was explosive. He wants more. But I'm not the girl that gets a man like Elijah in front of the altar in a bow tie. "You want to be…friends with benefits?"

"No." With a scoff, he drags my stool closer and gets right in my face. "*No*, Addison. I'd like you to be my girlfriend."

What? If it were possible for humans to fly, I would be soaring through the bar right now. Just clutching my chest and turning revolutions above everyone's heads. But my brain knows this is *bad*. This man can't help but do the right thing. He wants to sleep with me and this is how he manages it without feeling guilty. That's all it is. Wanting guilt-free sex doesn't make him a bad person—it makes him a good man with physical needs.

But where will this leave me when his appetite is satisfied? It will leave me kicked to the curb, just like my mother. Out in the cold someday soon, looking through the windows of the mansion, watching Elijah's real life unfold. The life he was always meant for.

"Okay," he says slowly, scrutinizing me. "There's a lot going on up in that head. You're wondering why it took me so long to pull my shit together, right?"

"Elijah—"

"What happened with the wedding, Goose..." He shakes his head. "I don't know if I ever got over it, you know? When you're always trying to do the right thing and something huge like that blows up in your face...I don't know if I can explain it. Except to say, I haven't worked my way through it yet. I'm trying."

He's telling me. Oh God. He's telling me he's not over Naomi. I mean, I already knew. But hearing it from his mouth while his hands are on me is devastating. My flying second self plummets to the floor and lands in a heap of protruding bones and wails of pain. I can't be this man's girlfriend when he's still in love with his ex-fiancée. I *can't*. A vision rises unbidden in my head. A side-by-side of Naomi and me—a screwed up version of "Who Wore It Best?" She's in a sash and tiara, waving to an adoring crowd. And I'm hocking goods in the market with a cockney accent and soot on my cheeks. Okay, that's pretty far-fetched, but it still hurts.

Get it together, girl. I'm not going to abandon my carefully constructed plan. I've already put my expansion efforts for the decorating business on hold so I could see my personal quest through to the end. The night I walked into the mansion for the first time, everything changed. My path shifted and all the lines I'd been casting into the waters of Charleston were reeled back in. Even though it hurt.

I vowed to myself I would leave Elijah better off than when I found him and that's exactly what I'm going to do. It's how I leave the past behind.

Eventually, it's going to be how I leave *him* behind.

A woman with any interest in safeguarding her heart would run away now. Run far and fast. There are deep-rooted needs inside me for Elijah, though, that keep me glued to the seat in front of him. Those needs urge my mind to justify being his girlfriend for just a little while. Long enough to collect a lifetime of memories to sustain me.

"What would this mean? Would you move into the house?"

Victory flares in his shadowed brow. "Yes."

My pulse flutters and skips in my neck. "You're prepared for the media fallout?"

"The media can do their worst as long as you're safe." Both of his hands skate up my thighs now. "You'll have a bodyguard to ensure that happens."

"Oh, you're having fun flexing that mayor muscle, aren't you?" My hips are starting to get antsy on the seat with him so close. So big and in charge and honest and *gorgeous*. But I need to set the guidelines for this relationship. I need my head to pilot me, not my heart. "I have some caveats."

"That so?" he drawls, frowning.

"Yes." I sit up straighter. "I want to keep my own room. Separate from yours."

His scowl deepens. "Why?"

Because that king-sized sleigh bed where you're destined to sire your heir makes me nauseous. "There's nothing wrong with a girl wanting to maintain an air of mystery."

"You maintain more than most," he says slowly. "What else?"

I brush a non-existent piece of lint off my shoulder. "We can still see other people."

Like ex-fiancées or comparable local debutantes.

"No. *Hard* no." His hands tighten on my thighs. "I broke the speed limit to get here because I thought you might *laugh* with someone else. We see each other and no one else, Addison. What the hell are you playing at?"

"Okay," I breathe, taken aback by the fury in his eyes. "Okay, fine. I'll modify. I-if you decide this has run its course or you've changed your mind, there are no hard feelings."

His voice is soft when he speaks. "And if you change *your* mind? Why are you only applying this rule to me?"

"Oversight," I blurt. "It's for both of us."

Elijah is quiet so long, I think he's changed his mind. Or he's going to try and negotiate the bedroom rule. So I'm relieved when he finally leans in and kisses my forehead, then brings his mouth within a whisper of mine. "Let's go home."

CHAPTER FIFTEEN

Elijah

*Dancing to the beat of her own drum and shaking up
Charleston's stuffy upper crust. The mayor-elect never knew
what hit him. Getaway Girl for the win.*

—TheTea.com

*Opinion: Bar-hopping Getaway Girl does not "getaway" with
lack of dignity.*

*If she's governing the mayor-elect, does she in turn govern our
principles?*

—Southern Insider News

CELL PHONE CAMERAS lift and snap as I guide Addison from the bar. I should probably be concerned with tomorrow's gossip section. Should probably be wary of the black sedan idling behind the SUV waiting for us at the curb. It's most likely a photographer who will snap a shot of us walking into the house together—and that picture will be printed beneath some suggestive headline that will make me see red...but what I'm really concerned about, despite all the noise around us, are Addison's caveats.

I deserve the distance she's trying to put between us, don't I? After the way I checked out the first time we slept together, she's probably throwing up barriers to protect herself. Yes, she's just being cautious. I really dislike that I've given her a reason to be skeptical of me, though. She might have agreed to be my girlfriend, but she immediately whittled us down to roommates who fuck before returning to their own rooms.

This is what I wanted, right? Walking into the bar tonight, I didn't plan on asking Addison to be my girlfriend. Commitments and expectations were supposed to remain by the wayside. My course of action changed when faced with her big, beautiful eyes and the husky voice I've been going crazy missing. When I said the title out loud, it felt right. It feels distinctly *wrong* that she didn't even want it. So am I satisfied that she's giving me exactly what I wanted? Sex and companionship without the faulty trappings of couplehood? No. I should be. But I'm not.

I wave off the driver and open the back door for Addison myself, helping her climb in and following behind. The closed door cuts off all sound and when it's just us, my stomach settles. *Stop looking for a problem.* This is exactly where I want to be, going home with Addison, her hand beneath mine on the seat.

"Maybe you should call and warn your father," she murmurs, scanning the interested bystanders lining the curb. "His morning oatmeal is going to be ruined."

I pick up her hand and guide it to my mouth, kissing her knuckles. "I should have asked for my own caveat."

She looks up at me through her eyelashes. "It's not too late."

Yes, it is, says a voice in my head. Referring to what, though? "People disagree about the color of the sky. As sure as the sun comes up, they're going to form an opinion about us. Maybe they already have. And it's going to be wrong." I move closer to her on the seat as the SUV pulls into traffic. "We're the *only* ones who know what's going on here."

Addison turns in the seat and curls her fingers in my collar, tugging my face close to hers. I go in for the kill without hesitation. A week. I haven't kissed this mouth *in a week*—and before that, I didn't taste it for *months*. How did I stay away when it was right in front of me? It's cool, sugar-mint paradise. Her head falls back and I surge closer on the seat, taking her chin and pulling it down, down, so I can explore every corner, driver be damned. Her head falls back with a whimper that would tent my fly, if I didn't already have an erection to beat the band.

Satisfied that her mouth will stay open wide for me, I let my hand slide lower than her chin. I can't touch her fast or thoroughly enough and God. God bless this girl. She arches her back and gives me options. I drag my hand down her tits and plump them high in her neckline, squeezing, one by one. When I release her mouth so we can breathe, we both look down at my knuckles where they rest on her belly. So close to that pussy I've been craving.

"Sorry for distracting you," she whispers. "Your caveat is...?"

Knowing she's not the least bit sorry, I breathe a laugh against her cheek. "When you hear or read something that makes you doubt what we've got..." I rub our damp lips together, setting her off purring and shifting on the seat. "Close your eyes and think of my tongue in your pretty mouth. Think of us on the bed making ornaments. Do whatever you have to do to get through the moment and back to me. Agreed?"

I hear her swallow. "Aye aye, captain."

Since the bar was so close to the house, it takes no time at all to pull up out front. We don't get out right away, staring in silence at the massive three-story, its palm trees swaying in the nighttime wind. Behind us, the black sedan flips off its lights and waits. Tomorrow there will probably be more black sedans and journalists hunting for the money shot, asking questions. I'll handle it then. Public interest has touched every damn thing in my life. It won't touch this thing with Addison. It will try, but I'm going to make sure it loses.

The driver opens the door and I climb out, offering my hand to Addison. "Is the lady of the manor ready to retire for the evening?"

With her head high, she takes my hand and hops out, throwing a wink at the black car. "Not a chance."

I'm still laughing as we walk up the pathway, my arm sliding around her waist halfway up the steps. She leans her head into my shoulder and I squeeze her tighter, a goose egg forming in my throat. "I missed you."

She winks up at me. "You're cooking tomorrow night."

When we reach the door, I let her go and lean against the doorframe, watching as she digs the key from the purse. There's a little tremble in her hand as if she's nervous, but her smirk tells me she doesn't want me to know it. Complicated woman. Doesn't she know I would crawl over hot coals to reassure her? I keep my observation to myself as we walk inside and lock the door behind us. Met with the sudden fall of privacy, my body acts on its own, flattening her against the door. Letting her feel my hard cock.

I drop the briefcase and tangle my hands in her hair—

"Curtains," she breathes. "All the curtains are open."

"Right." My head hits the door above her with a groan. "Wait. When did we even get curtains?"

"*You* hired someone."

"That's right," I hedge. "I forgot."

"No, you didn't. You've *bullied* me into being comfortable here."

I swoop in and capture her mouth in a hard kiss, smiling against her lips when she moans, giving me a slow wiggle.

"Guilty."

She runs her hands up my chest and starts to remove my tie. "Two window treatment designers—*both* named Lenore—"

"Liar."

"Hand to God. They came yesterday and annoyed me with a bunch of questions."

"Like what?"

"They asked me about my aesthetic." She sighs. "They didn't find North Pole Chic acceptable."

"We better get these damn curtains closed, Addison," I growl. "You're standing there being cute and pouting and shaking. A thousand things at once and they all make me need to get inside you more. To *fuck*."

Her eyelids flutter and close, pink climbing her cheeks. "Bossy man."

With a concerted effort, I peel myself away from her perfect curves. After one final, teasing meeting of tongues, we move to opposite sides of the room, throwing heavy cream curtains over the windows, careful not to leave even a sliver of glass visible. When I've closed the final curtain, I turn around to find Addison stripping her dress off in the middle of the foyer. At some point, she turned on a soft lamp and it glows behind her, the light playing on her hips and thighs as the dress comes off. The sandals are kicked off next, her bra unsnapped and tossed toward the staircase. And she's left in nothing but a barely-there black pair of panties.

She crooks her finger at me and I just go, shedding my jacket along the way, hastily pushing the buttons of my dress shirt through their holes. I've only managed about half the row when I reach her, but they're forgotten when she climbs me, the sexy, goddamn siren. One second she's standing, the next she's got her legs hitched around me hips, her mouth open on mine. "Not complaining. At all," I grind out, taking hold of her ass cheeks. "But I'm going to need more time to look at you standing around in your unmentionables."

"Pervert." She uses her thigh muscles to climb higher, dragging her hot pussy over my cock and a strangled curse leaves me. "I have a nice little treat for you, Captain," she murmurs at my mouth. "Find somewhere you can lie back and unzip your pants."

Whatever I say in response isn't even English. It's a combination of *thank you* and *what?* And her name, too, possibly. Blood is pounding in my ears and the pressure behind my zipper is so uncomfortable, it hurts to walk. But I do it anyway, obviously, leaving the foyer and entering a front room that—thank Christ—has been furnished. I drop down on a chaise lounge, gritting my teeth when gravity presses Addison down on my erection, her thighs tight around my waist. Not just Addison, though. Enthusiastic kisser, naked except for her panties Addison, for the love of everything holy. She's even more unrestrained than I remember, whimpering and fucking me through my pants.

"You want your treat now?" she asks, discarding my tie and unbuttoning the rest of my shirt, slowly. "I *really* want to give it to you."

"Sugar." I dive in for a taste of her neck. "I want anything you have to give me."

Finished with the row of buttons, she pushes my shirt open. Time passes in a thick beat—tick, tick—before she scrapes her nails down my chest. Hard. Right over my nipples. Pleasure and pain go nuclear in my middle, my cock swelling beneath her. "Jesus. Jesus *Christ*."

"I'm sorry, Captain. Did that hurt?" Addison slides off my lap and lands between my thighs, her fingers wasting no time wrestling with my belt buckle, my zipper and finally my briefs, freeing me from the waistband. "I promise I'll make up for it," she purrs, wrapping her lips around my cock and sucking deep. Deep, long and hard, her tongue flickering at my head when she reaches the top.

"*Yes*, Addison," I groan, my hands shooting to her hair, getting lost. There's no description for what she does to me. The slow, rough way she runs her thumb up the underside of my dick, up and back, like a hypnotist. I'm caught between marveling over the fact that she clearly *loves* giving me head and hell, just savoring the experience. In the end, the former heightens the latter until I'm falling back on my elbows to let her work. Goddamn. She strokes me with both hands, twisting, wetting me with adoring licks until I'm so slippery and tight in her grip, it already feels like I'm inside her pussy. My hips pump off the lounge, desperate grunts grinding free of my mouth. My cock has never been so thick or hard and it's all about her worshipping it, her eyes squeezed shut, her cheeks hollow with the effort to clean me out.

My hand scrubs down my stomach, because there's only one thing that can make this better, but Addison beats me there. She hums, taking me deep into the vibration of her throat...and she does it. She cups my balls, weighing them in her palm and I hold my breath, the air rushing from my lungs when she begins a tight massage.

I don't recognize the groan that comes out of me. It's from inside a cave or deep in the forest and I have no control over it. "That's what I need, sugar. Ah *God*. You're making me need to fuck so bad. *Shit*." She gives my balls a long squeeze and my thighs shoot wider. "Feel how heavy? That's my treat for *you*. I'm going to pound everything inside me into your pussy soon as you're done sucking."

The man who says these things to a woman isn't me. It's a version of me that only comes out to play with Addison. Would I ever have known he was inside me if I hadn't met her? Coming apart and being put together at the same time—that's what this is. Look at what such filth does to her, her thighs pressed together, her sweet little tits jiggling as she sucks my cock, struggling her way to the base. My God, I've never *wanted* this badly. Needed to lick every inch of Addison, sweat and all. I want to absorb her.

"I'm losing my mind, Addison." I wrap her hair around my fists and lift her head away from my lap. "This is what it's like to have a man obsessed with you. Do you like it?"

CHAPTER SIXTEEN

Addison

Message received loud and clear.
If this mansion is a-rocking, don't come a-knocking.
—TheTea.com

H E'S OBSESSED WITH my body. *Just* my body and the magic
it makes with his.

And I can give him that magic. I can rule him for right now.

"No. I don't like having you obsessed," I rasp, using his
thighs for balance to stand. "I love it."

Elijah sits up and reaches for me, but I shake my head.
Watching him wipe sweat from his forehead and upper lip with
satisfaction, I peel my panties down to my ankles. Nice and slow.
With a harsh sound, he once again reaches for me, but I use all
my strength to push him backward on the lounge. He could
easily turn the tables and manhandle me, but he's too excited to
see what I'll do next, that big chest shuddering with anticipation.
That thick trunk of flesh—still shiny from my mouth—lies rigid
on his abdomen, veins running in every direction and bisecting.
Pulsing. Needing relief.

My lust being given unlimited power sends a thrilling shud-
der down my spine.

I love this man.

There's no sense in tiptoeing around something so rooted in fact. Buried so deep in the soil of my being. Despite the love that has been growing since day one, though, he makes me suffer. I want to praise him and torture him at the same time.

I've been holding back since the beginning when it comes to this man. But I don't have to right now. Not with my body and touch—and the freedom is staggering. Yes, praise and torture are exactly what I'm going to give him.

I drop forward, catching myself on the edges of the lounge, crawling up Elijah's big body until I'm straddling his hips. "What was it you said, Captain?" I tease him with an almost-kiss, leaving him groaning as I drag my tongue across the breadth of his chest. My teeth catch a nipple and tug, jerking his hips off the lounge. "That you're going to 'pound me'?"

My tone is a cross between sex line operator and baby talk. There's no doubt that he loves the way I pout my way through the question while rubbing our naked bodies together. His neck muscles are strained, eyes unfocused. "Yes. *God*, yes. I just want to *pound* you."

I let my wet flesh settle lightly on top of his erection…and I skim up and back…touching him just enough to make him choke. "But what if I pound you first?"

With a growl, he reaches down and begins to stroke himself—fast and hard—so that his knuckles graze my clit again and again until I let loose a sob. "You keep pouting those lips at me," Elijah warns, "I'm going to wrap them around my cock again."

His threat makes me shake. *Shake. Do it*, I almost cry out. But having this man at my mercy is too intoxicating. I'm not giving it up so easily. I take his wrist and pull his hand away from where it pleasures his flesh, pinning it down to the left of his head. I do the same with his right and watch his eyes go molten at my breasts swaying so close to his panting mouth. What I do next is nothing short of hedonism. A giving in to the needs of the body. I slide and grind on his hard inches until his flesh pushes apart my feminine lips. And I rub myself from root to tip with a shameless moan.

Elijah strains beneath me, a string of epithets leaving his mouth. "Sugar, you're going to make me come carrying on like that," he grits out.

I press my lips to his ear and force a little whine into my voice, even though it takes all my concentration. He's so big. So big and perfect and mine for the night. "But I'm wrapped around that big part of you, just like you wanted."

"Sink me in deep or shut your little *mouth*." He frees his hands, slapping the right one down on my backside, shocking us both. But the flicker of worry in his gaze vanishes when I react like a complete heathen, diving for his lips like they're the gates of heaven. Oh my God. Oh my God, Elijah just spanked me. I'm so wet between my thighs that I'm dragging myself all over his erection in an attempt to drown in the kiss and grind on his lap at the same time. He's too tall for me to do both with any success, so I'm reduced to a desperate up and back slide that kicks off a rough rumble in his chest. A warning that trouble is coming, because I'm being a bad girl by not obeying. And when did I lose control of this situation?

His *mouth*. I can't accept enough of his tongue, can't touch enough of it with mine. His hands aren't being the least bit gentle with my bottom, bruising it with brutal fingers and jerking me up and down on his erection. Every once in a while, he lets go with his right hand to deliver another resounding smack and it makes me increasingly mindless. Racing toward my orgasm and his. "You want the real thing?" he says, giving my backside a sound slap, then taking a fistful of my hair. "Or are you going to play on it all night?"

"Want it. Want it."

I only feel his hand between us for a second, before the entire swollen length of his manhood rams home, stranding me on the brink of climax, my thighs shaking like leaves. "Elijah. Elijah. *Elijah*."

"Addison," he shudders out, lifting me up with his hips. "*Fuck* me."

Those two words remind me of my goal. To praise and torture and make myself a lasting memory for this man. I've got him right where I want him and I'm going to ignore the fact that he's so beloved and beautiful he's making my chest hurt. I'm going to ignore that and be the best he's ever had. When he's pleasuring himself in the shower a decade from now, he's going to remember the girl who knew his secrets, his needs better than anyone. "You're so huge," I manage, riding to the tip of his arousal and lowering myself back to the root with a whimper. "I bet it gets uncomfortable with that big bulge in your shorts, doesn't it? Poor baby. I bet you need to adjust yourself on camera all the time, but you can't. You just have to leave it crammed up behind your belt until you get somewhere private."

I can't describe the way he's looking at me, except to say it's exactly what I'm craving. I'm a blessing, a curse, a mystery and his only means of satisfaction. Sweat rolls down the side of his temple, his hips giving a mean upward thrust. "Final warning, Addison."

"Let me play," I lean down to whisper against his mouth. "Just for a while?"

Let it never be said that Elijah Montgomery Du Pont isn't a gentleman to the core of his being, because he can't deny my request any more than he could spit on the sidewalk. With his chest rising and falling rapidly, he reaches back and grips the top of the lounge, bracing himself. "Some part of it gets pinched between the crease of my pants and my thigh. Every damn time." He raises a damp eyebrow at me. "You happy now?"

I love you. I almost blurt it out right then and there. But I press my lips together at the last second and ride him instead. It works to distract me immediately, the insane pressure of him throbbing against my walls. The friction of him leaving me, sinking back in. My nipples trail up and down his chest as I work my hips forward and back, pressing down tight on his sensitive balls and earning myself grateful exhalations of my name. "What would everyone say if they knew…their mayor is so big and thick, it hurts to sit down?" I loosen my hips and bounce-bounce-grind, over and over, until he's speaking in another language, his knuckles white where he grips the lounge. "You shouldn't be allowed in polite company with this big thing dangling between your thighs, Elijah. Especially when it gets hard. Shame on you, Captain Du Pont." I bite down on his nipple, laving it with my tongue. "You better apologize."

The muscles of his body bunch head to toe. "*Addison.*"

I stop moving.

"Fuck," he explodes. "Christ. Oh, fuck. I'm sorry."

Having some mercy on him—and myself—I bring our bodies flush and let him devour me with a frustrated kiss. And I go for broke riding him, gasping when his fingers dig into my hips and encourage me with nothing short of savage brutality, hot air bursting from his nostrils, grunts vibrating his body and mine. "God. You're hitting me in all the right spots, baby," I murmur against his mouth, my lower body beginning to clench, *clench*. "All at once."

"Guess it's worth the discomfort when I sit, isn't it?" Before I know what's happening, Elijah rises and flips our positions, stealing my breath as I land on my back. He falls on top of me, pressing me down into the lounge and driving deep—*hard*—between my thighs, muffling my scream with his hand. "I don't fuck around with final warnings."

I come, screaming and thrashing, on his first thrust. It's brought on by a million little things, like his beard brushing my cheek, his scent greeting my nose, his full weight on top of me. Something I've always fantasized about. His fat, heavy sex. Yes, that, too. It presses in, seemingly from all sides, Elijah's hips circling and milking the orgasm from my body. Rolling his lower body against mine when I teeter down the other side of the peak, his mouth and tongue at my neck, licking and biting and sucking.

"Oh my god. Keep going. Elijah, *please.*"

"Apologize for being a cock tease when I haven't fucked you in a week." He drags his teeth down the side of my neck, sinking them into my shoulder. "*Apologize.*"

"Sorry! I'm sorry."

My legs are seized in rough hands, knees yanked up around his waist. I've been allowed to have my fun with the captain and now I'm his plaything. He doesn't spare a second using me, either, grunting into my neck as he pounds me, just as he promised. Stars wink behind my eyes, my limbs turning restless as another crescendo builds inside me. "You need to cream again, do it *soon,*" he growls. "Can't be patient. Not when you're offering up that tight pussy to me on a platter."

I find my nipples and squeeze them between my knuckles, dropping my thighs open wide. *Almost there. Again. Again. Please.* In the end, it's watching Elijah's jaw lose power, his eyes going blind that shoots me over the edge once more, my back arching off the lounge as euphoria strikes.

"*Addison.*"

I take his thrusting buttocks in my hands and yank him deep, crossing my ankles at the small of his back. "That's right," I gasp. "You want to fill me to the top, don't you?"

"*Yes.*" He bares his teeth against my mouth, opens my knees wide and pumps one final time. "This is *mine.*"

"Always," I whisper, floating into paradise when he collapses on top of me, his breath pelting my neck. My bones have disintegrated, my thoughts scattered on the wind. Before any unwanted reminders can intrude, I savor the moment, recording it with my heart. I bury my fingers in his hair and drag them along his scalp, a dreamy smile transforming my lips when he sighs and presses closer. As if to say, *feels good more scratching.* I give in and trail my fingers through his hair, rearranging it and smoothing it back to its original position. His fingertips begin to trail up and down my side, his mouth laying kisses on my collarbone, chin and neck.

When a swelling starts inside my rib cage, I know I've let the affection go on long enough, though. I can't get used to this. It will kill me to walk away. Or I'll start to hope for something he can't give me. With regret running in my veins, I kiss his temple and nudge him, sliding out from beneath his giant body.

I paste a saucy expression on my face, standing up and stretching my arms up over my head. "We done good, Captain."

A line appears between his eyebrows as he sits up, running his gaze up my naked body, landing on my face. "We done better than good."

"Yeah. We did," I whisper, reaching out to rub my thumb along his lower lip. "I have to be up early. Kiss me good night?"

He almost knocks me over, lunging off the lounge and sweeping me up in his arms, my feet leaving the floor. For a heady string of seconds, he does nothing but look me hard in the eye, our foreheads pressed together. What is he seeing? Oh God, I'm too exposed. It's too soon after I let my guard down to reinforce it as much as usual. He's so mighty and confused and satisfied all at once that my head finally gives in to the swoon and falls back, my mouth opening to be devoured. Our tongues tangle and his hands start to slip lower, but I pull back, breathless. "Good night, Elijah."

My back burns under his attention as I collect my things and leave, taking the stairs two at a time on the way to my room.

CHAPTER SEVENTEEN

Elijah

Look out below!
—*Charleston Post*

S LEEP DIDN'T COME easy last night.

It was the first time I've slept in the master bedroom and I spent a lot of time staring up at the domed ceiling. There's no dome on the roof of the house, so I have zero clue where the dome...domes. Around three in the morning, I got so restless, I almost climbed up to the top of the damn house to solve the mystery. But I found myself walking toward Addison's room, instead. She'd closed the door, so I stood there a few minutes trying to justify opening it.

Maybe *she* knows what's up with the dome? I could just nudge her awake and ask her. Might be fun to see a peeved Addison rub sleep from her eyes and tell me off.

No might about it. That would definitely be fun.

I'd paced some more, trying to find an excuse to open the door. I could think of several selfish reasons, including wanting to know what she's wearing, if she's warm enough, if there's any physical way I could fit into a twin-sized bed with her. Not that I would try it without her inviting me, but I'd just like to know. For logistics' sake.

Now, I flip off the shower faucet in the master bath, letting the water drip off my face. I don't give a shit about the dome in the bedroom. I just want to know why the closer I get to Addison, the further she scoots away. She doesn't want to be my girlfriend? Fine. I hate it, but I understand her skepticism after the unorthodox start to our relationship. Now I have no choice but to be patient, prove to her I'm steadfast and wait for her to trust me enough to attempt...this. Living together, walking through the front door holding hands, splitting cooking duty. Same as we did before, except now we're sleeping together.

Again, I remind myself this is exactly what I wanted. Why do I feel like either foot is on a weighing scale and leaning too far in one direction is going to screw me?

I push off the marble wall of the shower, ripping a towel off the rack and drying myself off. No doubt about it, I'm good and annoyed. Which is pretty damn amazing, considering I had the kind of sex last night most men don't know enough to fantasize about. I sure as hell didn't, until that night in my office. Addison is...abandoned, adventurous, naughty as all get out, sweet as an angel, and occasionally, perfectly silly when we're fucking. All those things wrapped up in this too-sexy package that can't quite hide its little tears. Tears I have no idea how to locate and repair, but I *need* to find for my own sanity.

I wasn't exaggerating when I said I'm obsessed with her.

I'm one hundred percent obsessed with my best friend.

When I'd given up on justifying my actions last night, I'd opened her bedroom door just to get a look. She wasn't in bed, though. No, she was outside sitting on the floor of the balcony, her arms wrapped around her drawn in legs. She was so still, I got to wondering if I'd fallen asleep and was dreaming her sitting there, hair carrying like streamers on the wind. I'd backed out of the room to the sound of my hammering heart—and it hammers again now as I get dressed in my black suit, blue tie and initialed cufflinks.

Why does everything seem so precarious? One minute last night, she's looking at me with a total lack of guile and the next...she's practically tripping over herself to get away.

I'm getting answers out of her. And I'm getting them today.

Mind set, I leave the room and its confusing dome in my wake. I'm relieved to hear her in the kitchen when I get halfway down the stairs, meaning she hasn't gone running yet. It's Sunday, so she's not working in the market. Normally I would take Sunday off, too, but I have a speaking engagement this afternoon and official correspondence with the state government that has to be sent by tomorrow. If I want to make dinner for Addison tonight, I have no choice but to plow through.

When I walk into the kitchen, I find Addison standing at the coffee maker in spandex running shorts and a T-shirt. One that provides a good amount of coverage. Thank you, God.

She turns and sends me a knowing smile over her shoulder. "Morning, Captain."

I nod back with appreciation. "Morning, Goose."

My annoyance is already taking a rapid nosedive as I move farther into the kitchen, picking a mug out of the cabinet and joining Addison at the coffee pot. A sense of rightness settles over me as we go through our patented routine. She pours us both a cup. I add the sugar to each mug. She adds the milk to them, while I stir it in. The difference between now and when we lived together as platonic roommates is...my cock plumps to the smell of her, filling out the front of my pants. The heat from her hip makes me wonder if she's sporting bruises from my fingers. When I glance over and find her nipples hard, I drop the spoon with a clatter, turn Addison and press her up against the counter.

"See? What did I tell you?" she breathes into my mouth, shifting her sexy body against my erection. "Not fit for public."

That sexual guilt she likes to inflict prods my gut with need, but I don't let her distract me. I take her chin in my hand and hold her steady. "Why won't you sleep beside me?" Her smile drops like an anvil and she tries to push me off, but I cage her in, our bodies flush. "Don't give me that bullshit about keeping the mystery alive, either."

"You probably snore," she blurts. "And…I'm not a cuddler."

"That's all you've got? I *probably* snore and you aren't a cuddle enthusiast?"

Sparks shoot from her eyes. "That's right."

"Knowing when you need space is a hobby of mine. I'll know when you want to stretch out on your own side of the bed, Addison." I nod once. "I'm demanding you try."

She gasps. "*Demanding?*"

"You heard me. And you're fucking beautiful all day, but especially in the morning."

"I—" Her mouth opens and shuts. "Wait. What?"

I tunnel my fingers through her hair, definitely messing up her ponytail, but I can't keep my hands off her. "And if I snore, I'll find a position where I don't."

"How do you not know if you snore?" She hiccups. "Didn't N…N-Naomi…tell you?"

Everything goes very still. Except for my pulse, which is going a thousand miles an hour. What the hell? A few days ago, she had no problem saying my ex-fiancée's name—smiled while she did it—and now she looks equal parts devastated and defiant. And then I remember the day I showed up with the movers. How she went pale when they opened the door to the master bedroom.

I'm an idiot. I am a giant, unworthy, lumbering, idiot man.

"You won't sleep in the same room as me because it was supposed be her room?"

"Both of your room. And...*no*." She scoffs. "I don't care. She picked out every piece of furniture in this house, Elijah. I wouldn't be able to go into *any* of the rooms, if I was...if that bothered me."

She's lying. She can't even look me in the eye. Holy shit. "I wasn't thinking. I'm a man and one piece of furniture looks the same as any other to me."

Affection—or perhaps feminine sympathy over my very male plight—collides with her panic. But she shoos it away. "I said that wasn't it."

This time, when she shoves me away, I go. One step. Even though I don't want to. I want to pick her up and beg and kiss her. Addison grabs on to her freedom without hesitation and stalks away, however, putting the island between us. Her chin is set and stubborn, but she's twisting the front of her T-shirt. When I walked in here, she was her usual confident self and now she's a cornered animal. All because I'm calling a bluff that should *not* have gotten this far.

My head drops forward. "Oh, sugar."

"Stop it." She points at me. "Stop that."

I turn on a heel and leave the room, because if I have to look at her upset anymore, I'm going to require a straightjacket. It has been a while since I got the tour of this place and I barely remember which door leads to the backyard, but I pick a direction and I commit, dammit. I commit. Turns out, I choose right, probably because the Good Lord knew I needed a break. The glass door leads out onto a brick patio, which I haven't seen since the original tour. But I don't take the time to do more than acknowledge the wrought-iron furniture and freshly trimmed hedges. I've got my eye on the shed and there's hell buzzing in my veins.

"What are you doing?" Addison's catches up to me as I throw open the shed door and search the darkness for what I need. "Elijah, answer me."

There. Every house has one. Leaning up against the corner of the shed is an axe. Being careful to keep it away from my girlfriend—because that's *damn well* what she is—I throw it over my shoulder and march back toward the house.

"You better not be doing what I think you're doing." She jogs alongside me, giving me her best stern voice, which she usually reserves for me leaving the seat up or adding too much garlic to the marinara sauce. "Don't you dare bring that axe upstairs."

I turn the corner at the end of the back hallway and climb the stairs, ignoring the gasps of outrage following me. And the stomping, too. There's definitely some stomping.

"Don't you dare bring that axe into that bedroom, Elijah Montgomery Du Pont." She kind of squeals my last name and I can't hold back a chuckle. "That bed probably cost five figures. You can't destroy it. You *can't*. Put down the axe or I'll…"

I pause at the entrance to the bedroom. "You'll what?"

She searches the ceiling for an answer. "I'll wear the pink bra. I'll wear it to the market and sell ornaments in it all day long."

Forget what I said about the Good Lord giving me a break. "I would like to see you try that, Addison Potts. I would *love* to see you try. I would go through that market like a motherfucking hurricane."

"You said motherfucking."

Since that doesn't require an answer, I kick open the bedroom door, take two steps and bury the axe in the center of the headboard. I don't have to turn around to know Addison is standing in the doorway with her mouth hanging open. But I do turn when she *still* doesn't join me in the room. "Look at you," I shout, ripping off the bedclothes and tossing them aside. "You won't even set foot in here. Why didn't you just *say* something?"

Her shadow shifts on the wall, but the lack of creaking floorboards tells me she's still hovering in the entrance. "If saying something leads to you destroying innocent furniture, that showed good judgment on my part."

With the bed stripped, I move to the floor-to-ceiling windows and pry one all the way open to a symphony of groaning wood, since it hasn't been used in God knows how long. Then I return to the bed and drag the mattress off the box spring. Even for me, the king-sized mattress is heavy, but it would have to weigh as much as a tank to deter me.

"You can't be serious," she breathes.

"Come into the room and I won't do it."

She hesitates on the threshold.

I shove the mattress out the window. "The box spring is next."

"You are a *lunatic*." She takes a step into the room, her face painted with color. "I'll sleep in the stupid bed, all right? Please, please, just don't destroy it. It must have been special at some point."

A man with a level head would quit while he's ahead, but it's becoming very obvious I don't have a level head where Addison is concerned. And I'm angrier with myself than anything for lying here all night like an asshole and not seeing the answer that was right in front of me. "Sorry, Goose. It has to go," I say, pulling the axe out of the headboard. "Any idea why this ceiling is domed?"

"What?"

"Not important." I'm in the process of picking a good angle for my first swing when Addison rushes around the bed. "Elijah, no—"

"Back up, Addison. Please. You're the only thing in this room I care about."

I listen to her shallow breathing move farther and farther away. After a look over my shoulder to confirm she's out of the axe's range, I lift the metal tool over my head and swing it down, splitting the headboard clean down the middle. The axe drops to my side, hanging in my hand.

It's odd…the lightness that follows me turning my bed into fire wood. I destroyed it for Addison, but until now, I wasn't aware of the pinched nerves *I've* been living with. Failure, falling short of expectations, disappointment. Hell, shock. Those things were never supposed to happen to me. But they did. And I think being blindsided by them on my wedding day hit me in ways I didn't realize. In ways I don't want to think about right now. Maybe ever.

When I drop the axe and turn around, Addison is already on her way to me and I'm more than happy to pour all my focus into her. Just her.

CHAPTER EIGHTEEN

Addison

This booty doesn't need memory foam.
It's already unforgettable.
#mattressgate
—Twitter @DuPontBadonk

I'M ABANDONING SHIP.

When a man chops a bed in half for you, is there any other choice?

My legs have the consistency of liquid and like the Grinch on Christmas morning, my heart has grown to three times its normal size. All full of Elijah. Bursting. *Bursting.* This beautiful, idiotic man who is going down in history as the mayor who threw a freaking mattress out the window. For me. Just so I would sleep beside him.

We're lunging for each other and I've almost reached him when I force a reality check. He's not over the wedding. Not over his ex. Things don't change overnight and it hasn't even been twenty-four hours since he admitted he's not over being left at the altar. But what if...what if there's a little possibility that Elijah could learn to love me, instead?

I'm so scared to even *begin* to hope, I have to press my lips together to keep a sob from escaping, but a second later I have to open them, because Elijah's mouth is on mine. Our lips fit together like a door lock cylinder, holding, both of us breathing through our noses. He stoops down with a groan and my legs obey his silent command, lifting to circle his waist. And the kiss turns hot, earnest, one hand loosing my hair from the ponytail, the other sliding down the back of my shorts to squeeze my bottom.

I cup his face in my hands and drop off the ledge into his texture, his taste, the hoarse sounds he's making in the back of his throat. We're walking somewhere, but I can't find the willpower to take my tongue out of his mouth. A responsible inner voice I didn't know I had tells me I'm making him late for work, but that enormous part of him lifting and rubbing between us definitely needs me now. *Now.* I need him back so bad, too. He has to keep stopping on his journey to wherever to give me a thorough enough kiss.

Finally, I sense us entering a room and my back lands on softness. My bed in the guest room. Not a beat passes before we're rushing to get undressed. As I watch Elijah shed his jacket and open a few buttons on his shirt, I'm flushed head to toe, growing wetter between my thighs by the second. My body has no choice in the matter, because he's determined, focused, shoulders flexing, tongue skating over his lips. A God-man towering over me. I've only managed to kick off my running shorts and underwear when he lands on top of me, our mouths colliding in a moaning dance of tongues.

He draws up my shirt between us, his right hand skating over my sports bra—and he lifts his head. I'm so disoriented from lust, I don't realize right away why he's stopped kissing me.

"Pink bra," he rasps, taking a handful of my right breast. "Were you planning on running along the Battery in this?"

Uh oh. I try to distract him by rolling my hips, but apart from his eyelids dipping, he doesn't bite. "I'm wearing a shirt over it."

"Were you planning on *keeping* it on?" he asks, circling a thumb over my peaked nipple. "Or were you going to strip it off soon as I walked out the door?"

My best friend knows me too well. He can see the answer in my eyes. "Women run in sports bras all the time. It's not unusual."

The words are barely out of my mouth when Elijah yanks the bra up, allowing my breasts to bounce out. If he didn't already know I was turned on, he would now. My nipples are in such tight points, they ache. So much that when Elijah touches one with the tip of his index finger, my back arches without consent. "One layer between these sexy tits and the world is not enough for me. I'm settling for two. You're *provoking* me with one."

"It has nothing to do with you," I manage. "I just don't like a sweaty shirt sticking to my skin."

Elijah settles more firmly between my legs, the bulging fly of his pants rocking up into the juncture of my thighs. My thoughts go foggy, my lips pressing together to keep from begging for Elijah to unzip and take me. "You give me a lot of grief about my size," he says, rubbing our lips together. "If I didn't wear briefs underneath my dress pants, people would see everything I've got. Would you like that?"

Jealousy and possessiveness claw me like a feral alley cat. "That's not funny."

"No. It's not." He leans down, running the very tip of his tongue around my areola. "If I can be uncomfortable and needing to adjust myself in slacks all day, sugar, you can deal with a sticky T-shirt." I don't like being told what to do and Elijah damn well knows it, but he covers my mouth when I start to voice a protest.

"We could keep arguing. Or you could open your legs like a good girl and get a nice treat." He removes his hand and kisses me long and hard, slanting our lips together until I'm writhing beneath him. "Which is it going to be?"

"What were we arguing about again?" I whimper.

Our wet lips brush. "You think you can talk your filth to me while I'm tonguing that pussy?"

My lungs evacuate in a rush. Elijah is going down on me. Is this real life? "I n-never back down from a challenge."

His eyes, still so heavy with lust, hit me with a serious look. "Will you sleep beside me tonight?"

"Where? You won't fit in here and—"

"I'll handle it. Yes or no."

"Fine," I whisper, my heart speeding into a gallop. "I'll sleep with you."

We stare at each other until smiles bloom on both of our faces. "It took the morning, but I do believe we just got on the same damn page." He has no idea I'm on thirty different pages, too, but I don't have the heart or the courage right now to tell him. "Let's stay on it, okay?"

I pull my lips into the pout I know will distract him. "Can I have my treat now?"

"God, yes." Elijah's growl starts a purr in my middle and his lips track down my sternum to meet it. I can't believe this is happening. I'm naked from the waist down, my bra hiked up near my collarbone…and Elijah is still fully dressed in his stuffy mayor clothes. It's every fantasy I've ever allowed myself, but a million times better, because I can feel the rasp of expensive material on my thighs, my belly. He still hasn't shaven, so the scrape of his beard awakens screeching nerves that run amok in every direction. "In the spirit of staying on the same page," he says in a low voice, kissing me right below the belly button. "I should confess this treat is really for me."

My eyes slide shut, my tongue loosening as sensations roll over me in waves. I reach down and twist my fingers in Elijah's hair, guiding him lower. "How long have you been thinking of putting your mouth in places it doesn't belong?"

"Longer than I should have," he grits out, pressing his panting open mouth over my naked flesh. Right on top of it, his head bowed. As if praying. "Sometimes when you roll your eyes at me, I want to pin you down and slap it. *Lick* it." A stuttered moan sneaks out and Elijah looks up at me with awed hunger. "You're going to love it, aren't you?"

Why is he making me wait? I'm so wet it should be illegal. "*Yes,* Elijah," I moan, shifting my hips. Until something about his hesitation pierces my need. "Have you...done this?"

Elijah's gaze flashes to mine. "Not with you. Not with someone who needs it so fucking beautifully." Strong hands push my thighs farther apart. "Not with someone I want to taste so bad I'd go insane without it."

My throat tightens. "We can't have that."

"No. We can't. I'm already destroying beds—who knows what I'd do if I lost any more of my mind." Eyes fastened on me, he slowly drags his tongue through my feminine lips, groaning as he goes. "Oh, fuck. That all for me, sugar?"

I think I scream in response, because there's no more hesitation from Elijah after that. He's a man possessed and his sole purpose is searching for the spots that make me gasp—and staying there. God love the man, he *stays* once he strikes gold. His arm reaches up and bands around my hips and he *yanks* me closer to his mouth, using the flat of his tongue to treat my clit like a queen. Rubbing, flickering, rubbing.

"Sh-shit. Oh my G-God." Elijah must have harnessed his tongue's powers and mine—for good, because forming sentences is harder than usual. Am I going into shock? "Yes, *that*. *That*. Yes."

He slides two fingers into me and I wince a little because I'm tender from last night. I don't need gentle, though. I need to lean in to that touch of soreness and beat it—and as if Elijah is reading my mind he starts driving into me with his fingers. Hard. *Fast*. In this mindbending contrast, he goes light on my clit with his tongue, sucking the bud between his lips and rolling it like a jeweler would handle the Hope Diamond.

My hands fly up and tangle in my own hair, my back coming off the bed in an upside-down U. "You like how I taste, baby?" I moan, apparently regaining the power of speech. "Is it making you need to come when you should be working?"

A guttural growl is my answer as his middle finger hits that spot deep inside me. I suck in a breath and hold it, releasing it in a whimper when my orgasm begins to build. And build and build faster than ever before with Elijah stroking my G-spot and his tongue trapping my clit against his upper lip and dragging side to side slowly.

"*Elijah.*" My thighs fall open, my pelvis lifting up in a silent beg. "You're so good, so good. I'm going to ask you for this all the time. Would you like that?"

Glazed eyes and a languid head nod are a resounding yes. His fingers surge deeper still, exploiting that place I'm going to forever associate with this man. He owns it.

"Will I roll my eyes at you for being late coming home...and stomp up the stairs in my littlest skirt? I'd have forgotten panties all day, Elijah. Are you going to let me get away with that?"

It's hard to tell because his words are muffled by my body,

but I think he calls on his maker. I don't realize my eyes are closed until I open them to the view that sends me sailing past the finish line. It's that tight, high and thick backside of Elijah's rolling slowly as he humps the bed. His dress pants are stretched over two hard buns that are *more* than capable of bursting the seam, especially with his erection testing the slacks in the opposite direction. Bump, bump, bump. His butt muscles bunch and loosen, bunch and loosen. He's so turned on from going down on me, he's trying to gratify himself with the mattress. Knowing he's self-conscious over that gorgeous hunk of ass only serves to make me hotter, because he's too lost in the act to care that it's on display. I've never seen anything so beautiful in my entire life.

"I'm going to come," I say on an exhale, my abdomen twisting lower and lower, light burning holes in my sight. "I-I'm going to come—oh *God.*"

It's not the sharp, pummeling climax from last night. It's different and equally brilliant. It passes through me in a devastating ripple, seizing my muscles and taking the breath in my lungs prisoner. I don't remember when I wrapped my thighs around Elijah's head, but they're locked around him now, my whole body shaking like I'm on a vibrating bed in a motel room. When the best/worst of it has passed and laid waste to my senses, Elijah climbs me, one hand busy on his zipper.

"One pump is all I need," he grinds out, sweat dappling his forehead. "Just one pump after watching you come."

It's more like two and a half, but they're the most savage thrusts my body has ever experienced. Elijah shoves inside me with a possessive shout, then fucks me a full foot up the bed, bracing his hand on the headboard just in time to keep me from getting a concussion. I think I'm prepared for the next one, but it's delivered with his full weight on top of me, my knees pinned up near my shoulders—and I'm not prepared, *not prepared*. An orgasm catches me off guard, thanks to his heavy hips grinding down on my sensitive clit and I scream his name, burying my fingernails in his glorious ass. I'm still spasming when his hips hitch mid-pump and he curses low and long in my ear, his giant frame stiffening, heat flooding me in heavy spurts.

"Goddamn," he rasps into my neck, his body still tense, the climax still holding him in its grip. "Little sugar pussy is too tight for its own good. Jesus, it was so *sweet* for my mouth."

"You own it, baby," I whisper in his ear and feel him stiffen again, listen to him groan through an aftershock of pleasure. "All for you."

"*Addison*." His mouth moves in my hair. "Mine."

I close my eyes and nod, knowing it's the absolute truth.

I'm his. Even if these dangerous new hopes are unfounded and he can't really be mine. I'll be in love with Elijah Montgomery Du Pont until I take my final breath on this Earth.

CHAPTER NINETEEN

Elijah

Snag Getaway Girl's Flirty Nighttime Look!
—Avant-Charleston

A look back at the Du Pont/Clemons courtship:
A far more dignified time.
—Southern Insider

I'M TWO HOURS late. But I just made Addison come so hard I'm going to have permanent scars on my ass, so I honestly don't give a good goddamn. As expected, there are news vans parked outside City Hall, lying in wait to ask me all manner of personal questions. I knew this was going to happen when I left the bar with Addison last night. Not to mention I've got nine voicemails from my father and various news outlets—and still I would leave with her all over again.

I take the final swig from my coffee mug I nabbed on the way out the door and take a few moments to collect myself. If I get out of the truck right now, I'm going to be the poster child for getting laid, because I cannot wipe the damn grin off my face.

Okay. Deep breath. You retired a captain in the United States Army. You are the mayor-elect of a major metropolitan city. Not some knucklehead college student who got lucky.

Grin is still there.

Who could blame me? This morning was a victory. I recognized a relationship problem, I solved it and I left my girlfriend in a messy-haired stupor. I've never seen her smile at me the way she did when I finally climbed out of bed. It was something akin to…cautious optimism, but that definitely can't be it, right? I destroyed a perfectly decent bed just so I have a shot of waking up beside her. I'm cooking her dinner tonight. She's met my parents. I can't keep my hands or my mind off of her. We're living together.

She *has* to know I'm dedicated.

Ignoring the weird cinch in my side, I nod once. Yeah. She definitely knows.

I check the rearview mirror and find the grin is still intact. There's no way to shake it, is there? I'm going to have to brave the frenzy looking like I just went for broke pleasuring an incredible woman. Because that's exactly what happened. I've always tried to be a giver during sex in the past, but there were unspoken rules put in place without discussion. Boundaries created in the name of respect that I had no trouble following because the women I was with before…they never inspired this kind of unmitigated lust. I want to do all manner of filthy activities with Addison. Now. Yesterday. And we don't need to have quiet sex with the lights off in order for me to still respect the hell out of her.

Oh yeah. The gentlemanly restraints are coming off. If I never found Addison, I wouldn't have known how good it felt to lose them. With her. Only with her. I'm aching to take her from behind. It's a position that has always turned me on the most to think about, but I've never even suggested it in the bedroom. Maybe it was intuition that it would be met with reluctance or my manners guiding me, but I have no such worries with

Addison. She probably has things she wants to do to me, too, and *damn*. I'm ready, willing and able to participate.

God, just the thought of her little tush shaking while I slam in and out of her soaking wet pussy…it's a thought I really need to stop having, unless I want a picture of me with a boner to make the front page tomorrow morning.

I take the handle of my suitcase and exhale long and steady before pushing out of the truck.

"Captain Du Pont, why did you throw a mattress out of your window this morning?"

"Broken spring."

"Are you officially living with Addison Potts?

"Yes."

Flashes go off.

"How long have you been seeing each other?"

I don't answer that one, because "last night" doesn't sound like the right answer, even though that's when we officially started to date. I'm not so sure I haven't been seeing her since I moved into her apartment, though, and fooling myself into believing we were just friends. We are friends. Best friends. But that doesn't explain how often I've thought of her, fantasized about her, how my heart would kick up into my damn throat every time she answered the door.

Holding on to the memory of Addison framed by Christmas lights, I push through the fray, keeping my features carefully schooled.

"Are you dating Clemons' cousin to get back at her for canceling the wedding?"

"Addison Potts' mother was the mistress of Naomi's father. There's some talk he might be Addison's father, as well. How—"

"How does the Clemons family feel about you dating Miss

Potts? Are you telling us this is all a coincidence, Captain Du Pont?"

"Is she pregnant? Will there be a rushed engagement?"

Christ. I've already arranged for Addison to be escorted to and from work by a security detail, but even two armed guards can't keep these ridiculous questions from being hurled in her direction. She's not accustomed to them like me.

"Naomi Clemons is back in town. Have you spoken to her?"

Okay, now that one I wasn't expecting. I check myself for some kind of reaction and find nothing more than…mild surprise. I'm glad Naomi is all right, returned to her family, and I hope to apologize someday for going through the motions as we got closer to the wedding. Or possibly since the beginning of our relationship. But I'm more concerned about Addison having to field this question from reporters. If she was insecure about the bed I destroyed, how is she going to feel about Naomi being back in Charleston?

Can't we get through one day together without something trying to disrupt us?

I set aside the news of Naomi's return and focus on getting through today. Being with Addison, holding her, ignoring anything that makes us question our relationship—that's how to deal with disruptions. Having made it to the door, I turn and nod to the reporters, several of whom I catch trying to film my ass. "What would I do without you all being so concerned about my love life?" I wink at their ripple of laughter. "If you're so invested in its success, send Addison flowers and tell her they're from me. I need all the help I can get."

They all go off like car alarms as soon as I leave, throwing questions at me through the door, but I only wave back at them while passing through security. Something about the tension in the lobby tells me my father is upstairs and that theory is confirmed a few moments later when I pass Preston in the hallway. Being that there's no love lost between us and I have no intention of faking otherwise, I start to pass him with a tight nod. I'm forced to slow, however, when he addresses me.

"I guess it's safe to say Addison won't be needing my tour guide services." He checks his phone, then slides it back into his suit pocket, tapping it into place with a finger. "Too bad. I was *really* looking forward to showing her around."

Red bleeds into the edges of my vision. "You're not on a first-name basis with her. Miss Potts will work just fine." I step into his space, satisfied when he drops a few shades of tan. "Not that you'll have the chance to call her anything."

"Oh, I'm sure we'll run into each other sometime." He backs away from me with an infuriating wink. "Charleston is a small world."

When Preston disappears down the stairwell, it takes all of my willpower not to go after him. I manage to calm the boil of my blood by recalling Addison's sex-limp body in bed, the feel of her fingertips tracing the knots of my spine. Her breath on my neck. She's my woman. Preston could never be a threat to that. He's pissed about not being asked to join my advisory council and is just trying to get under my skin—and jealousy over Addison is his only effective tool. No way I'm going to let him threaten the contentedness I left the house with this morning, though. Not happening.

As soon as I've managed to set aside the encounter with Preston, I enter my office. As usual, my father has the television turned to the local news station, my entrance to the building playing on a loop. However, he's no longer sitting at the desk—which is now mine—opting for a slow pace in front of the windows.

I expect him to launch into a lecture about the past, Addison and me, public perception. Et cetera. Things I don't give a damn about. Especially not when she's making me so happy, I barely know what to do with myself.

The fact that I'm not going to suffer any bullshit must be showing in my eyes, because my father's weathered face breaks into a smile. Making me even more suspicious.

"Good news. There was an opening on tonight's *Fastball* panel and they want you." He waves a hand at the television. "We'll ask them not to discuss this in too much detail, but your actions of the last twenty-four hours have definitely caused a stir. Like it or not, gossip and scandal boost ratings."

The sinking disappointment that I might not be able to cook dinner for Addison is only responsible for half of my irritation. "My actions? Look, I admit throwing the mattress out of the window wasn't my finest judgment call. Apart from that, I collected my girlfriend and drove her home."

"Your scantily clad girlfriend, Elijah. The daughter of a home wrecker."

Those words drive a fist into my solar plexus. "You need to leave."

"Not my words." He points to the window. "Theirs."

"*Who?*"

"The Tea."

There's no humor in my laugh. It's resentful. Toward anyone who wants to taint the best thing in my life. "That's a gossip website. It's not even worth mentioning."

"A gossip website with a million readers." He massages the center of his forehead with a sigh. "Elijah, I actually do like her. She's...nothing like I expected. Throwing large objects out of my window is something your mother might have inspired me to do, once upon a time." His mouth flattens. "But I want to retire knowing your success is guaranteed. They want a family at the wheel they can look up to. You look at Addison and see one thing, while they see the sins of her mother. Or a gold digger." He takes a folded newspaper off my desk and holds it up—and there's Addison from last night, dancing. With Lydia. A huge, beautiful smile on her face. "Hell, they see what the newspapers print. Addison out dancing and drinking in a cheap dress."

If I could go back in time, I would never mention the stupid pink bra. I would just suffer in silence while she wore that damn thing, even if it killed me. "You have the nerve to throw the word cheap around, when you're letting some exploitive, low-rent website do your thinking for you?" I move around the desk and take the newspaper from his hands, scanning the first few lines. Slowly, I start to relax, the morning's lightness returning in waves. "This story isn't negative. They...*love* her. She's, 'dancing to the beat of her own drum and shaking up Charleston's stuffy upper crust. Our love-struck mayor-elect never knew what hit him. Getaway Girl for the win.'"

"Give me some credit, son. I've been doing this a while." He stabs the desk with a finger. "What seems like positive spin today is exactly what they'll hate her for tomorrow. And in case you forgot, the stuffy upper crust are your *donors*. They take these headlines as an insult and you condone them by dating her."

"This is the last time I'm going to say this, so listen very carefully. I do not care what the public thinks of my relationship. We make each other happy. If there's a donor or a website or an entire goddamn public who takes it upon themselves to judge her, so be it. It won't change *my* judgment. And if you can't see she's incredible—if you can't evolve with me and stop living solely for public approval—then get the fuck out."

My veins are flowing with heat and I'm about ready to flip the desk we're facing off across. This isn't some fight an adolescent has with his dad. This is a man telling another man what the hell is up. It's a line in the sand and if he crosses it again, I'm done. It's a fact.

Finally, my father circles the desk and sits down in one of the guest seats, gesturing for me to take one behind the desk. "One of the panelists on *Fastball* likes to lean hard on education issues. You should have your ducks in a row." He rolls his tongue around his mouth. "We could work on some talking points, if you're done tearing me up one side and down the other."

Feeling my night with Addison slip further out of my reach, I drag a hand down my face and get to work, promising myself I'll make it up to her. And I know exactly how to start.

CHAPTER TWENTY

Addison

Special Delivery at the Mayor-Elect's Mansion.
Does Getaway Girl Already Have Control of the Credit Card?
—TheTea.com

Getaway Girl's Other Mode of Transportation.
Hint: It involves a paddle. Click to get her aquatic workout!
—Avant-Charleston

While the Mayor Is Away, the Getaway Girl Will Play.
Addison Potts Spotted with Two Men.
—Southern Insider News

Profile: Addison Potts and the Grandmother's Legacy She
Quietly Upholds.
—Charleston Courier

I GIVE UP my frantic purse search with a wounded animal sound, no choice but to face the facts. I've lost my earbuds. This morning, when I left the house to go kayaking, I plugged them deep into my ears, turned up the volume on The 1975 to full blast and heard none of the press's questions. I was tempted to give them all the middle finger as I dove into the back of the shiny government SUV, but something made me smile and wave instead.

It might have been the bone-deep sexual satisfaction. But I think that's only part of it. I want to make an...effort. If Elijah is going to take a gamble on ex-party girl turned Christmas ornament saleswoman, Addison Potts, the least I can do is be kind to the people who could help or hurt his career.

Inside my chest, my heart starts to wrap against my ribs.

Elijah *is* kind, isn't he?

Elijah is everything.

Whoa, girl. These extreme cases of swooning have been catching me off guard all day. And with a bevy of reporters lying in wait, being off my game is not helpful. I can't help it, though. Allowing myself the tiniest dash of hope that Elijah and I could be the real deal...it has broken an emotional dam and allowed all my suppressed feelings to come flooding in. Before now, I'm not sure I let myself acknowledge how in love I am with Elijah. Now that I have, I'm scared of its magnitude.

Realizing I've been sitting in the back of my Elijah-appointed SUV staring into space for long minutes, I shake myself. "Um..." I lean forward to the space between my bodyguards, two friendly ex-military men who take up the driver and passenger seats. "You guys don't happen to have an extra pair of headphones...?"

"No, ma'am," they say at the same time, before the passenger turns and smiles over his shoulder. "You ready to go, Miss Potts?"

I blow out a breath and look out at the sidewalk. At least two-dozen reporters anticipate me leaving the vehicle, cameras at the ready. A few weeks ago, there was an occasional run-in with the press. Now, it's constant.

Kind. I can be kind. No, I *want* to. That girl who showed up at the church all those months ago, hoping to cause a stir? I don't harbor that same resentment anymore. Of course some of it still exists, but my resentment was for the upper crust as a whole. The representation of the family that shut out my grandmother because of her daughter's behavior, without holding my possible birth father accountable *at all*. Elijah is part of that circle, though. He loves people who are members of it and I trust him. So I'm letting go of any leftover anger a little bit at a time. "Sure, I'm ready."

"Wait for us to come around and let you out."

"Will do," I mutter. I've spent less than a day with a security detail and I already know the drill. After Elijah left this morning, I floated downstairs and made a second attempt at coffee. I'd only taken my first sip when Ricky and Kyle knocked on the door, informing me they'd be escorting me where I need to go for the foreseeable future. Yes, even if it's just a jog along the Battery. Yes, even to buy tampons. Yes, even kayaking. Thankfully, I convinced them to remain on the shore while I snuck across the river to Drum Island—sorry, boys, there's only room for one in a kayak—but they didn't like me giving them the slip.

Once again I failed to spread my grandmother's ashes, still stowed in my backpack. I thought this time I would be able to let go. To set her free. I'm opening myself up to the potential pain that comes from loving Elijah. I'm allowing myself to free fall. I thought letting those barriers drop would make it easier to open the Mrs. Claus canister and let the wind take her, but...I still couldn't do it. There's still something holding me back.

After a rap on the window, it opens. Members of the media crowd in around my two security guards, taking pictures and calling my name, fighting for my attention. Flash. Flashflashflash. My hair is in disarray from the wind and I'm wearing yoga pants and a loose, wide-necked top with a bathing suit beneath. Definitely not the uniform for a mayor-elect's girlfriend. But I climb out, anyway, because I have no choice. *Just get to the gate.*

Remembering my resolution to try harder for Elijah's sake, I squeeze my backpack straps tight and smile, even saying excuse me as I pass. Whoa. Points for Addison. One morning in bed with Elijah and I'm a whole new person. I wonder if he's going to see this on the news and be proud of me. I want that so badly. I want him to be as proud of me as I am of him.

"Getaway Girl! Look this way!"

"Miss Potts! Do you have an explanation for Mattressgate?"

I giggle into the back of my wrist and keep moving. "Captain Du Pont is very particular about back support."

That earns me some pleased laughter. This is easy. I can do this.

"Is it true Naomi Clemons is your half-sister?"

My skin shrinks head to toe, but having prepared myself to eventually get hit with this question, I don't falter. "Sorry to disappoint. Just cousins."

Contradictions are shouted at me. Nothing that can be proven without my consent. Nothing. I'm internally repeating that reminder when my attention is snagged by the loudest reporter. "Are you living here permanently? Do you have the ex-mayor's blessing?"

My feet try to tangle together, but Kyle is there with a hand on my elbow, pulling me along through the throng of people. "I, um…"

"Are you aware Naomi Clemons is back in town, Miss Potts? Have you seen her?"

"Has Elijah been in contact with Naomi Clemons?"

"Does she wish to reconcile with the mayor-elect? Does she regret leaving him at the altar?"

I lose all of my breath. It's just *gone* in a sickening rush. Ricky unlocks the gate and shoves it open, Kyle guiding me through, and I'm walking, but I can't feel my legs. Naomi is back. She's in Charleston? I don't know why the news is so shocking to me. This is where her highly influential family lives. Her whole life is here.

Elijah is here.

Does he know she's back, too? Does he...want to see her?

Has he already?

If two men weren't watching my every move, I would sink down onto the gleaming floor as soon as we walk over the threshold. But they're locking the door and checking windows and I'm just standing in the middle of the foyer, trying to act like I haven't been struck by lightning. With Naomi off in parts unknown, it has been easy to pretend Elijah can go on like this forever. Naomi's family runs in the same circle as Elijah's, though. It's only a matter of time before they're in the same room together and he...and he...

Remembers what wife material looks like. Behaves like.

Remembers all the times they spent together.

Remembers he loves her. No. He's never even forgotten. Didn't he imply so last night at the bar?

"Miss Potts, the house is secure," Kyle says. "Unless you need anything else, we'll be back bright and early tomorrow to escort you to the market."

How absurd. It's all so *absurd*. Elijah dating a girl who works in the market selling dick joke ornaments. "Okay," I croak. "Thank you."

Before following Kyle out the door, Ricky stops. "Don't let them get to you."

I huff a laugh. "Easier said than done."

He drums his fingers on the doorjamb. "I hope you don't mind me speaking out of turn, but Captain Du Pont is one of the finest men I know. He honors his commitments." His nod is firm. "If he made one to you, there's nothing to worry about."

Has he made a commitment? Walking through the now-empty house like a ghost, I admit he's trying. Hard. He wants me to be his girlfriend, even if I know the offer was an attempt to do the right thing. I'm the one who forced more casual terms. But Elijah is honorable almost to a fault. He would hold tight to a commitment to a runaway bride, too, wouldn't he? Especially if he still loves her.

Yes, he's physically attracted to me. Cares for me, too. But she wore his ring.

And now she's back within reach. Where does that leave me?

This morning, the walls of this house were an embrace. Just as suddenly, they feel temporary.

My phone jangles in my backpack and I twist around, digging the vibrating device from the front pocket. *Elijah.* Seeing his name makes my heart go off like a bottle rocket and I take several deep breaths to make myself sound normal. "Hey, Captain."

"Hey, Goose." His affectionate tone spreads through me like wildfire, banishing the cold. That's all it takes. One instant and I'm calling myself ten kinds of fool for doubting what we have together. It's unusual, yes. But it's more real than anything I've ever had in my life. "Are you home safe?"

Cradling the phone to my ear, I sit down on the stairs leading to the second floor. "Yes, I'm here."

"Good." A chair creaks in the background and I picture his big body leaning back, thighs in his classic, epic manspread. "Are you planning on giving the men heart attacks every day?"

"Only one person fits in a kayak," I mutter. "Are they reporting my moves to you?"

"If they consider a move to be unorthodox or dangerous, yes.

They've been asked to call me. Does that bother you?"

Honesty floats out of me like a balloon. "No. In a weird way, it's kind of…hot."

"Really." He pauses. "Would you still feel that way if you knew they've been following you for a while? Those morning runs you took alone, especially before you moved to my place, sugar…they made me nervous." His voice is right up against my ear, just like it would be if he were home. Gruff. Deep. "Then reporters started showing up at the market and putting you on television. I couldn't take the risk of something happening to you. I was worried you'd forbid the protection and turn my damn hair gray way before its time."

My blood has morphed into champagne, lust and admiration and pleasure tickling my insides. "I'm mostly disappointed in myself for not realizing I was being followed." I fall back against the stairs and tilt my head back toward the ceiling. "But it's kind of nice. Having someone…worry about me."

"I can't remember a time when I didn't worry about you." His low chuckle turns into a sigh. "I can't get home tonight, Addison. I'm sorry."

Despite his warmth and affection, the house expands around me, making me feel tiny. Or maybe it's the stupid conclusion I jump to. He's going to see her. He's going to see her. "Oh, okay," I manage, pushing shaky fingers through my hair. "Raincheck, then."

He's quiet for a beat. "You know, you have the right to ask me for an explanation."

"Do you want to give me one?"

"Of course I do."

Does Elijah know Naomi is back in town? He must. I only braved the reporters once today, but he's probably done it countless times while traveling between engagements. So if he knows, why doesn't he mention it to me? If he would just say, right here and now, that he's aware of Naomi's return to Charleston and doesn't give two shits one way or the other, my heartbeat could go back to normal. Or maybe he does give two shits. Maybe he gives ten. At least then, I'll know where I stand. "Well?" I say, holding my breath.

"I'm a last-minute replacement on *Fastball* tonight at nine." I can hear the amusement in his pause. "If you have dinner in front of the television, it'll be kind of like we're eating together."

"Oh." I fall back on the stairs, my eyes fluttering shut. "I'll have to put the politics on mute if I want to keep my appetite." I cover the receiver so I can sigh over his laugh. "Good luck tonight. I *might* consider saving you a plate."

"Might?" His hum carries down the line. "I think we can do better than that. Have you been upstairs?"

"What?" I tilt my head backwards to look up the stairs, making everything seem upside down. "Not yet."

"Go look in the bedroom. Tell me when you get there."

My smile is so big it hurts as I stand and jog up the stairs. "Did you finally install that sex swing you always wanted?"

"Sex swing." He snorts. A couple ticks go by. "Why? Is that something that interests you?"

My laughter bounces around the empty upstairs hallway. "We cannot afford to scandalize the media any further. They're still up in arms over Mattressgate."

"I can't believe you let me do that."

"*Let* you? You were carrying an *axe*."

I'm almost to the bedroom, my feet sinking into the rich, blue carpet runner.

"The reporters..." Elijah stops to clear his throat. "Are they bothering you too much?"

Here's my chance to tell him yes. *Yes.* But only because they're asking me if you still want Naomi. Put my mind to rest, Elijah.

But I say nothing of the kind. Because I'm too afraid he won't.

"They're harmless," I murmur, stepping into the bedroom and turning on the light. "Oh," I say, staring at what's in front of me. "Oh wow."

It's a new bed. Where the sleigh bed was rustic and old-fashioned, this one is modern. Swanky, even. There's an uphol-stered headboard that runs almost to the ceiling. It's gray with a tufted grid and the frame matches. It's huge and tasteful and gorgeous. Even the silver and midnight-blue bedclothes are different. Not a single throw pillow in sight, either. Hallelujah.

"Elijah," I whisper, going to the bed and running my finger-tips across the silky comforter. "How did you do this so fast?"

"Don't worry about that. Do you like it?"

I shake my head even though he can't see me. "The things I'm going to let you do to me in this bed…"

His groan is agonized. "I'll take that as a yes."

Unable to resist, I hop up on the mattress and lie down, sigh-ing at the perfect degree of firmness, the fluff of the comforter. It might as well be custom made to my tastes.

"You're lying on it, aren't you?" Another creak of his chair. "Sugar, I have to go on national television very soon."

"Then don't think about how I'll be waiting in bed for you…all warm and naked." I slide my hips around and moan. "Grateful, too. So…*very* grateful."

"Christ. I'm going to regret this, but there's more."

"More what?"

"Get off our bed." He let's his emphasis on *our* hang in the air. "And go look in the room at the other end of the hall."

I sit up and push the hair out of my face. "The meditation room?"

"Addison Potts, I do believe you just said that without a hint of judgment."

"Maybe I'm just getting better at hiding it." I slide off the bed, taking one last, longing look at the incredible piece of furniture before turning out the light. "Thank you for the new bed," I say quietly. "It's perfect."

"You'll be sleeping in it when I get home."

My smile is back to hurting. "Yes, Captain."

I'm not prepared for what I see when I open the meditation room door. I was so wrapped up in flirting with Elijah and trying to distract myself from dwelling on Naomi returning home, I didn't have the headspace to speculate. But when I nudge open the door and see my neatly stacked tubs of Christmas ornament supplies, I plop right down on the floor.

"Addison," comes Elijah's voice in my ear. "Are you there?"

"Fine." I use my shirt sleeve to swipe at my eyes. "I'll save you a plate."

His laugh creeps down the line and makes a home in my ear. "Thank you, sugar."

I blow out a breath and stare at the ceiling, willing the moisture leaking out to go away. "Elijah?"

"Yes?"

I lied about the reporters. They're not harmless. A couple of well-aimed questions have the power to devastate me because I have no idea how you feel about your ex-fiancée. Or where I stand in relation to her. Am I your live-in hookup? Are you doing these lovely things for me out of guilt, because at the end of the day, all you want from me is sex and companionship?

"I'll save you the snowman buttons to glue on," I say, instead. "Good night."

He's quiet for a few seconds. "Night, Goose."

CHAPTER TWENTY-ONE

Elijah

Mayor-elect wows panel on Fastball.
Getaway Girl responsible for his renewed convictions?
—Charleston Courier

Mayor betrays his political roots on Fastball.
Getaway Girl responsible for his flagging sense of tradition?
—Southern Insider News

ADDISON IS FAST asleep when I finally walk into the bedroom around midnight. She barely takes up any of the bed and yet, the sight of her there is like a knockout punch. The tie I unknotted on the way up the stairs slips from my fingers, landing on the floor. My military training demands I pick it up, but I ignore the impulse and keep moving, keep stripping off my clothes and leaving them in a trail, needing like hell to get into the bed beside her.

When I draw back the covers, I see that she is, in fact, wearing nothing but her birthday suit and my cock wastes no time saluting her with enthusiasm. God, she's a sexy little thing, all rosy and curled up around a pillow. And I'm the man who gets to look. I'm the man who has the privilege of being trusted enough to walk into her bedroom without asking. To get naked and lie down beside her. My pulse is clanging in my ears over the wonder of that. Over the pride it gives me. I've wanted to sleep beside her for a very long time, I realize.

"You were with me tonight," I say into the darkness. "I needed you. And you were there. We're a team, Addison. Do you realize I'm never letting you go?"

Her fingers twitch on the pillow, her eyes blinking with sleep. "Elijah?"

I can barely hear her over the racket my heart is making. "It's me."

She pushes up onto one elbow with a drowsy smile, her tits swaying like the sweetest fruit. "You were amazing tonight." A yawn takes her by surprise—and so have I. Sleepy Addison is less mean, more full of compliments, is she? That's good to know. "I'm proud of you for standing up for those schools. The ones that aren't performing. They just need their curriculum overhauled and some strong leadership."

I choke a laugh into my fist when she repeats what I said on the panel tonight almost verbatim. "There you go again. Proving you were fake-sleeping all those times we watched *Meet the Press* on your couch. You like politics."

"I like anything if you're a part of it," she murmurs, sinking back down into the pillows with her eyes closed. "Come to bed."

"Coming." Need and affection are vying for the lead inside my chest, but I'm frowning as I climb into bed beside my girl. This half-asleep Addison reminds me a lot of flu-riddled Addison who I carried from the market all those weeks ago. She's unguarded right now as she was then, telling me things I'm not sure she'd want me to know if she was fully awake. But why does she feel the need to be guarded at all?

"Are you going to lose the election now?"

"No. And you don't worry about things like that."

"I worry about it all the time," she whispered.

"Why don't you talk to me about it?"

"Because that's not why you keep coming back."

As much as I know this girl, a part of her continues to be elusive. She only shows me glimpses of her deepest self when she's too weak or tired to keep her barriers up. After her refusal to sleep in the other bed, I now realize she's not all that secure where Naomi is concerned. And the only thing I can do to prove those insecurities are unfounded is to stay the course. Keep showing her how much she means to me. Actions not words. Earlier on the phone, I almost told her my ex was back in town, so she wouldn't be blindsided. I let the opportunity pass, though. I don't want to discuss my past failure. Even thinking about it causes me a headache and I'm not sure why. It's like a blurry unknown that I'm reluctant to bring into focus.

Here's what I know for sure. I don't want *anything* about it to touch the present. Because if I fail with Addison, I won't come out the other side of it alive.

With the vivid memory of carrying Addison in my arms revolving in my head, I slide over next to her, the blood singing in my veins when she lets me tuck her in against me. Her head uses my shoulder as a pillow, her feet slide between my calves—and it's goddamn heaven.

"I thought you didn't like to cuddle," I rasp against her forehead, throwing an arm around her waist and bringing her even tighter still against me. "Remember that?"

Another adorable yawn, right into my throat. "I *don't* like it."

"You don't?"

"No." Her lips twitch. "I'm just humoring you."

"Hmm." I brush my fingertips down the curve of her spine, laughing quietly when she whimpers and snuggles closer. "Did you make ornaments tonight?"

"A little. But I didn't want to miss you on television." She sighs. "You looked so hot."

Now I *know* she's half-asleep. "Did I?"

"Mmmhmm. All stubbly and intense and full of conviction. I was waiting here ready to seduce you, but the new bed backfired." Her voice is dreamlike. "It's too comfortable and now I can't move."

"We'll both be here in the morning, sugar. And the morning after that. And the one after that." I plant a kiss on her hairline, continuing to trail my fingers up and down her back. "We have all the time we need."

"Do we?" she whispers into my neck.

"*Yes.*" Alarmed, I pull back to find her studying my collarbone. "Addison, if something is bothering you, talk to me about it. I'll go get the axe."

She opens her mouth and closes it. "I just..." Long seconds pass. "I tried to spread my grandmother's ashes today. Again. And I couldn't do it. I guess I'm just feeling thrown off."

"Let me come with you next time." When she starts to comment, I put a hand over her mouth. "I know. There's only room for one in a kayak. I'll rent my own."

"You would do that?" she asks, when I take away my hand. "Would you wear your suit?"

"I own clothing besides suits."

"Sorry, I forgot about pajamas." I tickle her ribs and she writhes against me, teasing my poor cock into a state of protest. But when she casually drops her next question, I'm distracted from my building need to roll on top of her. "Do you want me to buy new clothes?"

"What?" I tip her chin up. "No, Addison. I don't. Please don't tell me you've been reading TheTea."

A puff of her breath feathers my lips. "The Tea?" Her voice is small. "They've been...talking about me?"

Shit. How did I manage to screw up crawling into bed with my adorably sleepy girlfriend? She looks stricken and it's my fault. Jesus. I have to fix this. I frame her face in my hands and wait until she focuses on me. "I will never care about some ridiculous website, Addison. They don't make money by reporting people are happy. So they look for anything they perceive to be negative and they blow it up."

"But it hurts you. It hurts your job."

"I don't want *you* hurt. *That's* what I care about." Those words are stone-cold truth. I've managed to get Addison living in my house, sleeping in my bed—safe and in my care—and now some faceless bloggers make her question the fact that she's good for me? The hell with that. I've just gotten a taste of what real happiness feels like. Not *only* happiness, either. Excitement. Lust. Looking forward to waking up so I can talk to her, make plans with her. No one is taking that away. I just have to protect her from the ugly side of being in the spotlight. I have to *protect* her, period, before she decides this life is more trouble than it's worth. Christ, if she left me...

What if the press becomes too much and she leaves me?

Panic hits me in the jugular. "Do you want to lay low for a while, until they move on to someone else?" I trace her cheekbone with my thumb. "You don't have to come to the inauguration on Saturday. I can come home to you afterward."

Down the hall, I hear the tick-tick-ticking of the grandfather clock as silence passes between us. "Yeah, maybe that's for the best."

"Okay." I drop kisses on her cheeks, eyelids, nose. "Okay, we're fine. We're fine?"

"Of course we are."

I only catch a glimpse of her troubled eyes, before she trails a hand down my belly and wraps a fist around my stiff cock. "Fuck," I groan, pushing my hips into her touch. "I need you so damn bad." Her tongue strokes into my mouth the same time her fist pumps my flesh. Hard. Tight. I almost erupt and spill all over her hand, but manage to keep myself contained. Barely.

"You worked so hard today, baby," She jacks me off faster, biting my bottom lip between her teeth and tugging. Then she hits me with that voice—pouty seductress—and it turns my dick to sweating steel. "I can think of a nice, wet place for you to let go of all that stress. Would you like that?"

Yes. *God*, yes. A warning tugs at me, though. Too easy. Something about how we transitioned to sex after our conversation is too effortless, but she's mewling against my lips, her outer knee sliding up and down my thigh like an invitation. I'm physically incapable of turning it down. Actions not words, right? Didn't I decide earlier today that I could prove my devotion to Addison with actions?

I roll her over and meld our mouths together. She realizes about halfway through the kiss that I mean business. This isn't sex. It's a fucking claiming. Her surprised moan makes my head spin, her hesitant hands on my back make my heart pound. By the time I drag my mouth away, she's pink faced and shaking. Looking at me like we just met.

"Show we where your man puts his stress."

Her lids fall to half-mast as she spreads her thighs, revealing that gorgeous pink pussy slit. "Do you need to be rough with me tonight, Captain?"

"*Yes*," I growl, reaching between us to guide myself to her opening, dragging the head over her clit a few times before working it inside. We both seem to be holding our breath as I thrust deep, her hoarse cry of my name giving me savage satisfaction. Almost. Almost...because there's something desperate there, too, I can't name. "Addison," I breathe into her mouth. "It's just us. Don't let anything else matter."

"B-but there's so many other things that *do*," she whispers, breaking off on a sob when I attack her neck, using my tongue and teeth to exploit her sensitive skin, rolling, rolling my hips and taking her smaller body with me on a ride each time. "*Elijah.*"

"Addison." I cage her head with my forearms and press our brows together. "Be here with me. Feel what you do to me. *Believe* it."

She nods. She nods, squeezes her eyes closed and kisses me, her body shaking with the force of my drives, one after the other, honey-drenched slaps filling the room and accelerating, our bodies straining and twisting. Her fingernails dig into the flesh of my ass, her palms molding me in that savoring way of hers, a groan kindling in her throat. "God, the things I want to do to this butt. I spend way too much time plotting how to get my hands on it."

Jesus. Never in my wildest dreams did I think I'd be grateful for my ass one day. But I am. Ever since Addison started biting her lip and checking it out, usually when I'm wearing sweatpants, I've stopped untucking my shirt or trying to hide it from cameras. Let them look. My woman is a fiend for it. "Your hands are on it right now. What do you want?"

Excitement lights up her eyes. "Turn over for me?"

"Fuck, I take it back. I didn't know I'd have to pull out of you." I punch deep and moan. "This pussy is so hot and tight around me, sugar."

Her index finger slides down the crease of my ass, putting

pressure on my back entrance and I suck in a breath. "Please, Elijah?"

Lord almighty. She hasn't put her finger there since the first time. Sex between us is so damn mind-blowing, I haven't had the chance to want her to do it again. Right now, though, with her pressing down tight and the memory of losing control of my own body rifling through my head, I can admit…to wanting it. Needing her to occupy me that way.

It hurts. *Bad.* But I slide my cock out of Addison's incredibly wet pussy and let her crawl on top of me, her thighs straddling mine. I was already so close to coming, I have no recourse but to pump my hips against the bed, my hips moving faster when Addison's hands glide over my cheeks, her thumbs pressing into the fleshiest part of me. "Mine?"

She has to ask? She's got me so hot, I'm humping the fucking mattress. Even knowing she's watching me move from behind, there's no self-consciousness. Or the need to be a gentleman and hold back. She's freed me from those restraints and turned me into a beast. Her beast. "Damn right, it's yours—"

I break off in a growl when Addison's teeth sink into my right cheek. *Hard.* It hurts enough to make flashbulbs go off in front of my eyes, but exhilaration rips along my nerve endings, stealing a roar from my mouth. "Christ, sugar. *Christ.*"

"Want more?"

"*Yes*," I rasp, reaching down to fuck my own hand. How could I respond any other way to the satisfied purr in her voice? She loves what we're doing—is turned on by her open invitation—and that knowledge makes my cock begin to drip warm, sticky moisture. Gives me no choice but to gratify myself while she licks her tongue over the bite mark, blowing cool air on it. God I would love to see her face. I'm bringing a mirror to bed next time. I want all of her. To see every expression, see every touch, in addition to feeling it.

When I think Addison is going to bite the opposite cheek, I bury my open mouth into a pillow, already halfway to bellowing from the pain/pleasure. But the bite never comes. Instead her hands push apart my ass cheeks and her tongue drags long and hard up the middle, reaching the back entrance and pressing down *hard*.

My balls wrench up into my stomach and I explode off the bed, her name leaving me in a drawn out, guttural grunt. I'm in pain. The kind of pain that only Addison can cure, and when I turn and find her flushed and kneeling, her nipples in sweet little points, I lunge for her, knocking her backwards on the foot of the bed. And then I fuck into her so hard, she screams, her perfect pussy spasming around my aching dick while she thrashes, her body shaking like a leaf beneath me. "That what you been plotting and keeping to yourself? Being a bad girl with that tongue?"

She's twisting, twisting, caught in the peak of her orgasm, her eyes gone blind. "Yesyesyes. *Elijah*."

"You can do whatever the hell you want, long as it keeps this pussy good and wet."

"*Ohhh*," she moans. "Oh my *God*."

Right before she goes limp, she squeezes me down low and I feel myself start to erupt, my need flooding her as I punch, punch, punch forward and finish. Halfway through my relief, our gazes connect and I've never seen anything more beautiful. Freedom. She's freedom and light and...more. So much more. There are words sitting right on the tip of my tongue, begging to be put out in the world, but something demands I hold them inside. Don't let them out.

Minutes later, I fall asleep holding Addison, sweat cooling on my bare skin. Content. I've never been more at peace in my entire life, while somehow…*electrified* at the same time. Thank God I found her. Thank God.

That peace is shattered sometime later when I jolt upright in bed, covered in fresh sweat. I make a mental grab for the fading images, but can't land on a clear memory of the nightmare. All I know is I'm drowning under the weight of unimaginable loss. Or the terrible feeling of it. Where is it coming from? I reach for Addison and come up empty, finding her facing away from me, curled up on her side. So far away. Why so far away?

"Goose."

In her sleep, she turns over and reaches out. Our fingers twine together as I lower back down to the pillows. Just a dream. It wasn't real.

It wasn't real.

CHAPTER TWENTY-TWO

Addison

Naomi Clemons Goes out in Public for the First Time...
To Visit a Wedding Planner?
—TheTea.com

I TEAR A receipt from the credit card machine, holding it down for a customer to sign. Usually, I can tell when someone stops by Jingle Balls just to get a good look at me, maybe even a covert selfie without permission. But this sweet, older lady from Michigan has no idea who I am. She just wants a naked Santa Claus with Christmas holly covering his junk.

"Do you mind me asking where you locals get your pralines?" the lady asks, tucking her receipt into her purse. "If I'm going to waste the calories, I want it to be good."

"I'm not exactly a local. More of a transplant." I prop my hip on one of the display tables, wondering at what point that will stop being true. Or if I'll always feel like I have one foot in South Carolina, one in New York. "But Kilwin's is a safe bet. That's where my grandmother used to buy hers."

She takes the receipt back out of her purse, waving it at me. "Would you mind writing that down? I'd forget my head if it wasn't attached."

"Sure." I take a pen out of my apron and write the name of

the sweet shop, handing it back to the customer…just in time to catch a young man snapping a picture of me with his cell phone as he passes the booth. "Good luck. Enjoy your Santa *and* those calories," I say, with a tight smile.

If the lady notices the impromptu photo session, she doesn't say anything, rejoining her husband mid-aisle and moving on to a hand-painted scarf stall. I wave to Ricky and Kyle who are posted up in the corner of the market, close enough to reach me if anything happens, but not close enough to intimidate potential customers. Ricky gives me an apologetic smile, so he must have noticed the curiosity seeker taking my picture. I shrug back. Market security has managed to keep members of the media from approaching me inside the market, but there isn't much they can do about cell phones. Based on some of the snaps I've seen online and in newspapers, either the media purchases pictures taken inside the market. Or they're just breaking the rules and taking the pictures themselves.

Not headache inducing at all, right?

I almost made it through a full day without looking myself up on TheTea after Elijah told me about the stories. Big mistake. They managed to make my innocent girls' night out with Lydia look like a drunken orgy, finding certain angles of me in the vicinity of men—men I never even spoke with or acknowledged but "witnesses" claim I pursued. *Mayor Arrives in a Jealous Rage to Collect His Naughty Party Girl.* It only went downhill from there. Everything from the length of my morning running shorts to speculations about my relationships with my bodyguards…it's never ending. It's probably never going to get better, either, as long as I'm dating the mayor.

Leading up to the inauguration tomorrow morning, Elijah's time at home has been rushed. He's overworked and exhausted, but he's still nothing short of amazing. He walked in the door last night, threw me up in his arms and carried me to the bedroom. God, he took me like a savage, rocking the bed against the wall so hard, I thought we might take it down. His fingers left bruises on my thighs, my backside. Whisker burns decorate every inch of me that's hidden by clothes. Dinner sat forgotten on the stove until we dragged ourselves downstairs around midnight wrapped in blankets, eating a picnic on the kitchen floor.

I'm so in love, I wonder if I spread my arms and wished hard enough, flight would be possible. Impossibilities don't exist when my whole being can be taken over by hope. This incredible man is my very best friend. He's my lover. My protector and ally. I can live without him telling me he loves me, can't I? I can live without him reaching that final level of feeling for me. In exchange for being held in his arms at night and getting his silly text messages, I can endure almost anything.

He still hasn't told me whether or not he's aware of Naomi being back in Charleston. Every day, I will him to bring it up, to get rid of the elephant in the room. I want to put my master plan behind me, once and for all. To trust that this relationship between Elijah and me will grow and get stronger. But the longer he pretends as if her presence doesn't linger, the longer I leave the end game I devised boiling on the back burner. If I'm not meant to be with Elijah, there's a way to leave everything how I found it, but better. For him.

I sense someone entering my stall and turn to greet them, drawing up short when I spot the customer. It's Elijah's mother.

"Mrs. Du Pont," I say, resisting the ridiculous urge to curtsey. "I didn't expect you to…"

"Hello, Addison. And please, it's Virginia." She gestures to a petite woman with graying blonde hair I didn't notice before but know very well. My mother used to point her out to me in public, before she left and never came back. I was so young, but it's impossible to forget the hatred in my mother's tone as the woman passed. "Have you met Mrs. Clemons? Naomi's mother."

Cold fingers creep along my skin until I'm shivering. The woman betrayed by my mother and her current husband is standing right in front of me, her sharp gaze starting on the tips of my ratty sneakers and ending at my ponytail. Looking for a resemblance to her husband? "Hello, Addison." She holds out a brisk hand, her blue eyes unreadable. "It's a pleasure. You may call me Della."

I'm half frozen but still manage to complete the handshake. "Hi."

Virginia taps a bell and smiles, mouthing a filthy rhyme she reads off a decorative wooden sign. When she rears back a little at the dirty joke, I bring my chin up. I'll never be ashamed of my grandmother's legacy, even if it consists mostly of dick jokes. "Um. Did you come here to buy decorations?"

The two women share a private look.

"Sure," Virginia says slowly. "Maybe an inauguration gift for Elijah. You are coming tomorrow, aren't you, Addison?"

"No." I clear the cobwebs from my throat. "No, I...we thought it was for the best. The attention should be on all the good things he's doing. Not on...his relationship, right?"

Della is nonplussed. "Public focus is always on the relationship."

"Maybe in the beginning," I say quickly, cement filling my throat. "But eventually they lose interest and focus on something else..."

They wait politely when I trail off, but I do nothing to occupy the silence. What would I say? I'm not going to the inauguration because I'll make a misstep or wear the wrong thing and it'll reflect poorly on Elijah? That doesn't bode well for any kind of future at all. And if there is no future, what exactly am I doing with him? "Um." I shake myself and walk through the women, toward a different display. "Elijah would probably laugh if you bought him one of these as a gift. He glued the eyes on himself."

"My son glued the eyes onto a stuffed snowman?" She can't hide her genuine surprise. And pleasure, too, I think. "How on earth did you convince him to do that?"

"I didn't have to." Thinking of him sprawled on my old guest room bed, fingers connected by threads of hot glue, I smile. "He makes me save him the big buttons. Everything else slips out of his fingers."

A smile blooms across her face, but she subdues it quickly when Naomi's mother steps even with her. She's holding a Cookie Monster in a Santa hat. "I'll take one of these for Naomi. Cookie Monster was always a favorite when she was a little girl."

All the blood drains from my face at the mention of Elijah's ex-fiancée. "Sure," I force out, taking the ornament from her. "I'll just ring that up—"

"It's so nice having her back home." I receive a pointed look. "If everything had worked out the way it was *supposed* to, there would have been no question of *her* attendance at the inauguration."

"No, I'm sure there wouldn't have been," I respond, my voice hard. It's one thing to be intimidated by Elijah's mother, but I'm not backing down from this woman who clearly holds my mother's actions against me. I'm surrounded by my grandmother's memory and I'm not going to disappoint the only family who never let me down. "Playing the what-if game is a little pointless now though, considering she left the best man I've ever known at the altar."

"She knows it was a mistake," she hisses at me. "I'm sure it's only a matter of time before she gets enough courage to make amends."

Virginia jolts when her friend elbows her, dragging her attention from the ornament in her hand. "Yes, I'm sure Elijah will be...amendable to speaking with Naomi."

"Cold feet are not uncommon," slides in Della. "I think the mayor will be willing to forgive when it means he can have someone capable of standing by his side."

"Really? She couldn't do it in a church."

My snap back is greeted by the gasp of the millennium.

"Della." Virginia puts a hand on her friend's arm. "I think we've taken up enough of Miss Potts' time."

"Potts." Naomi's mother laughs without humor, passing Elijah's mother an encouraging look. "Now would be a good time to mention Elijah's low approval ratings."

"What?" My blood was only beginning to heat, but now it's back to being ice cold. I seek out Virginia's eyes, but it takes her a second to look at me. "What is she talking about?"

She straightens, any glimpse of kindness I thought I saw before long gone. "It's true. His numbers are worse than they've been since early in the campaign and..." Her nod is resolute. "There's some speculation that it's your doing."

I'm being swallowed by a giant suck hole. It's taking me down, down, stomach first. Please, God. Don't let this be true. I will do anything. "Are you sure? He was on television last week and they didn't bring up low numbers—or me—at all."

Della scoffs. "Well, of course not. *Fastball* isn't the venue for such a personal discussion. It's the public that matters, though.

It's the public they poll."

Elijah's mother is staring off down the bustling market aisle. "I'm sorry, Addison. In their eyes, you're living in sin and flaunting convention. Such thinking might be old-fashioned, but my husband and now my son have made the decision to serve the public. Public opinion matters."

I want to pick up my things and run. Hide. I want to curl up and cry at the very possibility I could damage Elijah's career. But none of it makes sense. It does not make sense. Elijah comes home to me every night smiling. I can see him laughing in the pillows of our bed, dragging me over to him for long, lazy kisses. I can hear the resolution in his tone when he tells me he doesn't give a damn about the judgment of others. If I was tanking his approval rating, he wouldn't keep it from me, because I'd go nuclear when I found out, right?

So I'm not losing faith. *Fuck that.* These two women aren't going to waltz in here and demolish the trust and friendship Elijah and I have built together. It's ours and I'm not going to let anyone touch it. If he knew they were here saying these things to me, I know he wouldn't like it. That's why they're dividing and conquering. When he comes home tonight, I'll ask him if what they're telling me is true and we'll go from there. I *trust* him to tell me.

I have to. My other option is, believe that I'm actively hurting him—and that's unacceptable.

"The snowman is on the house," I say in a scratchy voice, taking it from Elijah's mother to wrap it in tissue paper, handing it back with a level gaze. "It's only fair, since you're related to one half of the manufacturing team."

"Thank you." I think I see the barest flicker of amusement in her expression as she inclines her head. "We'll let you get back to work."

Watching both of the women disappear into the crowd, I refuse to let the earth shift beneath my feet. I force it to firm up along with my lady balls. As soon as Elijah gets home tonight, we'll talk about this and he'll have an explanation. Everything will be fine.

I don't even consider the possibility that he won't come home tonight.

CHAPTER TWENTY-THREE

Elijah

Inauguration Day fashion!
What are Charleston's celebutantes wearing to the ceremony?
—Avant-Charleston

I hereby solemnly swear to stay thick and juicy.
—Twitter @DuPontBadonk

I LEAN BACK from my computer and massage my eye sockets.

How long have I been staring at the damn screen? Days?

A check of the clock tells me I've lost track of time—again—and I need to leave now or I won't make it home before Addison goes to sleep. But if I go home, I'll start my first official term as mayor in the morning with loose ends and plans without a solid foundation.

Dammit, I can't do it. I owe it to the people who elected me to *mean* what I say tomorrow. I'm not going to stand in front of everyone tomorrow without conviction.

Thinking of Addison bundled up under the covers makes me want to slam my head against the desk, though. That's where I want to be. *Need* to be. She's so sweet when she's half asleep. Even when she's digging her toes into my hips and urging me to go faster, that husky middle-of-the-night sleepiness in her tone has become my addiction. Lord, I crave her in all her forms.

Seductress, friend, tease, champion, partner in crime, mean girl, lover.

No wonder the news outlets have no idea what to make of her. She has the ability to be several incredible things at once—and they can't keep up.

Good. She's mine to figure out. *Mine* to pin down. No one else's.

With a half-smile on my face, I sort through the newspapers on my desk. Every morning, one of the aides drops them off, pertinent news stories highlighted. Addison is always a topic of interest, but depending on the news outlet, the coverage ranges from utter worship to outright derision. I loathe every single negative word printed about her, but it's the damn nature of the beast in politics. There are just as many negative opinions about me—mostly from the miffed upper crust—and before that, my father was the target of disapproval.

In a city the size of Charleston, making everyone happy is near impossible. Hell, my approval ratings reflect that, don't they? In one paper, my numbers are at an all-time high for any sitting mayor. In another, I might as well quit they're so low. Focusing on the job is the only answer. Getting lost in the bullshit will only distract me and drive me crazy.

I'm just about to pick up the phone to call Addison when there's a knock on my office door. Looking up, I'm surprised to see my mother framed in the doorway.

"Mom." I stand up and come around my desk, kissing her on her offered cheek. "What are you doing here so late?"

"I remember the night before your father was sworn in." She holds up a brown paper bag. "Macaroons are good for frayed nerves."

I take the bag and immediately dig in, popping a cookie into my mouth and she laughs when I make a big show of enjoying it. "Want one?"

"No, those are yours. I have plenty at home."

We fall silent after that, which is unusual. My mother usually talks a blue streak. "Is everything okay?" I ask, moving back to the other side of my desk.

She sits down across from me. "Having your father at home so much already has me at loose ends. I've cleaned every corner of the house—or supervised, anyway—I've lunched with every friend in my address book." She shrugs. "I guess I was just hoping to be helpful."

Having known this woman all my life, I know she's leaving something out, but I'm not going to press. I'm on the verge of telling her I've got everything under control and she should go home and get some sleep...when I stop myself. Ever since Sunday night when I told Addison she didn't have to go to the inauguration, I've wanted to go back in time and take it back. Not having her there tomorrow doesn't feel right. Not at all.

She's the most important part of my life and I want her standing beside me. I want everyone to see how *proud* I am to have her beside me. Being together means enduring the obnoxious questions from reporters and avoiding them can't become a pattern. No matter what they say, we should be able to look one another in the eye and know the truth.

"There is something, actually."

My mother sits forward. "Oh?"

"Yeah." I look at the framed picture of Addison and me, sitting near the phone on my desk. It was taken mere minutes before I was inside of her for the first time and *damn*, I have to admit the photo is pretty indecent, but there's something about her eyes that continues to draw me. She's nervous. Breathless.

Blissful. My memory of the night is wrapped tight in lust and the sensation of being caught off guard. Addison, though…her attraction to me isn't catching her off guard at all. More like that night was the culmination of it.

"Elijah?"

"Sorry." I cough the rasp out of my voice, but the spike suddenly lodged in my chest stays right where it is. "Addison was planning on staying home tomorrow. The sudden press coverage has been a lot for her to handle, but they're not going anywhere. We'll get through tomorrow, she'll see it can't touch us…and after that, facing them will be easier. She needs to be there. I need her there." I gesture to the paperwork on my desk. "I'd bring her myself, but I'm going to be here until the ceremony. And she needs to feel welcome by more than just me."

Color appears in her cheeks. "You're asking me to bring Addison *Potts* to the inauguration?"

Something about the way she says *Addison Potts* drives the spike further into my chest. But I ignore it. My mother and father are cut from the same cloth—old school to the bone. To them, the scandal with Addison's mother could have happened yesterday, it's so fresh. But I've witnessed them with Addison. They see the same extraordinary woman I do. It's only a matter of time before they set aside their doubts and accept her.

If they can't do that, then I'll *demand* it.

"At the very least, please encourage her to come. She already knows I want her there. Having it come from you might have more of an effect."

"Encourage her." One hand lifts to pat her hair. "I can do that."

"Can you?" I ask slowly, wondering if I'm making a mistake.

Her nod is more of a shrug, but it's an agreement.

I slide a finger across the screen of my phone and send Addison's contact information to my mother. "Thanks, Mom. This means a lot to me."

When I'm alone again in the office, my gaze strays back to the picture. To the girl sitting on my lap with so much naked vulnerability written on her face, I have to reach out and touch her, tracing my fingers over her lips. "Everything is going to be fine, Goose. Just have faith in me."

Addison

ELIJAH DIDN'T COME home last night.

Sometime around midnight, I got a text message.

Working through the night. Sleep tight, sugar. I'm thinking of you.

Over the last week, we've started talking more and more about his projects, the gazillion irons he has in the fire, so I knew going into yesterday, he might spend the night at the office. But that was before his mother and Naomi's mother dropped a house on me. All the insecurities I managed to keep at bay after the market encounter are running amok and I can't corral them, no matter how hard I try.

I'm pacing in front of the television, watching the coverage of inauguration day. There's an hour to go before the ceremony and God, I don't feel right dressed in leggings and a hoodie. Every time the camera pans through the gathering crowd, I notice the patriotic dresses and pressed suits. None of them know Elijah as well as I do, yet they're present on one of the most important days of his life. And I'm here. With granola crumbs stuck to my clothes.

I stop pacing and take a deep breath. There's no one keeping me here, is there?

No, there isn't. I have a nice dress upstairs that can pass for posh in a pinch.

My feet remain cemented to the ground.

Elijah told me I didn't have to attend, because he worried the reporters would make me uncomfortable. But…what if that's not the reason? What if he's aware of his approval ratings slipping and he's trying to save my feelings? Because that would be *such* an Elijah move. He can't fake how much he wants me. And I know he cares about me—it's there in every look, every touch. His career, though. He can't let it suffer, either.

Not for someone he doesn't love.

A knock at the door jars me out of my downward spiral. Knowing it's probably just Ricky and Kyle checking in, I jog to the door and glance through the peephole to confirm.

When I see who it is, I rear back with a frown on my face. "Um. Yes?"

"Addison, it's Preston." He stops there, as if it will be enough to make me open the door. Seconds later, he continues with a tight laugh. "You might remember me from election night. We were introduced by Mrs. Du Pont."

"I remember," I call through the door. "What are you doing here?"

"Mrs. Du Pont sent me to pick you up. She'd like you to be her guest at the ceremony this morning." I watch in a stupor through the peephole as he checks his watch. "We don't have a lot of time."

Hope tickles my belly. "She…wants *me* there?" I press a hand to my thudding heart. "Does Elijah know?"

"Yes and yes." I get the sense he knows I'm watching him, because he's all smiles now whereas before he seemed anxious. "I'm happy to wait out here while you get ready…"

Guilt is like a mule kick to my side. If this was New York, I would leave his butt on the stoop to wait without giving it a second thought. For all intents and purposes, he's a stranger. This is the south, though. I'm honor-bound by geography to invite him inside for sweet tea.

I finger the doorknob, but something won't allow me to turn it. This is Elijah's house. There are probably cameras outside. Inviting Preston inside when Elijah isn't home would be stupid. And I don't *want* to let him in, either. There's something about him that rubbed me the wrong way on election night and I have to trust my first impression.

"You know, I think I'll just drive myself," I say, backing away from the door. "Thanks anyway, Preston. Sorry for the inconvenience."

"You need security clearance," he drones louder, sounding kind of smug and impatient now. "Virginia put *my* name on the list. You'll need me to get in."

Dammit, he's right. Any other day, I could walk right into City Hall and go through a light security check, but today they probably have it sealed up like a drum. I can't call Elijah and bother him when he's reviewing his speech and preparing for the biggest moment of his life, either. I have no choice but to take the ride if I want to be there. And I do. I do so bad.

"I won't be more than ten minutes! Promise!" I call, already turning to sprint up the stairs, my socks sliding on the carpeted stairs. With the decision made not to invite Preston inside, I finally allow the excitement to trickle in. Holy shit. Maybe I wasn't imagining it yesterday when I sensed Elijah's mother softening toward me. And Elijah wants me at the ceremony, too. I was wrong about everything. How was I so wrong?

I still haven't moved my clothes into the master bedroom closet, so I take a hard right at the top of the stairs and dash down the hallway, mentally tearing apart my wardrobe. Black dress. Boom. Just throw the modest, black dress on, pair it with the pumps and swap my underwear for a thong to eliminate panty lines. I'm golden. That's all I have to do. Thank God my hair is washed. I'll brush it, clip it back and no one will know it was still messy from bed until eleven o'clock in the morning.

The transformation is completed in record time. I stop at the door to pluck my black pumps off the shoe rack, sliding them onto my feet for the first time in forever. Feeling armed and ready with my footwear in place, I'm out the door, keys and cell phone in hand.

When I get to the passenger side of Preston's idling Lexus, a few cameras go off from waiting vehicles and I hesitate. Getting a ride from this man is the right thing, isn't it? Preston might be kind of slimy, but he's a trusted member of their staff. We're only going less than a mile, aren't we?

"Addison." He rolls down the window and smiles. "We're going to be late."

"Right. Okay." Chewing my lip, I climb into the car and buckle my seatbelt, giving Preston a hard look when he makes no effort to hide his lazy perusal of my body. My fist bunches with the urge to deck him, but I force myself to relax. I just have to get through the ride to City Hall. There's an ugly voice in the back of my head, though, whispering he wouldn't be that disrespectful to Naomi. He would be ma'am-ing the bejeezus out of her. Rather, she would already be at the ceremony. "Can we go, please?"

His tongue is lodged in his cheek as he pulls into traffic on

King Street. I spend the ride with arms crossed so tightly, I start to worry for my circulation. Preston doesn't say anything as he weaves in and out of traffic, showing his identification at certain checkpoints. I'm grateful for the silence, but I can't shake the intuition that there's something he knows...that I don't. The closer we draw toward City Hall, the more my instincts begin to vibrate. People crowd the streets, watching giant projection screens that have been set up for the occasion. God. I've always known how Elijah's role as mayor was important, but seeing it happen live, is amazing. I'm so proud of him.

The magnitude of that pride makes this Lexus feel very small—very wrong—in comparison.

Elijah's reaction to his mother introducing Preston and me on election night comes roaring back, covering my face with flames. He wouldn't want me in a car with this man. He never would have encouraged this. What is going on?

When we reach the security gate that leads to City Hall, Preston already has his badge out to hand to the officer. Okay, this is fine. As soon as we're inside the gate, I can shake Preston and find a way to Elijah. Or if I can't reach him, at least I can watch him get sworn in.

My game plan is blown to smithereens when Preston rolls through security, circles the parking lot and pulls to a stop at the curb outside City Hall. There is a veritable mob of reporters, all of them filming the arrival and I know...I know in that moment that I've been had. Big time.

CHAPTER TWENTY-FOUR

Elijah

New Couple Alert?
—TheTea.com

"**C**APTAIN DU PONT, it's time."

I give the harried woman holding a clipboard my most patient smile, even though I'm the furthest thing from patient. "Yes, I realize that." A quick check of the clock tells me I should already have one hand on a Bible and my military sensibilities are protesting my lateness. "Have you been able to get a hold of my mother?"

A cursory consult of her clipboard and she nods. "She's on her way to the stage, along with your father, but she asked us to pass on a message."

There's a ticking in my temple. "What is it?"

Clipboard woman hesitates. "She says, she tried, but...Addison Potts won't be joining them. And she's sorry."

My optimism drops. Big time. "Really."

The woman holds up a finger, leaning into the headset and scribbling down a few more notes. "Sir, we need to go now."

Okay. Get over the disappointment. Addison didn't want to come to the inauguration in the first place. There are a million cameras and it was too much to ask of her so soon. I should be grateful that she's willing to brave the fray on a normal day. Standing behind me on the stage would have launched her into a much larger spotlight. One that would come with expectations and more media attention. I need to be more understanding and patient.

Still, my belief in her refuses to wane. I can't shake the feeling that she'll be here. Not when we've been spending more and more time talking about my job, the impact I want to have as mayor. I thought…today was important to her, too. No, it is. I *know* it is.

"Addison Potts. She's on your list, right?"

"Added last night, sir. At your request." Her smile is beginning to diminish around the edges. "I've asked to be informed when and if she arrives."

I'm due at the stage, but I can't get rid of this weight in my stomach. Would Addison turn my mother down without calling me with an explanation? It's not like her.

From across the office, I hear the woman's headset crackle and she presses a finger to the device, listening with an intent expression. "Captain Du Pont, Miss Potts has arrived."

"Has she?" Relief germinates in my chest, but it dies a quick death when I turn and look out the window, just in time to catch Addison stumbling to a halt in front of a dozen flashing cameras, another man's hand on her back. They're close, his body turned into hers, eyes regarding her with obvious affection. And she's simply standing there, letting him lean into her like they've just won Homecoming King and Queen. I'm so raw from the onslaught of jealousy, it takes me a rough series of breaths to identify the man touching my girlfriend.

Preston.

There a sharp pain in my jaw, as if I've been decked. "What

the fuck?"

"Sir?"

By the grace of God, I don't put my fist through the window, raining glass down on the scene below. But that's only because I'm frozen in place, my vision a sea of bright, sickening red. "Get on your headset," I grind out. "Have Miss Potts escorted to the stage by her security detail. They're waiting downstairs."

"Yes, Captain Du Pont."

"She's to be escorted *alone*. I can't make that clear enough."

As soon as I see Ricky and Kyle flank Addison and guide her along the edge of the building, I swipe the line of perspiration off my lip and turn from the window. My head is pounding, my steps laden with cement as I follow the woman downstairs and out the back hallway where a team of security forms around me, moving me toward the stage as a unit. I don't hear the cheering, but I know it's happening, because I can see hands clapping, mouths moving. Nothing can break through the ringing in my ears, though, and it builds louder and louder, the closer I come to the stage.

There she is. Addison stands beside where my parents sit, at least until someone scurries over with a chair. She drops into it, wide-eyed, hands clasped tightly in her lap...but all I can see are the high heels. It seems as if years have passed since she told me the stilettos are worn to meet men. It's the last memory I need right now. Climbing the stairs to the stage, her gaze locks with mine and I'm choked with need. Need to kiss her. Need to shout at her. Need, need, need. Colossal, undeniable need to consume myself with her. To get in her face and demand an explanation, just so I can tell her it isn't good enough.

Even as I force my mind back to the present and wave to the crowd, jealousy is still breathing fire in my throat. I can smell her.

I can taste her in the back of my throat. I'm not even one percent rational and I don't care. I'm at Point A and getting my hands on Addison to fuck those shoes right off her feet is Point B.

We can still see other people.

Didn't she try to make that one of our conditions for dating?

With my hand pressed to the Bible, I almost slur the words I'm repeating into the microphone, the added outrage is so sharp. The answer to her condition is still no. It will be *no* until the end of time, and as soon as we get off this stage, I'm going to make sure she understands that. Out of the corner of my eye, I sense her watching me closely, holding her breath. Anxiety radiates from her…and I don't like that. It breeds the same in me. A desire to soothe and reassure. But my head is too crowded with anger to allow sympathy.

The ceremony isn't long. When it concludes, I shake my father's hand and kiss my mother on the cheek. I do the same to Addison, some of the ice thawing in my middle when she curls a hand in my suit jacket, holding me close for an extra second. Letting her lips linger against my cheek. But I can't meet her eyes. I can't do it yet or I'll drag her off this stage.

I approach the microphone and stare at it like a foreign object, willing the words of my speech to come somehow, but they don't and I have no choice but to improvise. "Good morning. Thank you for coming," I say, my voice seeming to carry like a shotgun blast across the entire city. And it's amazing—*amazing*—that as riddled with madness as I am, I still gather strength from where Addison stands at my back. "I'm honored today to replace a man who has served this city most of his life, and done it with hard work, dedication and above all, loyalty. A man I'm grateful to call my father." Applause carries for long moments. "I will bring those same values to this office. Some of you will be

disappointed to hear I'm going to do things differently, however."
Silence stretches, cameras flash. "The results will change your
mind."

Minutes later, my speech is complete and we leave the stage
to a roar that matches the one in my head. People shout my name
and hold out their hands. I shake them, I smile, I pose for selfies.
It's like an out-of-body experience, when all I want is clarity. To
be free of the claws that are digging into my jugular. Having
received a detailed schedule of the day's events, I know security is
leading us to the private function room below the first floor of
City Hall to an invitation-only party. The first of many that will
last clear through until tomorrow. On my best day, parties seem
tedious, but right now they sound like torture.

My parents, Addison, myself and the security team finally
clear the back entrance of City Hall—the closing doors cutting
off the cheers—and I waste no time taking Addison's wrist. "We
need to talk."

"Yes, we do," she bites off, surprising me. "Lead the way."

An uncomfortable laugh from my father. "There are people
waiting to congratulate you—"

"Let them wait." I can't take my eyes off Addison now that
I've let myself focus on her. Goddamn her for being so beautiful.
For glowing and making me *ache*.

"Elijah—" begins my mother quietly.

"We'll be along in a while. Please take my parents to the
party," I instruct the security team without looking away from
my bristling girlfriend. What the hell is *she* mad about? If anyone
has the right to be pissed, it's me.

Reluctantly, my parents move off down the corridor, guided
by the security guards. I'm still holding Addison's wrist and I
should bring her upstairs to my office, but we're on the deserted

lower floor of City Hall and the closest private room is behind us. I've only been inside the small mail sorting room once or twice, but right now, it's everything I want. Close, convenient and empty. Works for me.

Seconds later, we're closed in the darkened room, the only source of light, a trio of fogged portholes near the ceiling. "Congratulations," she whispers. "Your speech was amazing. They were inspired, I could see it."

"I don't want to talk about the speech." I use my grip to yank her up against me. As soon as our bodies connect, her eyes flutter, that lower lip dragging through her teeth. "I want to talk about the fact that you came here with someone else." She opens her mouth to answer me, but an anger pocket bursts open inside me, and I add, "In your man-catching heels, too. Looks like you caught one."

No sooner are the words out of my mouth do I want them back. I want them back more than *anything*, because a shutter slams down over her face and she's suddenly unreadable to me. A puzzle where seconds ago she was the person I recognize most in the world. "Sure did. I was thinking he'd look great stuffed and mounted on my mantle."

"Now is *not* the time to play with me."

"No?" Her expression is one of mock innocence, along with her voice, and it's like fingers massaging my libido. "Do you want to play with me, instead, Captain?"

My cock comes to life, growing heavy in my briefs. "Explain yourself," I grit out, backing her toward a row of file cabinets. "Now."

"No," she fires back, gasping when I flatten her against the metal box, trapping her with my body. "No, I shouldn't have to."

"I should just trust you, shouldn't I? After you wanted to see other people? After you stood there and let him *hold you*?"

Confusion slips past her defenses before she can rein it in. "I only said that…a-about other people to give you an out, in case…"

"In case what?"

Her lips press together, her palms connecting with my chest to push me off—with more force than I expect—but I don't move an inch. Especially not when I see the sheen in her eyes. "Preston came to the door and said you wanted me here," she shouts, her voice cracking. "He said your m-mother wanted me here. It was stupid to get in the car, but I was so happy, I wasn't thinking. God. You *asshole*."

My mother? Jesus. There's so much to process here, but my attention snags on one tiny thread buried hidden in the giant quilt. "You were happy? I thought you didn't *want* to come."

"I know, right?" She throws up her hands, her breath catching. "I know. It's like, I've become this person who says one thing and means another. I *hate* it. But what I want might not be the best thing for you. So I lied. I feel like I'm lying *all the time*."

"Best thing for…" Confusion has me shaking my head. "The best thing for me is never going to be seeing you with another man."

Her feminine growl is issued toward the ceiling. "Elijah, if you're going to be a jealous idiot, I'm out of here."

She fakes left, then lunges right, moving past me, but I catch her around the waist with an arm, pulling her back against my front. "Do you think I can help it?" I rasp into her hair, conforming my lap to her backside. "When I see him, it's going to take all my willpower not to commit murder. You are *mine*."

There's a momentary softening before she slowly grows rigid again. "As much as I dislike him, it wasn't his idea to come get me. B-by the time I realized something was wrong, it was too late. There were cameras..."

"Shhh," I breathe into her hair, the distress in her voice prying my ribs open. "When I spoke to my mother last night, I told her I wanted you at the inauguration." Discomfort moves inside me, but I'm not sure which direction it's coming from anymore. "She must have meant well sending Preston over. Maybe she thought he could convince you?"

The excuse sounds hollow even to my ears and Addison's body shakes with a husky laugh. I can't see her face to know if it's genuine, though. "Yes." After a long pause, she nods. "It was probably just a misunderstanding."

I reach for some conviction. "She knows how I feel about you, Addison."

She wouldn't do this. I leave the words unspoken, because I'm not sure who I'm trying to convince anymore. Suddenly I can only think of my mother introducing Preston and Addison on election night. Listing all the things they have in common, encouraging them to talk. I hear my father complaining about his donors—his friends—not being happy with the directions I'm taking. Professionally *or* personally. And the ground beneath my feet isn't as solid as it was ten minutes ago, when I trusted the people standing at my back.

No. There's only the girl in front of me and with every second that passes, I sense her disconnecting. Fuck that. I won't allow it. I *can't* allow it. If I don't have her...I don't have myself. If I had to choose between making her happy and making this entire damn city happy, I would pick Addison without a second thought. Words are failing me, though, and Lord, I'm still jealous. I'm seething over the photos that people will see of Addison with someone else. The need to put a claim on her is closing in on me. It's more than that, though. I need to be close to her as possible. Even an inch of distance between us is unacceptable.

So I don't *leave* an inch. Keeping her ass pressed to the curve of my lap, I turn us back toward the file cabinet, watching goosebumps rise on her neck. "Elijah…"

My hands scrub down her hips and thighs, lifting her thin, black dress on the way back up. We're pressed together so tightly, the material being dragged up, up, higher and higher, is providing mind-blowing friction against my cock. She releases a sob and shifts against me, going up a little higher on her toes. Just as I reveal the tight globes of her bottom, separated down the middle by the strip of dark lace. "Christ, I've wanted you like this," I grind out, dipping down and thrusting up against her. Leaving the dress bunched around her waist, I slip a hand around the front of her body and massage the growing wet spot between her thighs. "I'm sorry, sugar. Going to use my body to show you how much."

CHAPTER TWENTY-FIVE

Addison

Former Mayoral Aide, Preston Hobbs, Left out of the Fold.
Hobbs the Very Picture of Displeasure While Watching Inauguration from Police Barricade.
—*Charleston Courier*

Sources Close to Mayor Laugh off Rumors of a Preston Hobbs/Getaway Girl Romance.
Source asked to be named as Lydia. L-Y-D-I-A.
—*Charleston Post*

M Y HEAD IS numb, but everywhere else is *alive*.
So I give myself over to the rush, whimpering at the firm press of Elijah's fingers on my clit. How they circle me with precision born of practice. Of paying attention. We've only been lovers such a short time, but he already knows how to make my body purr. How to make it tighten in some places and loosen in others. *Throbthrobthrob*.

I know the man behind me so well, too. His voice betrayed his doubts about what transpired today and why. But I won't confirm those doubts for him. I won't make someone he loves into a villain. Or weaken his ability to trust—it's one of the more beautiful things about him. And God, he might be clueless over how I feel, but there are *so many* beautiful things about him. I'm so aware of each and every one that I can't help but turn malleable in his hands and drop my head forward against the file cabinet.

Some might consider this giving in—and they might be right. But I'm not just giving in to Elijah. I'm giving in to myself, too. I'm taking as much of him as I can get. Greedy. *Greedy.* If what we have is only physical, I will exult in rocking his world. Giving him something he'll never get anywhere else. But I heard his words. *You are mine. She knows how I feel about you.* I hear those words and hope keeps me afloat. There's more here than sex and friendship. So I'm not giving in. I'm fighting in my own way.

I don't want to lie anymore. Not even by omission.

The decision comes with lightness…and a hint of nerves. Okay, more than a hint. So I give myself permission to touch now and talk later. My body rejoices in response, clamoring for what it considers the ultimate reward. Elijah's pleasure. Mine. Reaching that place together without a single reservation or apology.

"You've wanted me like this, Captain?" Drugging euphoria races through my blood, making my eyelids sag, my breath come faster. "Pinned underneath you on my belly so I can't get away?"

"*Yes.*" His fingers leave me to lower my panties with a rough yank. Then they're back. Flesh to flesh. Parting and worshipping me with thorough strokes. "I want to start you on your hands and spread knees, though. Your belly is where you'll end up when I get ready to come. I'll want to press down hard. Let myself go where it's tight and deep."

I wish more than anything that we were in bed right now. Away from the memory of what happened today and the endless responsibilities to follow. But every time Elijah rubs my clit, every time he grinds his thickness against my bottom, our surroundings blur a little more. "You're already so huge when you're inside me, Captain," I murmur, a thrill racing over my skin when he groans and starts to hump me in earnest, my knees bumping into the metal file cabinet every other second. "Do you think I can handle you from behind?"

"Dammit, sugar. Stop talking to me like that..." His words emerge hoarse. "I'm not even inside you yet and that bratty little whimper is tightening my balls up."

I brace my hands on the cabinet and glance back at him through my lashes. "Better get inside me fast, then," I say, dropping my voice to a whisper. "I want every drop for myself."

His hips ram into me with such force, I cry out...and the cry turns into a scream when his middle and index finger hook inside me and his teeth clamp down around my ear. "I haven't had my cock inside you in days," he grits, the pad of his middle finger jiggling my G-spot. "I try to be gentle with this pussy because she stays so sweet and wet for me. But if the taunting continues, I'll fuck her to hell."

My lungs are depleted of air. This is what I *live* for. Wrecking this man. Tempting the beast beneath his suit to the surface. "I needed you so bad last night. I slept with your pillow between my legs...and when I woke up—"

"Don't."

"I rubbed myself all over it. I called it by your name."

Excitement blares through me at an earsplitting level. It's threaded through with the sound of Elijah's zipper being ripped down behind me, his belt clanging. And I can do nothing more than wait, braced against the cabinet for what I earned. What I tempted. A wingtip shoves in between my ankles and kicks my feet wide. I angle my hips with a murmur of his name.

Hard, hot flesh finds my entrance, sinks in a mere inch—but

a *thick* one. I watch through the haze as one of Elijah's hands plants beside mine, the other arm anchoring me at the waist. I'm impaled in one filthy, grunting, nasty upthrust, my upper body forced against the cabinet, cheek pressed to the cool metal. The muscles in my upper thighs and loins wail in delight, my nerve endings invigorated with power. Need. *Love.*

With that love comes the responsibility to appease Elijah's hunger and I do it. *I do it* while my own simmers, simmers, begins to boil with every cursing pound of his flesh into my body. "You're so *deep* this way, baby." I squeeze my inner walls around him, sending myself closer to the beckoning crest. "Does that feel good?"

"Yes. *Oh God, yes.*"

"I bet you need to finish so bad."

"*Stop.*" The arm around my waist jerks me higher on Elijah's lap, leaving the toes of my high heels to scrape back and forth on the ground, my right shoe finally falling off. "Goddamn, sugar, it's tight. It's so tight."

"No, Elijah," I gasp. "You're just *big.*"

His forehead lands in the crook of my neck with a groan, his hips moving at a wild pace behind me, his abdomen rebounding off my backside with every savage pump. I've left the ground at this point, literally and figuratively, ticklish, restless pleasure beginning to attack me between the legs, making me sob and work my hips like a concubine.

"Addison, I'm going to fill you up. I'm going to fill you the fuck up, because you're mine. Head to toe. Morning and night. I don't share and I don't...I *can't* have you drifting away from me." The heel of his hand slams into the cabinet, rocking it back on its base. "*Mine.*"

His. This is the first time my heart and body have ever released at the same time. My sense of reality teeters and slips, my heart climbing into my throat. "I always have been. Always." The confession leaves me in a choked rush, Elijah's deep final thrust shooting me up into the atmosphere in a cloud of sparkling euphoria. My flesh quakes and tightens, milking him, coaxing his own climax and we meet in the middle, Elijah continuing to mutter epithets into my nape as he finishes, still going even as his release runs down the insides of my thighs.

There's no rest for my heart, though. It's still pounding as hard as it was mid-orgasm, still ricocheting off the glands of my throat. *I told him.* I said it out loud that I've always been his and now the dam is open. Closing it would be physically painful and…God, how many times did he say—out loud—that I'm his? Do I have anything to lose? He has to feel the same. He *has* to or I wouldn't be floating up near the ceiling right now.

Still breathing heavily, Elijah plants a kiss on my shoulder and buckles up his pants behind me. He doesn't move away, though, his heat still warming my back, his gaze sliding along the curve of my neck. I can feel it there.

I reach down and pull my panties back into place, letting my dress drop from where it has been rucked up around my waist. And when I turn around, Elijah smiles at me, his eyes searching mine…

"I love you," I whisper in a shaky voice. "Elijah, I love you."

Until that moment, I don't realize I've been living with tension in my neck, my back, my chest, but the bolts loosen as soon as the truth slips free. I could *fly.*

"I saw you standing in the front of the church—a-and I had to leave, because I couldn't stand it. I couldn't stand to watch you marry someone else. We hadn't even met." I lay my palms on my flaming cheeks. "When you got into my car, everything made sense, though. Not loving you would have been crazier than loving you at first sight. You're my best friend…and I love you. I always have. Before I knew you and…so much more after. More every day." I swipe at my damp eyes. "It has been really hard not to tell you."

I've been so caught up in finally releasing my feelings out into the light, it hasn't occurred to me until a heavy silence falls that Elijah hasn't responded. Those chocolate eyes that only a moment ago scrutinized me, looking for lingering signs of our fight? They're confused. Dark and troubled. *Shocked.* "Addison…"

Shocked?

Denial begins to creep into my stomach, but I beat it back. "Yes?"

His mouth opens and closes. He shoves a hand through his hair. "I want to say it back." Dark eyebrows draw together, like he's trying to puzzle something out. "I want to, but…"

All the world's color melts away, sliding down the walls, leaving everything black and white. Leaving me stripped of my skin and trying not to wheeze. "Oh."

He reaches for me, but I have the presence of mind to step back. Away from the man who is devastating me. Clipping the veins leading to my heart, one by one. "You and me…we make each other happy. I *need* you." His hand drops, his big chest starting to lift and fall, *fastfastfast.* "Why can't things stay exactly as they are? You say those words and now…"

"Now what?"

"Now I'm expected to say them back. And then we're expected to do a million other things until we lose sight of us. Just *us.*"

Oh my God.

Oh my God. I've just bled myself dry in front of this man, told him I loved him…and he's not going to say it back. He's not. Going to say it back. Because he doesn't feel that way about me. Here it is. Confirmation of my deepest, most awful fear. Oh my God.

I'm forcing him to let me down with these patented excuses, because he's a good man. But we both know the truth. It's lying on the floor between us like a hunted deer. He's not over the past. He's not over his ex, just as I've always suspected but apparently never accepted.

What happened with the wedding, Goose…I don't know if I ever got over it, you know? When you're always trying to do the right thing and something huge like that blows up in your face…I don't know if I can explain it. Except to say, I haven't worked my way through it yet. I'm trying.

Not hard enough, I guess. Or maybe he did try and I was just too impatient. Or their love is still too fresh. My knees wobble, trying to drop me to the floor, but I reach deep for the strength to stay standing. I reach further and find the willpower to swallow the scream. To lift my chin. What now? What now?

The plan.

When a person is adrift, they'll cling to any life preserver, even if it's half deflated and they'd rather just sink to the bottom of the ocean. But I'm a survivor, so I hold tight to the only route I can take, now that I've had my heart crushed on the rocks of a cliff.

My entire body jolts when Elijah frames my face with his hands. "*Addison.*"

How is he looking at me? Is that sympathy? Or is he haunted and suffering like me? I can't tell anymore, but I can't stand it. I just need a way out of this room. Out of this horrifying moment. "Elijah." I pat his hands and step back. "I love a party, but I'm going to sit this one out."

"No. You can't leave like this." Panic swells in his eyes, joining the denial already there. "Not with everything on the table and *nothing* worked out." His chest is lifting and falling faster and faster. "*Addison.* We have to resolve this."

"We'll work it out at home." I smile even though it must be pathetic. Even though I'm lying right to his face. "I'll see you at home."

In my utter desperation, my lie is the epitome of convincing, though, and he seems to buy it. He's not happy, but with the music beginning to blare upstairs, both of us know the new mayor doesn't have a choice but to leave. To talk and shake hands and receive congratulations for the next several hours. I'm banking on him living up to his responsibilities, as usual, because I have to get out of here and keep moving. I'll drop otherwise.

A voice comes over a loudspeaker upstairs and his name—along with his new official title—is called to the sound of booming applause and whistles. When Elijah's eyes slide closed, I start to step back, but at the last second, something compels me forward and I lift up, pressing a kiss to his mouth. With a broken sound, he tries to bury his fingers in my hair, tries to deepen the kiss, but I'm already on my way to the door.

"Looks like I'm the one all dressed up with nowhere to go this time." Over my shoulder, I toss back the words from the day he climbed into my car, followed by a genuine smile. I can't help it. He might have broken my heart, but I still love him. I've loved every second I've been given with him. "Later, Captain."

CHAPTER TWENTY-SIX

Elijah

Getaway Girl Mysteriously Absent from Inauguration
Afterparties
—TheTea.com

The Shoe Buzz Sells out of Black Stilettos Post-Inauguration
This Just In: Black is the New Must-Have Summer Color
—Avant-Charleston

THERE'S A STATE between sleep and wakefulness I get stuck in sometimes. My common sense swears I'm alone, the only one occupying my room. But the part of my brain that's dreaming causes me to see things. People. They want to ask me questions. To work. No matter how many times I remind myself I'm alone in my bedroom, I can't block out the dream.

That's how I feel for the rest of the day. Like I'm half asleep and being harassed by figments of my imagination. Only, unlike my dreams, I'm gutted where I stand.

Being on the receiving end of applause and back slapping and bullshit is unacceptable. Don't they know the most incredible person on the planet just told me she loves me...and I let her leave? How did I let her leave?

Worse, how could I not say it back?

The words were right there in my mouth and I kept swallowing them. Because I didn't want to lie? Or was it something else? Hours later, I've still got an axe buried in the center of my chest and the wound only deepens the longer it takes me to get home to Addison. Although I have no idea what's going to happen when I get there. Things can never go back to the way they were. The loss of the reality I lived in this morning is catastrophic.

For the last twenty minutes, I've been nodding at the state senator's son, but I can't recall a single word he's said. I think it might have been something about government subsidies? Or possibly a recipe for pork marinade. That could have been the last guy I spoke with, too. How long until this party ends? Every time someone leaves, two people seem to take their place. Reminding myself of the important job ahead of me doesn't help at all. None of it seems to mean a damn thing without Addison here.

When the senator's son launches into a story about his glory days on the gridiron, I drift back in time myself. To the only other time a woman told me she loved me. Naomi. I was walking her to her car after a date, wasn't I? My memory of where or when is hazy at best, but we'd probably been dating about two or three months. The appropriate amount of time for an announcement like I love you. I said it to her, because tradition dictates the man say it first—and we were all about tradition. She said it back. I opened the car door for her and waved her off as she drove away.

All of it was so easy.

"Excuse me." My mother's polite company voice breaks into the foggy memory. "Would you mind if I had a moment with my son? I swear he's talked to everyone twice except me and I'm starting to take offense."

The senator's son and my mother share a laugh, both of them capping it with a sip of their drink. "I know better than to argue with mama." An obnoxious slap on my back. "You'll be hearing from me. There's a lot we can do to benefit each other. Take care, now, Mayor."

"Thank you," I say, my voice sounding distant. "Same to you."

Now that we're left alone, my mother still says nothing. Which suits me just fine, because I've got a lot of questions. "Were you hoping the pictures of Preston cozying up to Addison would turn the public against her?"

"I don't know if hoping is the right word."

"There's a *right* one?" When several people turn to look at us, I realize I've raised my voice. Add it to the rapidly growing list of things I don't care about at the moment. "I want an explanation. I want to know why you'd try to damage what I've got with her."

She twists the glass in her hand, the corners of her mouth turned down. "Sometimes you do things out of loyalty to a friend, even when you don't want to."

"I don't keep friends that would expect those things of me."

"Well you *could*. Someday. People change. Priorities change when things like children and marriage and *appearances* come along." She stops to take a shaky breath. "Although, you're right. Ever since you were a young boy, you never compromised your beliefs. Ever. But we can't all be like you, Elijah. And I'm sorry. I was sorry before it even happened and I'll do what I can to fix it. I'll take responsibility."

"I don't need you to do that." I turn more fully to face her. "Addison told me Preston came to the door claiming I'd given him permission to drive her, along with yours. She'd already figured out it was nonsense and after I stopped behaving like a jealous moron, so did I. That kind of thing wouldn't have gotten between us. We're stronger than that." The more I talk about her, the more gut sick I am for missing her. Gut sick over hurting her. She's loved me since the beginning? How did I not *see* it? "God, even if she'd openly gone out with another man, I would have…I'd have knocked out the son of a bitch and informed her it wouldn't be happening again. She's…my Addison. She's complicated and she's mine."

I'm not sure how long I remain in the daze, but when I finally glance over at my mother, her eyes are close to overflowing. "I didn't know. I thought it was a passing infatuation, until we went to see her at the market and—"

"When was this?"

Pressing her lips together, she digs a small package out of her pocket and hands it over. "Do you remember how I like to knit at night?" I nod. "As far back as I can remember, your father has let me wrap the yarn around his hands. He'll sit there for hours and let me use him as a spool, even though he still doesn't know a rib stitch from a purl." As she talks, I unwrap the package and find a snowman inside, the buttons ever so slightly uneven, and I stop breathing. Not because I haven't seen thousands of these same snowmen, but because it's a slice of Addison where none existed a moment ago. Right there in my hands. "When she told me you helped her glue on the big buttons, I knew."

I run a finger around the button's rim and picture Addison handing it to my mother. She would have been standing there in her apron, sparkles stuck to her hands. Gorgeous. Unsuspecting. Why didn't she tell me about my mother's visit to the market? Because I didn't come home last night? Or has she been shouldering the unpleasant behind-the-scenes parts of our relationship alone? "You said 'we.' It was Della that went with you to the market, wasn't it?"

She nods and my gut twists over what it must have been like.

The woman who loves me coming face to face with my ex-fiancée's mother. "It hasn't been easy for Naomi's mother, you know. She's barely gotten over the humiliation of her husband having an affair all those years ago. Maybe even getting another woman *pregnant*. Now she's faced with embarrassment of what Naomi did to you. She wants to make it right. She wants…"

My head comes up. "What?"

"She wants a do-over." My mother shrugs. "Addison is a threat to that."

A do-over? As in, a second attempt to walk down the aisle? The idea is so ludicrous, I'm not even sure how to respond. I would no sooner put myself in that position with Naomi than I would skydive without a parachute. "Addison isn't a threat to anyone or anything. *She's* the one being threatened." My tone betrays my anger, which is reigniting. Goddammit. On top of what transpired between us this morning and being set up by my mother, she was ambushed at the market yesterday. Hell, she's been followed by reporters, had her name dragged through the mud. For what? Simply for being with me. And I couldn't even tell her I loved her.

"I need to go home," I say, stowing the snowman inside my jacket. "I don't want to be anywhere she doesn't feel welcome."

"She is welcome," my mother murmurs, laying a hand on my arm. "Go get her. Bring her back here so I can apologize in person. Please?"

"She's been maneuvered enough." I'm already headed for the door. "I'll let *her* decide when she's ready to hear it."

Addison

MAKE SURE YOUR umbrellas are in working order, Charleston. Or better yet, stay inside. This storm is roaring toward us like a freight train with the brakes cut...

I turn down the volume on the radio and press my foot down harder on the gas pedal. My Honda groans in response but does as she's told, protesting the added weight in her trunk as we trundle over the Arthur Ravenel Jr. Bridge. Beside me on the passenger seat sits the Mrs. Claus urn holding my grandmother's ashes. One more thing to check off my list before I go. And based on the darkening sky and the weatherman's prediction, I have about an hour before the heavens open up and rain down holy hell on this place I've called home for such a short while.

Ignoring the tug in my stomach insisting it's still my home, I take the turnoff for Remley's Point, unsurprised to find only one car in the parking lot. The rental hut still looks like it's open, though. *Thank God.* This can't wait until tomorrow. After what I've set into motion today, I can't stay in Charleston. Elijah's touch, voice, scent and the love he's burdened me with will stay forever, but I can't subject myself to torture.

There's a box in my trunk full of thwarted plans for the decorating business. Vendors price lists, sketches, résumés from local artists who I've been corresponding with about the launch and joining forces. God, I was excited to venture out into the great unknown of starting a business, carrying a flag for my grandmother and all she gave me, but that box full of dreams might as well be fire kindling now. I can't stay here and see it through. I *can't.*

No sooner have I parked the car do I grab the urn, tuck it into the backpack containing my wallet and sprint for the rental place. When I see they're sliding the window shut and turning off the lights, I run faster. "Wait," I call, catching the familiar young man's attention. "Wait, please. I need to rent a kayak."

He gives a cracking laugh. "Sorry, ma'am, but…ain't you seen the sky?"

"Yes. Yes, I know there's a storm coming, but it's not going to break until five." I duck down to read the clock mounted on the wall behind him inside the hut. "It's barely four. I can be across the river and back in half that time."

"Last time it took you two hours."

"I was lingering. I promise I won't linger this time."

There's a small hesitation, but he shakes his head. "Can't do it," he says, reaching once again for the window. "Come back in the morning and I'll give you a discount."

"Wait." I'm breathing like I just *swam* across the damn river. "Please. I'm leaving town today and I won't get this chance again." I hold up the backpack. "My grandmother is in this bag."

He whistles low and long. "I didn't see that coming."

"Like, in an urn…she's not, like, really small or something." Oh my God, heartbreak has completely derailed my common sense. My brain has checked out and I'm running on emotion. Confusing, nonsensical emotion. "Look, she used to kayak this route and I've tried to scatter her ashes *twice*—yes, I know it's illegal—but I couldn't *do* it. It just wasn't the right time. But I really need this closure, okay? I need it before I can leave. And I have to leave *today* or I might see them or—or he might try and find me and apologize for not loving me and I couldn't stand it."

His sigh is directed upward. "It's always about the opposite sex, isn't it?"

"Not for me. It was just this once and it'll *never* happen again."

"Never say never."

"Fine, I won't. Just let me rent a kayak. I'll be back by a quarter to five. Please."

The young man drags both hands down his face, then leaves the window. A few seconds later, I hear the back door of the rental hut open, followed by the now-familiar sound of a boat dragging along the dirt. Relief weakens my knees, but I lurch to the side and clear the hut, prepared to take the kayak from him. "Thank you, thank you, thank you."

He looks up at the sky. "Thank me by coming back in one piece."

Remembering the procedure from earlier visits, I dig in my backpack for my wallet and hand him my ID. I notice him do a double take while studying my ID, but I've already grabbed the front of the kayak and started jogging toward the launch area.

"Hell, I didn't recognize you before. Now I know I'm going to regret this," I hear him say behind me, sounding alarmed. "You're the Mayor's Getaway Girl."

I look back over my shoulder at him, but the wind whips the hair into my eyes and blocks my vision. "Not anymore."

CHAPTER TWENTY-SEVEN

Elijah

Run for cover, Charleston.
This sweet jiggle isn't the only thing making the ladies wet
tonight.
—Twitter @DuPontBadonk

I UNLOCK THE door to my house and throw it open, making a beeline for the kitchen. I'll check there first. If she's not making coffee or leafing through recipes, she'll be upstairs working on ornaments. Sitting cross-legged on the floor with her hair in one of those messy knots, frowning as she applies tiny sequins to fabric. She needs floor pillows. Why didn't I think of that before? Next week. I'll get her a million floor pillows so she can be comfortable.

"*Addison.*"

No answer.

The back of my neck is tingling. There's no light coming from beneath the kitchen door. Rainclouds are starting to gather in the sky, thanks to a building storm, so if she was in there, she'd need light. I check, anyway, refusing to acknowledge that the entire house is dark. It's all fucking dark and I'm kicking myself for not coming home sooner. She told me she'd be here—that she'd see me at home. At the time, I was still so stunned over her confession, I took her word at face value. Which was stupid. I can see now how incredibly *stupid* it was.

I throw on the lights in the kitchen, just to make it less cold. It doesn't help. Why is it so cold? I'm pushing back out into the foyer a second later, trying not to panic. I mean, why would I panic? My girlfriend—my best friend—told me she loves me and I didn't say it back and now she's not home. She's not home. Where the hell is she?

Holding on to one final thread of hope, I start up the stairs, begging her to be in the ornament room or dozing on our bed. When I find her, I have no idea what I'm going to say, only that I better make it good. I'm going to start with sorry. Sorry for not deserving her. Sorry she didn't feel comfortable telling me about what happened yesterday at the market. For behaving like an untrusting fool this morning.

God. God, she has exactly zero reasons to be here, does she?

What reason have I given her to stick around?

A knock at the door stops me halfway up the stairs. At first I write it off as rolling thunder, but no, there's a shadow beneath the door. Maybe Addison ran out to get something at the store or went for a run and forgot her key. Knowing I don't deserve to be so lucky, I jog back down the stairs with a prayer on my lips, nonetheless.

But when I open the door, it's not Addison.

Naomi stands in front of me, her fist raised to knock a second time.

"Elijah." Her hands cling to her purse strap. "Hello."

What follows her greeting is not subtle. I'm clubbed over the head so hard, the force splits my skull down the center. This woman framed in my doorway might as well be a stranger to me. And I know her as well *now* as I did during our engagement. During all of it. I spent those years of our relationship convinced what we had was love. Maybe I was convinced right up until a second ago, when I opened the door. And that's why I couldn't recognize what love *actually* felt like. I'd never experienced it.

Naomi and I didn't drift apart or fall out of love. We were never in love to begin with.

Love isn't duty and tradition and consistency. It's wild and unquenchable and inconvenient. It's messy and raw. It's what I feel for Addison. *I love Addison.*

I've questioned that love because it was so different from the first time. But the first time was only a forced illusion. Not the real thing. And I might have been able to make the distinction, if I hadn't been associating love with failure. A broken engagement. Disappointing family and community. Not seeing it coming. Failure. Jesus, I couldn't allow myself the possibility that I loved Addison because I was too afraid to fail again.

I was too afraid to fail when it actually *mattered.*

I love Addison. I love Addison so much the weight of it is crushing me.

"Elijah." Naomi ducks her head into my line of vision. "Are you all right?"

"No." My hand goes to the doorframe for support. "Naomi, I don't want to be rude, but this isn't the best time."

"Oh, of course, I—" With a confused frown, she digs through her purse. "I wouldn't have come, only you sent me the note."

"Note?"

"It was in my mailbox this afternoon." A beat of silence passes. "I'm guessing you didn't write it."

When she hands me the folded piece of paper, I recognize the bold, sloping handwriting immediately. I've seen it on countless shopping lists and notes stuck to the refrigerator. It belongs to my girlfriend. My girlfriend who professed her love to me this morning and got nothing from me in return. *Nothing.*

Dear Naomi,
I still love you. I know we can get past what happened. Please
come see me.
Elijah

Agony fills me like cement, wrapping and hardening around my lungs. No, this isn't possible. It isn't possible the situation is *this bad*. Addison can't really believe I'm still in love with Naomi when I would exchange ten years of my life to hold her right now, can she?

Of course she can. Until a few minutes ago, I didn't even realize my feelings for Naomi were nothing more than…respectful fondness. Comparing how I feel about Addison to Naomi is like measuring Kilimanjaro up against flat, lifeless earth. I avoided the topic of my ex-fiancée and the cancelled wedding like the plague. Didn't even acknowledge the fact that Naomi was back in town. And on top of everything, I missed my chance to tell Addison I love her this morning. If the shoe was on the other foot, I would assume she still loved her ex, too. The searing pain of even that *hypothetical* possibility almost doubles me over. Oh Christ, that's how she's feeling right now. She's suffering—she's been suffering—and it's all because of me.

A roll of thunder goes off behind Naomi and my southern manners prod me to invite her in, but I can't do it. Not when I die a little more every second I don't know where Addison is. "Naomi…"

She holds up a hand. "You don't have to explain." Her gaze snags on the note. "Engaged to be married and I didn't even know your handwriting. If that's not a sign, I don't know what is." Her laugh is quiet, a little sad. "Even so, I'm sorry about what happened, Elijah. How I handled it, especially. Driving like a bat out of hell to Florida until I couldn't go any farther. Honestly, I barely *recognized* myself—" She cuts herself off, face fusing with color. "Gosh, I've been going around apologizing to just about everyone. My mother, the wedding planner. Something about us just never felt right." She shakes her head. "Maybe I don't know what right is even supposed to feel like with another person. Maybe...that's what I learned in Florida. I'm not sure. I'm just sorry about the trouble I caused you."

"I'm sorry, too," I say, my instincts telling me I'm not the only one who's had a life-changing couple of months. "Someday, when all of this is long behind us, Addison and I would love to have you over for dinner. We'll laugh about it."

A blonde eyebrow goes up. "I wondered if it was true. You and my cousin." She looks past me into the house, a small sigh leaving her. "Everyone thinks I'm crazy, and seeing you in this house where we were meant to live...I think they must be right. Hopefully Addison is smarter than me."

"I'm hoping for the opposite. The smarter she is, the harder it's going to be to convince her to forgive me." I want to share in her laughter, but I can't. All I can think about is finding Addison and apologizing until I run out of breath. "Naomi, I really have to go."

"I understand. But there's just one more quick thing." She seems to be gathering strength. "I overheard my parents arguing. A *very* long time ago. Addison...she's not just my cousin, she's my half-sister. She deserves to know that. Will you tell her, please?"

Christ. Addison has been denied by damn near everyone, hasn't she? Never again. As soon as I find her, she won't spend another second of her life wondering about her place in this world. "Yes, I'll tell her," I say. "Goodbye, Naomi."

No sooner have I closed the door behind her do I resume my race up the stairs, but this time it's a million times more urgent. Somewhere on this planet, the girl I love beyond measure believes I'm in love with someone else. Until I find her and fix the misconception, my world is on fucking fire. "*Addison!*"

It's useless to check upstairs. If she sent Naomi a request to come see me, there is no way she'd stick around for that. But I slam into the ornament room, anyway, maybe just to reassure myself that she *was* here—

It's empty.

Not a speck of glitter decorates the ground. It's barren.

"No..." I whisper under my breath, turning and jogging back down the hallway to our bedroom. "No...no..."

She's not there. Her clothes are gone. Every little trace of her is gone. I tug the cell phone out of my dress pants and hit the speed dial for her number, like I did numerous times on the way home. Straight to voicemail. Not even her voice, just a generic operator greeting. God, is it too much to ask for one solid reminder of her?

Rain starts to patter on the window, light but ominous, not loud enough to drown out my heavy breaths in the bedroom. Where is she? Where the hell did she go?

On the way back downstairs, I dial Ricky, who answers on the first ring. "Hello?"

"Please tell me Addison is with you."

An uncomfortable silence passes. "Sorry, Captain Du Pont. We checked in at the house after seeing her on the news. She wasn't supposed to go anywhere today and I don't mind telling you, we lectured her a little. But she assured us she had no plans to go out until tomorrow." He clears his throat. "She didn't listen, did she?"

"No." My head is splitting in half. "Can you please go check her old apartment? It's empty, but she could be there." *Avoiding you.* "And I need Kyle down at the market. Maybe she had to cover a shift, or..."

I trail off when I notice her shoe rack is gone from its place of honor beside the front door. There are tiny, almost imperceptible holes where it used to be drilled into the plaster. After finding her clothes and craft supplies gone, I'm not sure why this final blow almost pitches me forward off the stairs, but it does. She really left. She left me.

"Captain?"

I swallow hard and open my mouth to answer, but nothing comes out. What if I can't find her? She covered all her bases in less than a day. Was she planning this? Did she always believe it would end this way? She would force me to get my post-jilted shit together and move into my rightful house, furnish it, then hand a better version of me off to another woman?

Jesus, that's exactly what she was doing. This morning's revelation might have been a last-ditch effort, but she always thought I'd move on.

"Addison, goddammit. No." My legs finally give up the battle and drop me to the steps, just as another call beeps in on the other line. A frantic check of the screen beats down my hopes of Addison calling. "Ricky, I have to go. Please. Please let me know immediately if you find her." Without waiting for his answer, I click over. "Hello?"

"Elijah."

I've known Chris long enough to gather—in three syllables—that something is wrong.

Slowly, I come to my feet, every inch of me bracing for impact. "What is it?"

In the background, there's shouting, a door slamming, an engine starting. "We just got a call in from the boat launch at Remley's Point. They rented out a kayak about an hour ago and the person hasn't returned. Name on the ID is Addison Potts."

Like something out of a horror film, a crack of lightning streaks across the front window, rain pelting the glass. Or is that hail? My pulse begins slamming against my eardrums. "Chris, don't tell me she's out on the river in this goddamn storm."

"There's a possibility she didn't risk it and went ashore somewhere closer, instead of crossing back the way she came. But the rental manager didn't want to take any chances, since she's pretty much a beginner." A crackle comes over the radio, but I can't make it out. "We'll find her, all right? She's a certified bad ass. If she got caught somewhere, she'll be fine until we reach her."

He's trying to calm me down, but I'll never be calm again. Not until I have her in my arms. "She's...it's her grandmother's ashes. She's spreading them before she leaves." Was she so frantic to get away from me, she's risking her life to tie up loose ends? No. Please. If I'm responsible for her being hurt or worse, I won't make it to tomorrow's sunrise. *Addison, I'm sorry*. Needing to take action even though I'm battling the urge to vomit, I throw open the door and run outside into the rain, ignoring the photographers that snap a dozen pictures of me from various vehicles. "Where are you?" I shout into the phone, praying Chris can hear me over the thunder. He repeats the address twice and I start running toward my truck. "I'm on my way, but don't wait. Get out there as soon as you can. *Find her*."

"We will."

His grim tone turns my blood turns to ice, but urgency and

adrenaline have me starting the truck, peeling out of my space. "I'll call the chief of police as soon as I hang up and get you more support. *All* of it." I take a hard right and merge onto 5th Avenue, gunning the engine and trying not to panic over the rough state of the river alongside me. "Chris, please. I can't fucking lose her. She's..."

I'm hit with a deluge of moving pictures. Only I'm seeing them now through a totally different lens. Addison pulling up outside the church and holding up a bottle of Grey Goose. I thought she was such a cowgirl that day. Spontaneous. but knowing what I know now...that she's loved me since day one...I see the hope in her eyes as she idles at the curb. The shock. The fear she was embarking on something she shouldn't.

I remember us locking eyes through the crowd the night she went dancing with Lydia, looking so gorgeous and alive. The night she finally became my girlfriend. I can see her mouthing the words *Oh God, Oh God* when she spots me at the bar, even though I didn't notice at the time. She loved me at that moment and I didn't soak it in all the way. I squandered it. Three words— words I've had inside me as long as Addison kept the same ones for me—and all of this could have been avoided.

All the hurt I put her through never would have happened, *goddammit.*

"*Elijah.*"

I hang up without responding to Chris, because I can't. All I can do is floor the gas pedal and roar my anguish into the empty truck.

CHAPTER TWENTY-EIGHT

Addison

A Black Cloud Tonight Over Charleston.
—Southern Insider News

I T'S HARD TO remember when it all goes to shit.

I make it to the island in record time, my arms straining from the effort of paddling without a breather. Making ornaments did not prepare me for this kind of exertion. I climb out of the kayak and drag it to shore just as the sky opens overhead. At first, the rain falls in giant, gloppy drops, so heavy it hits the river like small stones. There's a nervous turn in my stomach. Other stall owners in the market are always talking about the unpredictable nature of southern storms. How it can be sunny one minute and thundering the next. But I always assumed they were exaggerating since they embellish just about everything else.

Turns out, they haven't been embellishing about storms.

I barely have Mrs. Claus out of my backpack when the rain turns sharp. It stings the skin of my arms, neck, face. Little stingers that try to distract me from my task. But I don't let them. No, the distraction comes in the form of the rising tide. I'm standing on the edge of the island among the reeds, my rain boots sunk a few inches into the mud…and within a minute, the water goes from my ankles to halfway up my boots. I look around the island and realize it's slowly being swallowed from all sides.

"That's not good," I whisper.

Above my head, lightning streaks across the sky in a jagged line, as if to say, *no shit*.

While uncapping the makeshift urn, I look out across the river. Okay. It's not treacherous. A little choppier than usual, but no waves or anything that could capsize me on the way back. I can power through before the storm gets worse. I'm not usually outside during a thunderstorm, so of course it seems worse up close. I'm out of my element, but I have some practice under my belt and I know the direction to take back to the launch site. It's all good.

Focus on why you came here.

With a deep breath, I shove Mrs. Claus's head into the backpack and hug the bottom half of the porcelain figure to my chest. "It's time to say goodbye, Grandma. I'm sending you off in pretty dramatic fashion, right? I hope you approve." Rain is getting in my eyes, so I close them. "Mom let this place beat her. I didn't. It hurt me. H-he hurt me. But I put things back where they belonged and now I'm walking away knowing I did the right thing. When they think of our side of the family, it will be with respect. Grudging, but so what, right? *So what.* We're not less than. We're more than they expected. I hope. I hope."

The water has risen to the top of my boots now, so I take two giant steps back, water splashing up and drenching my jeans, along with the rain.

"I want to be selfish and keep you with me, but you would want to be free, wouldn't you? Thank you for loving me. Thank you for *everything*. I'll think of you all the time." I tip over the urn and watch the building storm carry away my grandmother, my breath catching in my throat at the swirl of gray in the wind.

"Goodbye. I love you."

There's a part of me that just wants to sit down and let the storm wail on me. I'm caught in the grip of loneliness and wouldn't the howling wind be the perfect distraction? But I can't deny the water in front of me is growing rougher with each passing second. It's manageable now, but if I don't get my ass to the other side of this river in fifteen minutes, I'm not sure what it'll look like. And the island is shrinking more and more the longer I wait, so staying and hoping for the weather to pass isn't an option. My only option is to get back in the kayak and *move*.

Elijah would be having a fit.

I'm not sure where the thought comes from, but it's not welcome. It makes me clutch my stomach on a childish sob. His reaction when I told him I went kayaking in the sunshine springs to mind. He didn't even like *that*. If he knew I was about to paddle across the Cooper River during a thunderstorm, he would...throw another mattress out the window.

Stop. I have to stop thinking about the one thing making it hardest to leave. Elijah genuinely cares about me. Enough to care for me when I'm sick. Enough to introduce me to his friends, his parents. Enough to split open a headboard with an axe.

If only it was enough.

He's probably with Naomi right now, I remind myself. I brought them back together. And it's that horrible mental jolt that has me climbing into the kayak.

The tide has risen so high that it takes almost no effort to push back from shore with my paddle. I'm on the river and turning, turning, heading in the right direction. Yes, the water is a lot bumpier than usual, but I'm not thinking about that. I can't think about it, because the rain turns violent. It slashes horizontal, pummeled by the wind, hurting my eyes and making it impossible to see in more than a squint. But I have to get across the river, there's no choice, so I aim my kayak toward the outcropping where the launch is located and I paddle with everything I'm worth. Every few seconds a thick swell pushes me off course, but I work double time to get back on the watery path and I push. I push.

Until the lights across the river blink—and they go out. *They go out.*

Did they lose power? I can't see the distant, reassuring glow of the rental hut anymore.

Far off to my right, the white lights of the bridge are nothing more than a blur. Maybe I can judge my location based on the landmark, though? Yes, I know the correct distance and as long as I keep the bridge to my right, I'm bound to hit land—

A wave slams into the kayak and I gasp.

Just like that the bridge is behind me. Which way was forward?

My legs turn freezing and I realize the wave has filled the kayak with water.

"No, no, no." My words come out in a chatter of teeth. "Keep paddling."

It takes me some time, but I manage to get the bridge back on the correct side of me and begin paddling again, harder than before. I'm going to make it. I *will* make it.

I don't expect a second, bigger wave.

Elijah

I MAKE IT to the police docks just in time, which is a relief and a curse, because I want them out on the river finding Addison.

Now. I want her safe *now*. My mind is caving in on itself, rejecting any kind of hope, projecting worst-case scenarios instead. I've never been swimming with her, so I have no idea how well she'd handle rough water. In this petrified state in which I'm currently living, all I can do is berate myself for never *taking* her swimming. All that wasted time, blind to the fact that I loved her, I could have been taking her to Isle of Palms to swim in the ocean. Could have taken her on vacations or hell, just gone kayaking with her, like I said I would. What have I been doing? Everything is a fucking blur, except for her face. I have failed. I have failed at the only thing that matters. Her.

We're in the police watercraft, speeding toward the section of the river where Addison should be. We're not the only ones, either. It's possible I threatened the chief of police's job if he didn't get every available unit on the goddamn river. Despite the storm, there's a police chopper bringing up the rear of our search party, his spotlight moving in patterns on the water. There's a second helicopter, too, belonging to a news station, but I'm willing to take all the help we can get.

God, it's so damn dark. I hate knowing she could be out here alone.

"This is it." Chris turns and nods to me from his position at the wheel and I grab hold of a metal overhead bar and lunge to my feet, looking out over the water, praying like a madman for some sign of her. Please. *Please.* She's such a fierce, beautiful girl and I wish like hell I could muster some faith in her ability to survive this, but I'm too terrified. I'm too aware that I've fucked up so badly that the universe might just deal me this final blow out of sheer disgust.

"*Addison!*"

Rain lashes my face in razor-sharp sheets, the boat lifting and falling beneath me in angry swells. I can't see. How can I find her if I can't see?

"Come on, Goose," I rasp. "Come on, please. Where are you?"

Out of the corner of my eye, I watch the chopper searchlight graze the very edge of something red and my heart lurches.

"Chris." I shove past two other officers, pointing in the direction I saw something. "There. *Go back*."

As soon as he turns around, the light on the front of the boat lands on what I saw.

It's a red kayak. And it's flipped over.

"No. *No*." I don't even give myself time to process that numbing fact before I shoot forward, attempting to dive out of the boat and into the water. Something holds me back, though. Chris. The other officers with us. They wrestle me back, but I fight them like an animal. I have to get to her. She's not gone. She can't be gone. I could have told her I loved her. We would be home right now cooking in the kitchen. She loves that kitchen and we haven't had enough time to use it yet. What the hell have I done? I lost her. I *killed* her.

"*Hey*." Chris's fist belts me across the face and sound rushes back in with a vengeance, attacking my ears. "Stay with us, man."

I'm just coherent enough to notice someone has taken the wheel from Chris. Turning my attention back to the water, I see we're circling the capsized kayak from a distance, rain splattering off the hull like crazy. Thousands of droplets being sprayed in every direction are why I don't see her at first. She's blocked by the darkness, the fall of rain and splash of the river. And I don't believe my eyes at first, because my heart has splintered with loss. But when I see an oar lift out of the water and wave up and down, I come back to life.

I try to shout her name, but it comes out in nothing but a choked whisper. Once again, I'm held back from jumping into the water. I allow it this time, though, because everything moves at once where before there was just fear and darkness. Radios crackle, cheers go up around us, even the rain seems to let up. Most importantly, the boat is moving in her direction and *she's alive*. She's alive and I'm falling to the side of the boat on my knees, leaning over to scoop her up into my arms.

"Come here. Come here, sugar. I've got you." Her water-logged clothes weigh her down, but nothing can keep me from her. As soon as I've got my arms wrapped around her shivering body, she's up into the boat, clinging to me in a way that makes me want to yell and rage and thank God. I want to go on holding her forever, but the tremors wracking her are so intense, I can hear her teeth chattering at my neck. Alarm gets me by the jugular. She's safe right now, but she might not be out of the woods and I'm not losing her again, so I move. I move, stripping the wet clothes off her and getting rid of my own, until we're left in nothing but our pants and her bra, modesty be damned when she needs me. "You're cold. Jesus, you're so cold. You shouldn't have done this. *Why did you do this?*"

Chris puts a blanket around Addison, and I yank her into me, closing my eyes when she moans over my body heat and struggles closer. "Elijah."

My heart twists. "I'm here. I'm never going *anywhere*." I can't get her near enough, but I try, her trembling like an ice pick to my chest. "I thought I'd already lost you. *I thought you were gone.*"

She shakes her head back and forth in the crook of my neck. "You shouldn't be holding me like this anymore."

"I'll hold you every day for the rest of my life," I say, my voice hoarse. "Or it won't be worth living, Addison. Don't tell me I shouldn't hold you."

I'm so caught up in the horror of the last hour, it takes me a few beats to realize what's going on here. She thinks I can't hold her because she believes I'm back with my ex-fiancée. That I still love Naomi. A truth she's been holding for months and *I* let it happen. The utter horror of this woman who makes my world turn thinking I love someone else is too outrageous to believe—and I won't allow another minute to pass with her under this misconception. With her not knowing she's the one who gives my life worth—always has been and always will be.

"Look at me."

She stays close, but lifts her chin and I see she still isn't hopeful. *Still.* And even though I'm the idiot who landed us in this mess, I can't tone down my outrage. Not when the woman I intend to spend my life with has doubts about me.

"Goddammit, Addison, *think.* It has been months since the wedding. Have I made even one attempt to go find her? No. No, I've been with you. Right where I was always meant to be." I jerk my chin toward the sky where two helicopters circle over our heads. "This is what happens when you leave me for *two hours*. You know why that is? If you think—and if you look at me dying over here—you'll know why. I *love* you. I'm in love with you. I'm sorry I almost didn't realize it in time, but the love has *always* been there."

I struggle for the right words, but it's hard when she's shaking so bad and I want her in our home, warm in bed with me wrapped around her. But she hasn't breathed since I told her I love her and I know she needs to hear more. All of it. Everything I've got.

"You have my heart. You have my soul. And you're the first and last person to ever have either one. I loved you *first*. And *last*.

I've only got this feeling for you. No one else. *Never.* Do you hear me?" I press a hard kiss to her forehead, then meet her eyes again. Eyes that are finally beginning to show hope. "I was a fool. I thought being your man and everything that came with it…meant I could lose you someday. Love meant loss, right? So I held one part of me back. But it was the most important part. I didn't recognize what it was, because I'd never actually *felt* it before. And I'm sorry. I'm so fucking sorry. I *love* you, Addison."

I'm not expecting it when she bursts into tears, because it's not an Addison response. But finally, there's not just hope. There's belief. She believes me. More than that, there's happiness and love and trust. As I hold her tight and whisper those three words, over and over again, into her hair…I realize there's even more of Addison that I've just unlocked.

I bring our mouths together and walk right through her door.

EPILOGUE

Addison

Mayor Gets It Right the Second Time Around
—Charleston Post

A Match Made in Southern Heaven
—Southern Insider News

Getaway Girl Charms at Gala in Bold Fall Colors
—Avant-Charleston

Can't wait to share the throne with my queen. Although we
might need a second throne...space wise...
—Twitter @DuPontBadonk

Three Months Later

MOST DAYS, I can't tell if I'm floating or walking on solid ground. Even now as I cross the intersection and blow a kiss to the photographer, I'm light as air. If I held out my arms and wished really hard, I think I could reach the clouds. Everything seems possible. *Everything.*

Six months ago, I came to Charleston only planning to stay a couple of weeks. Just long enough to get my grandmother's loose ends tied up, then back to Brooklyn. Now I can't imagine my life anywhere else. I have this man, you see.

I have this man.

And this man has me.

"Getaway Girl!" shouts the photographer. "Where are you headed today?"

"The market!" I call back, reaching the sidewalk. "Where else?"

His grin is a little more smug than usual, but I'm in too good a mood to speculate why. After a quick stop at Jingle Balls to pick up the cash drop and post the employee schedule for next week, I'm meeting Lydia and Elijah's mother for lunch. We've been doing it once a week for the last month and it's turned into something I really look forward to. Mostly because there's day drinking involved and when Virginia gets tipsy, she tells us stories about Elijah as a child. Turns out he had an imaginary friend named Albert. A zebra. And Virginia used to overhear Elijah asking Albert if he thought his butt looked big.

Priceless.

October is here and with Jolly Holidays Incorporated starting its maiden Halloween voyage, I no longer have time to work the booth. Although I plan to snatch up a weekly shift or two at the market in the spring—it makes me feel connected to my grandmother—right now the expansion has my attention and I'm firing on all cylinders. Taking a page from Elijah's book, I hired local. With some artistic guidance, my newly formed team was able to land several commercial contracts...including City Hall...and we're off to a roaring start. Walking through Charleston and seeing my handiwork in the form of scary window scenery, flickering lamps and orange fairy lights wrapped around trees? It's like I have all this happiness inside me and my outlet is to decorate the whole city.

It's magic. Wait until they see what I can do with Christmas.

I smile when I see the market up ahead, tourists coming in

and out of the buzzing within. It's probably a good thing I'm not working shifts very often at the booth anymore, because my Cooper River rescue gained national media attention, thanks to the news chopper that circled overhead when Elijah pulled me into the boat. And proceeded to strip us both down to the skin. And kissed me until we forgot about our surroundings.

Whoops.

At first, I wished that moment with Elijah were private. Just for us. I wanted to gather that proof that he loved me and keep it all to myself. But the camera captured something honest while we clung to one another in the boat and *nothing* has been the same since then. Of course Elijah still deals with his fair share of criticism and opposition—such is politics—but after that night on the river, our relationship stopped being a source of rampant speculation and became something to be celebrated. Not just by Elijah and me, but strangers, too. Elijah's family and friends. We never would have let rumors and gossip tear us apart, but it's a lot easier to be happy when everyone else is happy with us.

Speaking of rumors, it turns out I *do* have a half-sister out there. A confirmed father, too, not that I plan to do anything with that information besides…have it. The possibility has always been in the front of my mind and knowing for sure where I came from settled something inside me I didn't know was cluttered up. For now, Elijah and I are keeping the knowledge just to ourselves. Maybe we will forever. But who knows? Someday soon, I might very well have to invite Naomi to one of the lady's lunches.

If she ever stays in Charleston long enough to pin down.

Happy is such a thin word for how I feel. My days are spent doing what I love—a business I'm proud of—and my nights and weekends are full of Elijah. Over the summer, we went on kayaking trips, Elijah showing me parts of South Carolina I didn't know existed. One weekend in July was spent in New York so Elijah could see where I'd been, "while making him wait." We've put the giant kitchen to good use, cooking old favorites and trying new things. Most of the time we even make it through dinner without getting naked.

Okay fine, most of the time we *don't* make it through the meal, but we give it the old college try. It's just that…sex between us has exploded into another realm since all the walls crashed down between us. There are no secrets. No white lies or holding back truths. No confusion or pasts hanging over our heads. It's just his heartbeat thundering against mine, our mouths whispering words of praise and love…and filth…and an infinite amount of time to revel in each other.

God, I love Elijah. I loved him in the back of that church with my whole heart. But he's got my heart *and* soul now. My past, present and future. He's got them right in those capable hands I trust so much and they'll never be anywhere else.

As I step into the market, I can feel the weight of the soul he's handed me, too. It's a weight that presses on my chest in the most delicious way all day and all night long. Maybe it's been there since the beginning, this weight, but I wouldn't let myself accept it. I couldn't accept it, until that night in the boat. Now I can't live without it.

I'm only a few steps into the market when I hear…singing? It stops me in my tracks because it's so unexpected. There's no cacophony of voices or shuffling of feet. Everything is so still, too. No one is taking selfies or haggling over sales prices. There is a sea of faces on either side of the main aisle—some semi-familiar—and they're all still. They're looking at *me*. Smiling.

I follow the sound of singing farther down the aisle. It's a choir. They're harmonizing and the sound whips around the rafters, beautiful. So beautiful and clear. Putting one foot in front of the other, I start to notice things, like Christmas lights. Usually our booth is the only one lit up by lights, but they're on every stall now, twinkling white and blue, guiding my way toward the singing, which gets a little louder with every step. What is going on here? No one is moving in the usually chaotic market and I'm starting to wonder if I'm still wrapped in Elijah's arms in our bed, dreaming this whole scene.

It gets even more surreal when snow begins to fall from the ceiling.

Yes. Snow.

When I catch a flake in my palm, it's not cold and has the consistency of cotton, but it's falling around the entire market. And combined with the angelic singing and lights and smiling faces…I've been transported to the most incredible wonderland I could ever imagine. Faces are beginning to grow more familiar now, too. I recognize some of my artists, orange paint still on their noses from decorating store fronts. Chris is there with Sonia—and Lydia, too. They shift a little and I spot Virginia and Roy, dressed in their Sunday finest. I guess…

My heart starts to slam into my rib cage.

I guess lunch isn't happening now?

Until now, I didn't place the song they're singing, but I do now. It's "Carol of the Bells" and the choir is killing it. Melodic strains fill every corner of the market. The fullness and passion of it tightens my throat. I see the singers up ahead, dressed in blue robes, faces smiling.

And in front of them stands Elijah, the center of all gravity.

"Oh, what did you do?" I whisper, the words getting swallowed up in the music. But Elijah reads my lips and his smile is both tender and roguish at the same time. My pulse trips over itself and I walk faster, compelled to reach him as fast as possible. Once upon a time, I would have sauntered, played it cool or refused to obey the magnetic pull in his direction, but I don't hide anymore. I give and show and tell him everything—and the reward is Elijah doing the same.

I've almost reached him now. He's wearing a light gray suit I've never seen before. A black tie. Every inch the gentleman, but I know what waits underneath and there's nothing polite about it. My best friend. My lover. My biggest supporter.

My Elijah.

When I'm a few yards away, my heart leaps and I'm zapped by the current that always runs between us. I take a running step and launch myself into his arms—and the most amazing, deafening cheer goes up around us, temporarily drowning out the music. But it keeps going, the singers finally winning out again when the clapping and whistling dies down.

My face is pressed to Elijah's neck, inhaling eucalyptus and soap. He does the same, holding me several inches off the ground and sucking in a lungful of me, as if we didn't have breakfast together a few hours ago. As if he didn't tug open my robe afterward and command me to ride him, right there at the table. As if he didn't hold me and tell me he loved me long afterward, taking the time to do it right until I was wrapped a cloud of security and contentedness. Just like right now.

"The plan was to get down on one knee," he rasps in my ear, moving me side to side, nice and slow. "But I can't let you go for the life of me."

Moisture floods my eyes and I laugh, my heart soaring to new, even higher heights I didn't know were possible. He's proposing. He's proposing in front of everyone we know, including my grandmother. He's done it in a place and in a fashion where he knew I'd feel her most, like she's standing in the crowd with everyone else. "Don't. Don't let me go."

"I won't." His stubble catches me on the cheek and I shiver, going up on tiptoes and laying my head on his shoulder. "Everyone got to see me tell you I love you," Elijah continues, "This time it's just between us." I sense him gesturing behind my back and the choir sings louder, so loud that I'm the only one who can hear the gruff timbre of Elijah's voice as he speaks. "I want to be your husband, Addison Potts. I want to witness your wins and hold you after your losses. I want to be the father of your children. And your best friend. I'm man enough to ask you for the same. To tell you I *need* the same." I nod into his neck, tears blurring my vision. "I don't need these things because I'm supposed to. I need them because you *made* me need them with *you*. You were the love of my life before I knew what that meant. You showed me. And I want to spend every damn day showing you, too." He has to clear his throat before moving on. "Will you let me be your husband?"

"Yes," I whisper, before leaning back and pressing our heads together. "Yes, Elijah. Be my husband. Let me be your wife. I need that, too. More than anything in the world. Yes."

Our mouths meet, Elijah's taste and texture snaring me in their trap, as usual. And there's more cheering as my future husband carries me from the market, but I can barely hear it over the thundering of my heart.

"Getaway Girl!" shouts a photographer, lifting his camera. "Over here!"

"You're going to have to come up with another name for her!" Elijah calls back. "I'm never letting her get away again."

THE END

ACKNOWLEDGMENTS

I owe this book to a road trip I took with my family in Summer 2017. Charleston was my favorite of all our stops, because right there on the Battery, I had the most beautiful love story between two best friends form in my head. I spent the rest of the day distracted, walking through the inspiring streets of Charleston while plotting, but I couldn't stand to let the idea fade. I'm so relieved that it not only refused to fade, but grew in color and texture when I started to write—and finally met Elijah and Addison on the page. Huge thanks to Charleston and our tour guide for throwing out random facts about family feuds and southern politics on our journey.

Thank you as always to my family for loving and believing in me, even though I have a job that often seems to have an uncertain future. Thank you to Eagle at Aquila Editing for once again throwing me the right puzzle pieces to make a better, fuller picture. Thank you to Bailey's Babes for being excited about my, "bubble butt hero and dirty talker heroine," book. Here it is! You guys approve? Last but not least, thank you to the readers for picking up this book. I hope you loved it. And I hope you'll consider leaving it a review. Who knows…if I think enough people are interested in Naomi's lost two months in Florida, I might just have to write it.

Love to everyone!